P9-BBO-097

ANNIHILATION DAY

ALBANY PUBLIC LIBRARY
ALBANY, OR 97322-6945

THE MISSHAPES

ANNIHILATION DAY

ALEX FLYNN

The following is a work of fiction. Names, characters, places, events and incidents are either the product of the author's imagination or used in an entirely fictitious manner. Any resemblance to actual persons, living or dead, is entirely coincidental.

Copyright © 2015 by Stuart Sherman and Elisabeth Donnelly

Cover illustration by Sebastian Ciaffliogne
Logo and jacket design by Eamon O'Donoghue
Interior design by E.M. Tippetts Book Designs

ISBN 978-1-940610-15-3
eISBN 978-1-940610-58-0

First hardcover edition October 2015 by Polis Books, LLC
1201 Hudson Street, #211S
Hoboken, NJ 07030

POLIS BOOKS

Dedicated to the memory of Anne Audet Donnelly

I stood at the edge of a cliff, looking over the landscape. A carpet of blue and green stretched before my eyes. Fuzzy woods. Snow-capped hills. We had taken all day to hike up to this point. It was grueling. My backpack worried lines into my shoulders.

But things were going to be different now, at this point. The sun had set, and it was dusk. Purples, blues, and a stripe of pink lit up the canvas. I wanted to be part of it. I stood broadly, feeling the great rock beneath my feet. We were at the top of the cliff. It had taken thousands of years for this slab of rock to form; it was time for me to appreciate it in all its glory.

And then I stepped off.

ONE

MY HOUSE looked the same. Same windows shaped like jack-o-lantern eyeballs, same drooping rain gutters, and same red doorknocker like a dopey dog with its tongue stuck out, happy to greet me. I wondered if I looked the same. I didn't feel the same. The world, to me, felt different after everything that happened. The Hero Academy fight, Mom's return, followed by her disappearance, once again. The massive cover-up. I felt different, too. I had a tiny, beaded braid in my hair for proof. I had just been on the best trip of my life, spending weeks helping indigenous farmers in the Amazon rainforest. It was so beautiful, days in vivid yellow and green, nights that felt like endless blue. I ate the best coconut I'd ever had there, saw rainbow-colored birds the size of insects and was bitten by insects the size of airplanes. PeriGenomics had touched down, door-to-door service, dropping me and my bag of stuff off on the lawn — "Jump, Sarah!" they said — and then the propellers clattered back off into the sky, only to disappear, and I was alone. Returned.

I took the spare key from under the frog next to the welcome mat and walked inside the house. It was empty.

I felt a flicker of disappointment, even though I had known it was going to be empty. A few weeks earlier, after he stopped yelling at me on the phone, Dad said that he was spending the last half of August in Maine, camping and communing with nature. He was off the grid. "Look, you'll be fine," he said. "Johnny will be around."

"He can barely feed himself!" I replied, trying to will myself to get good reception even though I was on some ancient brick of a phone on a one-way street in a shadow of a town. "You guys need me, right?"

"It's not as if you gave us an itinerary, Sarah, before you just went on a helicopter ride with some PeriGenomics drone."

"You're a PeriGenomics drone," I pointed out, and we laughed.

So the red carpet that you secretly wish for when you return home was nonexistent. Just an empty house. Dad on vacation and Johnny who-knows-where. I had missed my family and friends when I was away, and I wanted to see them immediately to tell them all about my amazing journey. But the only one listening was the four walls of my small house in Doolittle Falls.

Dad said he would only be gone for ten days. I think this was day three. But from the look of the house, it had been abandoned for decades. Dishes piled up in the sink. Clothes all over the floor. The lawn half-mowed. Empty bags of chips and drinks all over the place. And the couch looked worn in, more so than normal. I could nearly make out the shape of my brother's body. He had pulled the video game console out into the living room, in front of the large TV, ready at a moment's notice.

I went up to my room and put my bag on the floor. My whole summer was in the bag. Postcards, seashells, a jar of sand, new clothes. When I got in the plane with Sam I only had the things on my back. PeriGenomics had let me borrow some gear, but in the end they took back everything that wasn't a PeriGenomics t-shirt.

I surveyed my room. Everything I left was there: the humidifier, my Black Zephyr poster, my computer, clothes, books. All of it. It was the same as when I left it. The bed was made, although I got the distinct impression that someone had been sleeping in it. As I walked over to inspect it I saw a few brightly colored drops of dried paint on the floor.

It could only be one person: Hamilton.

Johnny must have been using my room for guests. I was going to kill him. I went back downstairs, sent him a quick text, and I made a sandwich. As I stood at the kitchen counter, chewing, half-famished, I realized there was only one person I wanted to see. I called Alice. The phone rang and rang but no one picked up. I tried a few other friends but the same thing happened.

Where was everyone? I had this fantasy in my mind; they'd all be hanging out somewhere waiting for me to get back. They should've known I was coming back. Between calls and texts and emails, I'd practically sent out a virtual little trumpet boy to herald my arrival.

It was time to canvass the streets. I grabbed my bag and went outside into the thick summer heat. When I got to the pizza shop on Main Street, I saw someone running toward me, flailing their arms. It was Betty. She had spent the summer at the Academy retreat in Cuernavaca, Mexico, or, to be clearer, three weeks there and the rest of the summer scooping ice cream. I went for a hug but she grabbed me by the shoulders. "Hey! Betty! It's great to see you!" I said, a little confused.

"We need your help. Where is he?" she demanded. She looked at me, quizzically. Her hair was pulled back in a neat ponytail and she had on a black t-shirt and Capri pants. She looked like Audrey Hepburn dancing with bohemians in *Funny Face*. I felt epically bedraggled in comparison: ratty t-shirt with holes in it, cut-off shorts, and a braid that felt like it was disintegrating on my head.

"Who?" I asked

"Butters!" She was tense, like a soda can ready to pop. What had happened? Did the world threaten to end, again?

"Well, I've been back for about five minutes now," I said slowly. Maybe this radio silence meant that we were in the middle of a post-apocalyptic dream world. Maybe that's why I couldn't find anybody.

"I sent him to find you when we heard you were getting back. I should have gone myself. That boy is so distractible. And the Spectors! We'll never make it."

I looked at her, totally confused. "Betty, slow down. What's going on? Is someone after you? Is it the Hero Academy again? Did Dr. Mann resurrect himself in order to make a bigger, better machine?" It had to be something important. The last time she was this worried she was about to confess to me regarding George.

"No. It's bigger than that. The whole world depends on it," she said.

"What is it? Is the town under attack? Is Dr. Mann back?" We were standing still on the sidewalk, facing each other. She wasn't very good at getting me wherever I needed to go.

"No. Worse," Betty said. She looked at me with the most serious face in the world and spit out the truth: "Karaoke!"

TWO

S HE LOOKED at me. I'm sure my face was as off-kilter as a Picasso. "Okay, maybe I overstated it," Betty said. "The world doesn't depend on it. Just Butters' world. I'll explain later."

She grabbed me by the hand and we went on a walk to her car. We cruised through the town looking for Butters. The Karaoke state championship was happening tonight and Butters had qualified to represent Doolittle Falls' region, the Sleepy Valley. If he was in the top three he'd get to compete at the regionals in the New England Championship, and if he won that, he'd go on to the Karaoke nationals in Washington DC.

"There's a Karaoke nationals?"

"There's an *everything* nationals these days." Betty said. "Haven't you ever watched singing shows?"

"What does he get if he wins?"

"Fifty thousand dollars and a spot on *The Sing-Along*."

"The what?"

"Ugh. You really were off the grid this summer. *The Sing-Along* is the biggest reality musical show in the country. Everyone—Normals, Heroes, Misshapes, even supervillains—cover songs and the best singer gets a record deal with Titan Records.

"And Butters wants to get on the show?"

"Everyone wants to get on the show."

"That's awesome."

"It could be. It's still far away, and I can't even get him to the regionals."

"What do you mean?"

Betty explained to me that there had been a series of events leading up to the competition. Butters was calling it his curse. Before he performed, strange things would happen. Bouts of laryngitis. Downed power in the bars. He'd almost gotten hit by a tree. "I think it's the Admiral," Betty said.

"Admiral Doom?" I asked. "Why would he want to stop karaoke? Doesn't he have bigger plans, like his Doom Ray?"

"Not Admiral Doom, silly," Betty corrected, executing a perfect turn. "Admiral Skylark. He's in the competition as well, and he also has powers and money to recruit minions to help him."

Once we got off the main drag, I put my head out the window to see if I could spot Butters. The slow echoes of doo-wop filled the air. We followed it like hounds on a scent until we pulled over to the field where Butters was standing in the middle distance, belting "It's In His Kiss (the Shoop Shoop song)" with full back-up by the Spectors. Butters was okay. The Spectors were amazing.

We tumbled out of the car, approaching Butters from behind. "I don't want to interrupt him," Betty said, putting a finger over her lips. "He's nervous enough as it is." We watched him finish the song, then start again. He made the same exact gestures each time, never moving from his space. It was like he was caught on loop. When we got up to him we could see that he was singing against his will. While his whole body was into the performance, his small hands making large circles and his feet doing a tap-dancing soft shoe in place, there was fear in his eyes. We tried to talk to him but he kept going. We tried to move him but he was stuck, as if by glue, in place.

"Is someone messing with you?" I asked.

Butters nodded, almost imperceptibly.

We heard a loud, slow clap when he finished. Christie emerged from behind a lonely maple tree, a smirk on her face.

"Bravo. They figured it out. Bravo." She paused and looked over at Butters and the Spectors. "Again!" she shouted. "Less vibrato this time. If I wanted Christina Aguilera murdering a classic, I'd ask for it."

Butters opened his mouth. A tremulous warble whispered through the air.

I was going to shout something clever at Christie, so she'd stop it with Butters, but her mind control moves at the speed of thought, and by the time I finished, I'd be in Butters' chorus line, singing and dancing forever. I sent a bolt of lightning ripping through the sky. It landed with an enormous BANG twenty feet away from Christie, splitting a branch in the tree. Everyone jumped, clutching their ears and falling to the ground in a ball, including the Spectors. Butters stayed upright, with a marine's posture, still singing. Some debris from the tree hit Christie in the head and she yelped. Betty gave me a nod of approval.

"Why'd you do that?" Christie moaned. "It hurt."

"Consider it a warning," I said. "The next one won't be."

"I can have you doing—" she was about to launch into a spiel about how she could get me to do anything, absolutely anything. We had heard it before from the Glanton family.

I cut her off. If there was one thing I learned this summer it was how to talk big. Apparently, it's half of what they teach you at the Academy. "Hey Christie, the second I sense you getting into my mind at all it's done. In fact, right now, my hand's not on the trigger, it's over the muzzle. The shots have been fired, and I'm the only thing between you and the bullet. You move, you wake up in a year with white hair and some serious memory loss. Your call."

It was a bluff. A big one. I didn't have nearly that kind of power.

Or control. The tree thing was luck. I was aiming thirty yards east of it. But Christie didn't know that. She just knew that I was more powerful now, and I scared the hell out of her. Would it be worth it to test me? She wrinkled her nose.

Butters' body collapsed. Out of breath, he fell to the ground. Betty went over to him while I continued to stare Christie down. I felt like a cat locked in a neighborhood battle. She smiled at me and I smiled back, and we slowly backed away from each other, never breaking eye contact until she had shrank in my vision to the size of a peanut.

THREE

"**W**HY WOULD Christie waste her time tormenting Butters?" I asked. "No offense, Butters."

"You! Are! FORGIVEN!" the Spectors replied.

"Nice to see you," Butters said.

"She's just a sadist," Betty said. "It's probably just revenge for hearing 'Build Me Up Buttercup' during the fight one hundred times."

Butters, surrounded by his Spectors, smiled. They chirped, in unison, "Tweedle-dee-dee, Tweedle-dee-wop."

"What?" I asked.

"It was Skylark," Butters said. "He put her up to it. Paid her off."

"She probably would have done it for free," Betty said.

"Yeah. But the $250 helped," Butters said.

"But she doesn't need the money," Betty said. "She's soooo spoiled and her stupid family is going to take over the world."

"Money was probably just the excuse," I said. "Though I'm worried that this Skylark can use money or her natural cruelty to get her to do anything."

"He's a huge jerk," Butters said.

We passed a beat-up car with the words "Lofting Rodent and

Pest Removal" stenciled on the side. Alice stood at the front of the car with the hood up, white smoke billowing in her face. She stepped back to get some air. Her face was covered in grease and soot.

"Hey lady, need a ride?" I yelled out the window.

She looked totally shocked. "Sarah! It's you!" There was a flicker of something on her face, but it was wiped away by a big smile. "I actually do need a ride."

A car honked behind us. "Okay, I get it," Betty grumbled. "You have places to go in Doolittle Falls. Have to get to the hardware store before four p.m., right?" She beamed at Alice. "Let me pull over."

"Hey, we got that karaoke competition tonight," Butters said. "If we make it in one piece."

"I'm there with bells on, Butters," Alice replied. "As long as we can bring someone else, too."

"Who?" I asked.

"I promised your brother a ride. He's obsessed with Butters."

"Where is that jerk, anyways?" I asked. "He leaves the house a mess and rents out my room like it's on AirBnB."

"Just at Pete's Record Store," Alice said, pulling open the backdoor and smushing in next to Butters and the Spectors.

"Wait," Betty added, "is this many people in my car legal, technically?"

"Well, three of us are technically mental projections so I think we're okay," I said.

"Who you calling a projection?" the Spectors shot back at me.

We pulled over by the record store, where Johnny was outside, leaning against the brick wall. He was still limping a little from the bite he'd gotten last year but seemed much better.

"Hey, sis. Long time no see," Johnny said, and got in the car. He winced when he sat back down. "Where we headed?"

"Springfield." He smushed next to Alice and the Spectors, out of room, disappeared.

"Why Springfield?"

"We're off to the glamorous karaoke capital of Massachusetts," I said.

"You in?" Alice asked.

"Hell yeah." He kicked at the passenger seat. "Let's get this tour bus on the road." It was like I had never been away. Johnny was still exactly the same.

A long stretch of highway and country road was standing in the way between our car and Springfield. When we got the exit, a large blinking sign said it was closed. We had to drive another twenty minutes for the next exit, winding our way down rural roads to get back to where we were going, using Butters' phone to guide us. There was road closure after road closure, sign after sign that meant we had to redirect our route. We ended up on the last road into town from the outside world, passing only John Deere tractor stores and the occasional chrome-lined diner.

Butters exhaled, nervously. "It's like someone's trying to seal off Springfield.""Or trap us on this road," Alice added.

"I hope not," I said just as we began to slow down to a stop because of traffic. I craned my neck out of the window and there was a line of cars. It looked like a parking lot.

"What do you think? Just too many people trying to get in on the last road?" Johnny asked.

"Or some accident," Betty said, trying to peek around the large truck in front of us.

We sat for ten minutes. Occasionally the car would get the chance to crawl forward three feet. "Did you know," a Spector said, sitting on Butters' lap, "that your brain gets annoyed when you can't see the way forward in a car, and it's the same part of your brain that hates hearing other people's one-sided phone conversations?""Ooooh, I totally get that," said Alice. "It's like an animal instinct. You want to hear both sides and see where you're going."

"This doesn't feel right," I said. "Even with everything, why so many cars and why so sudden?"

"It's the Admiral," Butters said.

"All this for Karaoke?" Johnny asked.

"You don't know what people would do to win that spot on *The Sing-Along*," Butters said.

"Well, we're not getting anywhere just sitting here in traffic. You stay here, Betty. Sarah and I can go to check it out," Alice said. "We'll jump back in when the problem's solved."

We got out of the car and started walking ahead. I wondered why Alice volunteered me for the job. Was it because she believed in my powers? People looked despondent in their vehicles. Resigned to be stuck in traffic forever. Some honked in desperation. The whole time it was as if Alice wanted to say something but instead she made small talk about the back up. The amount of cars made it seem like one of those apocalyptic movies where everyone tries to abandon the city at once. But they were heading into a city. And, oddly, there were no cars in the other direction.

Then we saw the source. A tree. A big one. It was nearly as tall on its side than I was standing up. There were a few onlookers who had also gotten out of their car to inspect it.

I summoned all my strength and tried to create a wind strong enough to move the tree. Some leaves rustled and a couple of tiny branches snapped. A hat flew by me. It was at least gale force, but when I saw the tree barely budge a centimeter, I lost control and it died down to a light gust.

"That's a big one," a man said, picking up his Bruins hat. "Need a little more wind to move it."

"Probably took ten times that to knock it down," said another man.

I took another minute to size up the tree. Maybe Johnny could convert any water in it into alcohol and burn it down. But then we'd have a giant fire in the middle of the road and probably an explosion if he turned it into high-octane. I was fresh out of ideas.

A group of older grizzled men formed a conclave that was sizing it up and talking about their options. There were lots of "MmHmms" and "Yups" but little in the way of actual movement.

"I got a chainsaw in my truck but nothing that can handle something that size. Especially lying like that," said another man.

A younger man, in a plaid shirt and jeans, said, "Probably gonna take a road crew to clear that. Two-hour job. Maybe three."

"I can do it in thirty," Alice said. "And that's minutes."

They all turned their heads in shock.

"What are you doing?" I whispered to her.

"I got this. I learned a new language this summer. I think it might just come in handy."

"How do you suppose you'll do that, little lady?" said a man the size of a small truck with his thumbs wresting in his belt loops.

"Just watch and see," she said.

Alice walked to the edge of the forest on the side of the road and started making a gurgling noise in the back of her throat. It sounded bestial. Inhuman. And it kind of creeped me out. She looked down at the map on her phone, which seemed to be some app that identified local animal populations.

"There should be some near enough to hear, there's a lake two hundred feet in that direction," she said, pointing into the thick forest. I couldn't see anything but trees.She made some more odd noises and then a smile crept across her face.

"Thank god. There's one right there. Let's hope he brought friends."

She pointed to a small creature trundling through forest. It looked like a fat cat at first, with small thick legs but an odd tail. As it got closer I could see it didn't have a long, thin tail like a dog or a cat but rather a wide, almost triangular, one. It was brown with a flat face and large protruding teeth.

"A beaver, Alice?" She smiled.

Moments later, Alice was leading a small posse of beavers to the middle of the road to assess the tree. The men looked on in disbelief. Alice had the beavers set up to start gnawing through the wood. They called over more and soon there were three-dozen beavers gnawing at full speed, kicking up wood chips in every direction. The brown bark gave way to a reddish layer and then a pale yellow. They cut it by biting little sections, leaving small pock-like marks with each bite. They split the tree into sections that we took into the forest.

Each one was kind of slow, but working together they got through most of it in the promised thirty minutes, with the help of some of the men who weren't too proud to prove Alice right, and some other bored drivers eager to get out. Once the tree was gone, the cars started moving again. Betty pulled over, and we piled back in, making it into Springfield just under the wire so that Butters could perform.

FOUR

THE BAR was in Springfield's deserted downtown, a block away from the Basketball Hall of Fame, which was, legitimately, a building shaped like a giant basketball. Sadly, the karaoke wasn't in the ball, but at a chain restaurant called Wingdinigans. It had the faux kitschy front of a place called Wingdinigans. Booths circled the perimeter and there was a bar dead center. They had set up the stage and karaoke machine there, and people were crowded against the bar, teetering over the people seated at small round tables. When I made for a tiny table, a man in a striped green and purple shirt ran over to me.

"Excuse me, but it's twenty-one and over only for our drinking establishment. If you'd like, I can get a waitress to seat you at a booth."

"I get my drinks for free anyway," Johnny said.

The man glowered. I stared at my brother, wishing that he'd shut up before he wasted all our efforts.

We were exhausted from the whole trip and didn't have time to have a Wingdinigans manager stop us at the finish line. Butters was too busy mumbling to himself and running through his routine to notice any of it.

"The competition," Betty finally said. "We're here for the karaoke."

"Ohh," he said, drawing the word out. "In that case the registration is over there. Lower turnout then we expected. But if I see you drinking anything from the bar that isn't soda or water, you're out of here immediately. All of you. I should be carding ya," he continued, "but you got lucky tonight. Be good, okay?"

There was a stage with a solitary microphone on a stand up front, a small TV pointing at the mic, and a folding table. Three people sat at the table drinking enormous cocktails from Hurricane glasses, with fruit and umbrellas tumbling out of the perimeter. They had the look of "wacky" local celebrities, you know the sort: they host the morning zoo radio show, complete with fart sound effects, or the meteorologists that have a special hat for every holiday or pseudo-holiday. It seemed a little preposterous that we had used all our powers to get Butters here so the goofiest people in the room could decide his fate.

There was a parade of middling drunken singers belting their way through rock and R & B classics. Occasionally someone could actually sing really well, and it was impressive. The judges made semi-funny comments that we felt obliged to laugh at and gave out mostly fives and sixes. The performances ranged from one person nervously singing into the mic to people wildly flailing around like they were fronting some Eighties hair metal band. One guy, in the middle of an air guitar windmill, ate it on the mic cord and nearly took out the TV on the way down.

"Fire in the hole," the wacky DJ screamed, and he plummeted.

I was happy to be there, but as the night went on I got sleepier and sleepier. I think I was jetlagged. And something about hanging out with Betty, Butters, Johnny, and Alice felt off to me. I was so excited to see them but I couldn't keep up. They had jokes that I didn't know, and Johnny and Alice had started a band, maybe, and I think they were calling it The Third Policeman. "I bet you're totally influenced by Taylor Swift," I joked, and Alice waved me off at one point.

At least Butters looked as nervous as I felt. The Spectors filed their nails and rolled their eyes at the competition. They were really, really confident in a way that Butters couldn't even approach. I was jealous of them.

Finally the announcer called him up. Butters looked dorky in his pleated khakis and white button-down shirt. Especially surrounded by the Spectors, who had on floor-length sequined dresses in midnight blue with embroidered lace running from the hip to the bust.

"So, to be clear," I asked Betty. "That's all from his mind?"

"What do you mean?"

"The dresses, the hair, their attitudes. If that's all a mental projection, everything they do, say, and wear comes from him."

"Yeah, I guess. Why?"

"It's just funny. He's able to dress *them* so well."

"Hey," she said. "I helped him pick that out."

"A little Norman Bates," Alice said.

I started to laugh but the announcer started talking and Betty threw her hand over my mouth.

"Our next contestant is Matthew Butters. He'll be performing 'He's a Rebel' by the Crystals."

We all applauded and Johnny shouted, "Butters!"

Butters took the mic and corrected the announcer. "Actually, sir, it's Butters and the Spectors. Thanks so much." The music cued up, and Butters hit the first line with perfect pitch. He changed it to "She's a Rebel." The Spectors frowned for a second and then played along. Beyond being tortured by Christie, which really didn't count, I'd never actually heard Butters really belt it out before. He had a good voice. A really good voice. He looked so nervous, though. Like he wanted to fall into himself and disappear. Maybe that's why he chose the Spectors. They were all bravado; they covered up for his shyness."Ever hear the version by The Zippers?" Johnny whispered to Alice during the first chorus as the Spectors belted *She's a rebel and she'll never be any good.*

"No," Alice whispered back. "Who are they?"

"You've never heard of the Zippers? They were an awesome LA punk band. I got it on vinyl. Come over. I'll play it for you."

Alice's eyes darted toward me for a second before she whispered, "Awesome." The chorus ended and they returned their focus to the stage. Betty beamed as Butters sang, but even better, the audience was enthralled with his performance. People who had been talking loudly and spilling drinks stopped to watch. The judges put down their pens and just nodded their heads to the song. It was spectacular. The real spectacle was provided by the Spectors. When he finished we hooted and hollered and the crowd joined in. Everyone stood and applauded loudly except for one man, who had a large black bouffant and was wearing a strange looking robe or cape thing. He just sat, drinking tea, and watched Butters awkwardly take in the applause and then stand there, shaking, while he waited for the judges' votes.

He was given tens by two of the judges and a 9.5 from the last one. Everyone booed the 9.5 loudly. Butters was clearly in the lead, and there was only one performer left. He would make it to the next round.

"Can you believe that nonsense?" the lead Spector, the one who always insisted on standing in the middle, said. "It's probably because he changed it."

"What are you talking about," the shorter Spector said. "It was the same, Doris.""The same? *She's* a rebel. *She.* It's he's a rebel Beverly. She. He ain't no Gene Pitney."

"And you ain't no Darlene Love," said the last Spector, the tall, skinny one."Maybeline, I swear one of these days I'm gonna step out and leave your sorry sacks behind."

"What the heck is stepping out?" I asked Alice.

"It's when one of the singers in a group steps out from the chorus and does a solo. It mean she's thinking of leaving and striking off on her own. Like Diana Ross stepped out from the Supremes," Alice said. She noticed my confused look and added, "or Beyonce and Destiny's Child."

"I don't get it. How could she do that? Like, on a molecular level?" I whispered to Alice.

Alice just shrugged. Butters was too busy getting accolades from strangers while the Spectors grumbled. The manager kept an eye on him and every time he got a drink he refused it under the glare of his stupid eyes.

The Spectors were still bickering with each other. At least I knew their names now. "Talk talk talk," said Maybeline. "You ever stop out I'm gonna eat my stockings.""Nice one, Werner Herzog," Alice joked and all the Spectors stopped to stare at her before evaporating in a puff of smoke as Butters returned to the group and handed out free Cokes. Johnny raised his finger like a man of class, offering to spike the glass.

Then the announcer called on Admiral Skylark, and the man with the bouffant stood up, combed his hair, pulled out a pocket mirror and looked at himself, then slowly strutted to the stage. Under the lights I could see what he was wearing. It was a floor- length cape made out of bright white feathers and matching white pants and shirt. His face had a deep fake-tan orange and he appeared to be wearing dark eye makeup.

Was this Butters' arch-nemesis? Was this his enemy?

"And now, for our last performer, Admiral Skylark, who will be performing 'When Doves Cry' by Prince," said the announcer.

Admiral Skylark stood in front of the microphone, his arms at his side, his head down. The song began with a solo from some instrument I couldn't identify, maybe it was a keytar with its strange Eighties electronic blooping. A drum kicked in, and as soon as it did, Skylark raised his hands and doves started pouring out of his hands and his chest. They shot outward to the audience, who ducked in unison, but before they reached anyone they disappeared in a rainbow explosion of spectral light.

Just as the audience got their bearings again he started singing. They went nuts. It made the applause for Butters seem like golf claps. As he sang he made birds disappear and explode into choreographed color displays that accompanied the song. When the final solo started, he raised his arms and transformed into a large red phoenix that grew brighter and brighter with flame as the solo got more intense.

Then, suddenly, he disappeared into an enormous fire, which flashed a brilliant orange that blinded the audience. A black light blurred in front of my eyes until it gave away to Skylark appearing like a phoenix, his cape now a radiant orange-red, his pants and shirt black, singing the last note of the song lingering on the speaker.

Pandemonium broke out. He got straight tens across the board to roaring applause. Butters quietly grabbed his second place trophy and fifty dollar gift certificate to Wingdingans and tried to sneak out. But Admiral Skylark brushed away adoring fans to get to him at the door.

"Nice job there," he said. "A little sharp on the bridge but your singers were great."

"Why, thank you," the Spectors replied, brushing off his praise like it was nothing before Butters had them disappear.

"Not so bad yourself," Butters said.

"Good thing you could make it. I heard a lot of the competition got stuck," he said, chuckling to himself like it was an adorable joke.

"Funny thing about that," Johnny said, but Alice pulled him back.

"Well, I'll see you at regionals," Butters mumbled, trying to leave.

"Oh yes," said Skylark. "I look forward to it." He gave us one last leer and we were out the door. I looked ahead at Betty, who was comforting Butters, who looked as overwhelmed as I felt. How was he going to top Skylark's performance?

FIVE

I HAD SLEPT on the whole ride home from karaoke and didn't
have a chance to catch up with anyone. I gave Alice a call.

"Oh, I was coming over later anyways," she said. "Band
practice."

"What band?" I asked.

Five minutes later, her car pulled up outside. She knocked on the
door vigorously. "Girl!" she yelled, running up to the door. I gave her
a hug. "I'm sorry I went away with no warning," I said.

"Oh, I was there at the quarry with you. The minute I saw that jet
touch down I knew it was going to happen. I mean, who would say
no to a summer practicing heroics with Sam."

I smirked. She was right. I wouldn't have given up my summer
with Sam for anything.

"It was fun."

"I bet it was. I want all the gory details."

"I wouldn't call them gory per se. Lots of hot nights in the jungle
and a few intimate moments," I gloated.

"Intimate moments. What are you, the movie rating board? I bet
he didn't ever wear a shirt. Did he wear a shirt?" Alice asked.

"Sometimes. It was funded by PeriGenomics and they like their employees in professional attire," I paused. "But, yeah, keeping a shirt on him is like keeping a leash on a cat."

"And how's Freedom Boy?" she asked pointedly.

I didn't really have a good answer for her. I slightly stuttered. How were things with boys? Freedom Boy was out in the world. There was something with Sam—we kissed, at one point—but just as soon as it happened, it was like it disappeared. Now I was back in Doolittle Falls and both dudes were elsewhere. "We're chill. We have an understanding," I said. "Both Freedom Boy and Sam." Alice rolled her eyes.

"I'll believe that when I see it," she said, shaking her head. "When are you ever chill about anything?" I thought about it for a moment. The sky clouded over. No, being chill wasn't really in my skillset.

"Do you want to hear about my summer? Everything's changed, it seems." Alice said this quite seriously, and then broke out into a laugh. Her blonde hair had a purple streak in it, and it looked really cool. "No, seriously, nothing happened, I wish I went with you. All I've been doing is running around from restaurant to restaurant, creating various détentes for the sake of peace. And clean food."

"And your band?" I asked. "Did you guys come up with a name yet? I think Swan Squad would be killer."

"Oh that. It's just Johnny and me and anyone else we can find with a semblance of musical talent playing our instruments off key in the garage. But, you know, we hope to get better. I've gotten to spend a lot of time with your brother."

"Why?" I said. It felt a little weird hearing her talk about the band so casually. I go away one summer and my best friend and my brother are hanging out in a band. It's like I didn't even exist. But I decided to be resilient and move past it. Changing the topic, I made a joke. "Do you know how much pan-flute I heard this summer?"

My phone buzzed. It was Johnny. *I'm selling tourist stuff right now if you want to see me*, he wrote. *Welcome back.*

You could make a lot of money off tourists in Doolittle Falls. Especially if they were Hero fans looking to press the flesh in person. Hero Maps sold in the stores. Small buses would drive by estates in Marston Heights pointing out houses. The chamber of commerce ran all sorts of events and usually called it stuff like Summer of Heroics, like nightly showings of Docs projected in the town park. Obviously not any GrappaMan films. It was the usual Freedom Man popcorn fare. *Freedom Men In History. Freedom Man Versus the Dragon. Freedom Man Versus Nature Man, Freedom Man Versus Society Man, Freedom Man Versus MechaFreedom Man Freedom Man, the Hero's Hero.*

"Hey, Johnny's just sent a text. He's on the main drag," I told Alice. She nodded, sinking into the lumpy sofa, her boots pointing in the air.

"He's made so much money this summer between his t-shirts and Hamilton's painting. Our band's made no money, though. There's a million tourists around. You heard about the Freedom Man movie, right?"

"Yeah, I head a little about it," I said, which was a partial truth. I knew there was going to be a movie. I'm a human girl; I do read celebrity blogs. The details had been skimpy, and I'd been in the jungle for a month with no Wi-Fi or cell reception. There was still mail in the jungle and I'd heard nothing about it from Freedom Boy himself, despite his occasional letter. But I didn't want to admit that. "Should we go see him?"

"I guess. Sure. Let's walk over," Alice said. Apparently, there's been no parking in Doolittle Falls ever since the open Harpastball practices started.

I grabbed a hat on my way out. I wanted to go incognito for now. Even if Alice knew the deal with me and whatever dude flew in my orbit this week, I didn't want to ruin it by actually running into either Freedom Boy or Sam. I didn't want to risk it.

SIX

W E WALKED downtown and Alice filled in the blanks on the movie. They'd been hiring people around town for the film, which would be shooting on occasion in our own Doolittle Falls."

"Did you get a job on it? Do you want one?" I asked.

"I was going to see if they needed a small animal wrangler. Nothing worse than a squirrel ruining a great shot. I want to trick out my drum kit. But they need people for everything. Extras. Background damsels in distress. Crew jobs. Hamilton was trying to get a job painting sets."

"I'm stuck, Alice." We walked. She looked over at me. "Does a squirrel really ruin a shot?"

"Well, let's just say that if a certain someone *doesn't* get the position, there might be a few million dollar scenes ruined because of poorly placed mice."

She grinned, her teeth flashing. "You haven't even told me what the film's about."

"I thought you said you'd heard about it," she said.

"Well, only a little. And you can't trust that online stuff. Besides,

I've been Thoreauing it up with Sam in South America and that guy acts like any celeb or Hero news is beneath him," I said. "Hey." I jabbed her shoulder. "Tell me. Is it another in a long line of Freedom Man Saves The day features?"

"Umm, not quite," she said. With her left hand, she grabbed her right hand's pointer finger and started pulling at it. She was using her finger like a worry doll. "This is the big one. I can't believe he hasn't been in touch."

Playing dumb, I asked her, "Who? What are you talking about?"

"Freedom Boy," she said. "Your sweetheart. Or ex-sweetheart."

"We're chill," I said, playing it cool.

I was chill as possible. Freedom Boy was busy.

Alice, with some reluctance, filled me in. The upcoming film wasn't a Freedom Man film, but a Freedom Boy film. It was the long awaited transition one, the one rumored to be happening for years on end. I knew what it was supposed to be—the one where Freedom Man hands over the reigns to Freedom Boy. In other words, Freedom Boy was about to become Freedom Man, or Freedom Man Jr., or Freedom Man 2, or really Freedom Man the fourth. He was going to fight Admiral Doom and win the Battle of Innsmouth for good. It was slated for an Annihilation Day release, and the working title was *Annihilation Day: The Rise of Freedom Boy*, but when posters went up for the movie around town, it had a nickname: "Bluff."

"That doesn't sound too bad," I said, lying through my teeth. "No worse than any other Freedom Family celebrity vehicle."

"Yeah, but there's this one other thing," she said, and before she could finish, I saw with my own eyes what she was about to tell me. We had just hit downtown and passed our first Hero Paraphernalia store. There was a giant poster in the front window, framed by toy Hero figures and plastic versions of Hero weapons.

It was a blown-up cover of *Maximus Magazine*, a glossy magazine directed at teenage boys with a lot of news about Hero fights and Docs and scantily clad models. On the cover was a giant grinning picture of Freedom Boy, and under his arm was Dangerous Girl, with her tiny Lycra-clad waist and enormous chest heaving through the boob window in her top. Above them, it said, "Freedom Boy finally becomes a Freedom Man." The magazine screamed 'more photos of Dangerous Girl inside and an exclusive on the filming on *Annihilation Day.*'

My jaw dropped. I did not feel that chill anymore. Freedom Boy was a liar. He told me he was spending the summer in Europe and taking a relaxing vacation after all the drama of last year. And the whole time he'd been preparing for this movie and gallivanting around with that flying pair of boobs. Before I could start ranting to Alice, she grabbed my hand and dragged me down the street.

"There they are," she said, ignoring the poster and my fragile mental response.She was right. Just around the corner, Hamilton was slouched against the outside wall of Boscoe's Pizza wearing a shirt that read, "Undiscovered Genius." He was surrounded by his art: giant canvases of graffiti-style paintings of Heroes doing mundane tasks. Johnny was next to him in a shirt, which he also made, that said, "Minor caught loitering." He was selling his "This is Not A Red Shirt" t-shirts out of a large beat-up brown box and a shirt with a screen-printed image of the Freedom Family Logo with "Freedom Man Was Hero To Most, But..." scrawled over it.

Main Street was a mixture of fancy restaurants, grimy but awesome places like Boscoe's, Hero-themed stores, and weird places that sold overpriced antiques. But I was happy to see that the bookstore, Pete's Record Shop, and Buzz Man were still around. The line was out the door at Buzz Man, probably tourists hoping to catch a Hero in motion.

As we approached Hamilton and Johnny, Hamilton was busy talking to a woman who looked like a model and had the legs of a newborn foal and her boyfriend, some old dude dressed like a giant baby in primary colors. He was interested in Hamilton's work, but the lady kept trying to subtly drag him away.

"What's up, prodigal daughter?" Johnny said. "Enjoy your night of sleep?"

"Hey brother," I said to Johnny, and squeezed him back. "Sorry about the snoring."

"What are you two up to?" Alice asked.

The girlfriend took the opportunity of distraction to drag the guy away. By the time we sat down against the wall with the guys, the couple was halfway down the block. "I was just about to make a sale. That guy wanted to buy the painting of a hero pissing against a wall holding a forty," Hamilton said, pointing to a canvas that had a man in a green suit and red cape holding an enormous beer.

"Yeah, but the lady didn't like it," I said.

Hamilton smirked. "Everything I do is for the ladies, you know." I didn't believe him for a second, but I liked his attitude. "Hey, Sarah, did you cut your hair? You look different. I like it."

I hadn't touched my hair in the Amazon. It probably looked crazy. But I liked that Hamilton was paying attention.

"How's sales?" Alice asked.

"Never took you for a capitalist," Johnny replied. It looked like they hadn't sold anything. But they said that they had been selling their wares for only a week, and the weather had been all over the place. Hamilton and Johnny made a big show of doing inventory.

The only reason Hamilton was allowed to hang outside Boscoe's, Alice explained, was because he worked there as a delivery boy. Whenever there wasn't a delivery, Hamilton could hang out front and sell his work. Johnny was in charge when he had to drop off pizzas. Hamilton had convinced Boscoe that the paintings gave the place some 'class.' The only other artwork Bosco seemed to like were gaudy murals of Sicily, which were painted on every spare scrap of wall of his pizza joint.

"What's with the shirts?" Alice asked Johnny. "Of all the crap you can sell here, why the red shirts?"

"Well, I figured there's probably going to be a lot of extras hanging around for the documentary. If they buy a shirt they stand a better chance of not getting killed. You know, red shirts always getting phasered on *Star Trek*."

Alice laughed at this. "You know you try to act cool, but deep down you're a nerd," she said. "Neeeeeeeerd. I'll buy a shirt and a slice of veggie for myself and Sarah."Hamilton added, "And a painting."

"I'm already out eight for the shirt. What's the cheapest work of genius you have for sale?"

Hamilton got up and scanned the assorted paintings. He reached behind a large canvas with a flying dog dragging a man through the air, and produced a small 8x10 canvas. He put it in Alice's hand.

"Ten bucks," he said. The painting was a fake portrait of all of us in our Halloween costumes, meant to look like a documentary poster, with the words 'The Misshapes' stenciled below it in Marquee lettering. It was incredible. I could tell from Alice's response that she wanted it.

"If you don't want it, I'll buy it," I muttered to her. Hamilton gave me another smile.

"Sold," Alice said.

Boscoe opened the door a crack and thrust out his large bald head. "Hammy-Ton. We have deliveries. Fifteen minutes or less," he said, then plodded back toward the large metal oven.

"Crap. I'll tell you what. Man my gallery, and whatever we get for the night is yours. I'll swing by when I'm done."

"Deal." Alice thrust money into his hand.

He ran back through the store and emerged seconds later with pies stacked up to his chin.

"I'll see you later at the dinner?" he asked me.

"What?" I asked back.

"Well, I was sorry about not meeting you when you got back in and with all the craziness of karaoke I figured we should have a welcome- back-Sarah dinner. It was going to be a surprise," Johnny said.

"Oh, like you letting Hamilton use my room?" I said.

"How'd you…" they both said.

"Paint on the carpet." I smiled. I could be observant.

Hamilton smacked his head with his hand and Johnny glared at him.

"Yeah. For that too. It's tonight at Jr's," Hamilton said.

"I guess I'll see you there," I said to Hamilton, and he took off with a spring in his step.

We sat outside trying to sell shirts. An hour passed. No takers. Johnny packed up shop. I had one more thing to look forward to tonight: Walt Jr.'s world-famous disco fries and breakfast food, fit for a hero or a supervillain.

SEVEN

A S WE turned the corner to my house, I heard a distinctive whooshing noise above me. Freedom Boy landed gently on his feet in front of my house and flashed his million-dollar smile.

"This putz?" Alice muttered. "Put me down for team spinster if that's the ideal man."

"Bye, Sarah," she said. "Bye, Freedork Boy" She waved. She got in her car and drove off, yelling, "See you at the diner later! Love ya!"

Freedom Boy looked at me. His green eyes twinkled. "Hi," he said. "It's been a while."

"Sorry about my friend," I said.

"She's protective. I get that. I would be too."

"Why? Do I need protecting? I thought that was your job," I replied.

"It is," he replied. "There's nothing to fear when Freedom Boy is here."

"New catch phrase?" I asked.

"Just trying it out," he said.

He seemed at a loss for words. I think Alice must have knocked him off his game and my less than warm repartee had him confused. He usually came prepared with snappier dialogue. Though it was refreshing to hear him using contractions. Perhaps his acting coach had finally rid him of that nasty tic.

He put his arms around my waist and kissed me. It almost felt like we were dating, like I should be the girl in the magazine, as I felt his strong hands on my back. When he pulled back and looked me in the eyes, I didn't feel anything, though. I remembered how he looked on the Maximus poster.

I wriggled away and put my hands on my hips. "So, how's the movie going?""Great. Just getting started. They are still writing some of it."

"And Dangerous Girl?"

With that question, his smile dropped.

"I meant to talk to you about that."

"When?" I asked. "Before you went on your walkabout? Or before you sent postcards from Europe? I try to be cool but it's really hard to come home to posters of you and some chick."

"Look, Sarah, this only happened in the past few weeks. I had nothing to do with it. One minute my dad sends me away, and the next he drags me back and the movie people take over."

Whatever. I just wanted it to be over. "Where does the danger gal fit in here?""Only for the film. They always do these things for publicity and promotion. She's actually a cool person."

"Well I know she has ventilation if that's what you mean." It was mean, I knew it, and I felt like a jerk the minute the words came out of my mouth.

"Don't be like that, Sarah. You know how the gossip rags can be. When you meet her you'll see she is actually not some stupid trollop like the magazines make her out to be." Fantastic Boy defended Dangerous Girl lamely. It sounded like a relationship that would last for the length of the contract.

"I'll meet her? What do you mean?" I said. I squinted. I didn't really want to play paddy cake with the new couple. And I wasn't so sure if I wanted to fall into some old weird tortured dynamic with Freedom Boy. There were so many boys in the world. "That's what I came here to tell you. I heard you were back and I had to see you." He seemed a bit robotic. He had dark rings around his eyes. Maybe he was being run around by his family and the movie shoot. "I have news," he said, standing on my lawn. "Good news?"

"Well, Sarah Robertson, I can't see you so much with this film filming. But I thought of an alternative. Would you like to work on the new Freedom Man feature?" "Sure. Need a caterer? I've done that before."

Freedom Boy smiled and it was like one thousand spotlights just trained on his face, highlighting his cheekbones. He had the look on his face when he made big announcements or just saved the world. "Apprentice to the head Weather Designer, Steve Kirby. Also known as the Black Zephyr."

"What? That's amazing," I yelled. I couldn't hide my excitement. The Black Zephyr was my hero.

The Weather Designer was one of the most important crew jobs for big-budget documentaries. Most films couldn't even afford one. It was a job for people with powers like me, people who could control the weather for the duration of the film's shoot. They made things look good; they made all the hectic set-up worth it. I never thought I could do it and now I can see the best in the world do it.

"Should I take that as a yes?"

I wanted to blurt out *yes* immediately, but then I remembered the Dangerous Girl pictures and the lying about the movie. Well, not lying, but pretty damn big omission. I crossed my arms on my chest and gave a resolute "Maybe. I'll have to see if I'm free."

"Well let me know. It won't be for some time, unfortunately. Probably not more than a day on set," Freedom Boy said. "I know that Doolittle Falls is excited, but most of the filming will be in Malta." So he was leaving again. And for Malta, an island off the coast of Italy.

What would tiny little Doolittle Falls have in comparison? Or me, even after everything? How could I ever measure up to Dangerous Girl?

His wrist beeped, and he looked down at a tiny digital watch. He pressed it once and before I could ask when he was going, he said, "Got to take this," and just like that, Freedom Boy flew into the sky, on another do-gooder mission. Or, more likely, a meeting with his producers.

EIGHT

A FTER MY run in with Freedom Boy, I was glad to be reunited with my friends at the diner. At least with them, I knew where I stood. Or sat, rather. I was crammed into a round silver table with Hamilton, Johnny, Butters, Rosa, the Spectors, Betty, Alice, Kurt glowering in a corner, and Wendy. They all looked flushed and healthy and they had questions about my summer adventure. I tried to explain the most exciting day over some disco fries.

"I was standing next to Sam on a pile of sand bags. It was humid. Sam was slicked over with sweat but he didn't seem to notice. We had to focus on our enemy. The angry face of Hurricane Randy bore down upon us. Its black billowing clouds unleashed bolts of lightning into the dark sky. Each bolt illuminated the massive interior of the dense cloud. The rumbles from the thunder sounded like trucks in the distance. The only thing standing between the small trailer park behind us and imminent destruction was me and Sam." I took a sip of my milkshake and narrowed my eyes. "We were going to save the world."

"OOOOOH Sam, shining like a light!" The Spectors chimed in. I blushed.

"Stop the storm, save the world?" Johnny said, waving a fry in the air. "It all sounds pretty melodramatic to me. Angry faces, billowing clouds. It was just a tropical storm." He took a sip of his Coke. "News said it was little rain."

"Will you stop interrupting me, Johnny?" I said. "It was a hurricane when it made landfall, okay? Part of the reason it was a Tropical Storm was because of the work Sam and I did."

"And the other Heroes," Hamilton said.

"And, you know, nature, the greatest Hero of all," Johnny added.

"Let her finish," Alice said, dipping a fry in a small dish of gravy. "It's just getting interesting."

"The storm was growing. The wind started to pick up. Slow at first, just enough to rumble a few cans around, and then faster and faster. The sand on the beach started to blast in our faces. I had to squint to see. Small grains felt like fire on our bare flesh. The thin metal walls of the houses behind us started to shake like sails. I thought they would topple at any moment. I heard all this rumbling."

"Burning down the house!" The Spectors sang, and Butters smirked. This wasn't a spontaneous number but a planned music cue.

"Sounds like a rhumba," Betty said. "Storm sounds are the scariest."

"They really are," I blurted. I was terrified. My foot tapped a little just remembering that storm. It had the potential for so much destruction and we slowed it down. "The houses were shaking. They sounded like tractor-trailers on a bad road, growing louder and louder as the storm approached. I knew if we didn't weaken it, at least on our front, we'd die. But the storm kept growing. A drop of rain fell on my nose. And then more and more. Soon drops turned into torrents, and I was soaked." I took a gulp of breath. Everyone was staring. "Even in our waterproof clothes the dampness got in. Wind pulled at our jackets, pressing them tight against our skin. The last remnants of light dispersed as the storm took over the sky, filling it with its inky blackness. Sam and I were alone facing the monster. We were supposed to have reinforcements. Several other anemoitians were supposed to come to back us up but there were called away to help other areas along the coast."

"Anemoitians?" asked Hamilton.

"Weather controllers," Alice whispered and gave me a glance to say keep going. "Wait, wait, wait. Where were these other anemoitians? Why was it just you and a junior Hero? No offense, but shouldn't the big guns be there?" Kurt blurted.

"They were at the 'important' places," I replied.

"Oh, I get it. Rich people. They sent the real Heroes to protect the coastal mansions from damage and the JV squad had to actually save people," Kurt said.

"Sure. Can I just finish, though?" I asked.

I didn't like having Kurt around. Not after what he did last year. I didn't know what Johnny saw in him or why they kept talking to each other. After what he did to the Aqua Kid... it was scary. And yet my brother still hung out with Kurt, even though the incident at the river had just made him grow angrier and cockier and more gloom and doom about the world and liable to go into speeches about the world's inherent crappiness.

Worst of all, he wasn't wrong. That's why I shivered. Kurt scared me because he was so close to having a righteous cause, but he was like a gymnast who blew the landing every time. People who are almost right, who walk the line of truth but turn sharply before getting there, are the most dangerous people. But I hated that this time, Kurt *was* right. There should have been Anemoitians beside us to fight the storm. They were saving property instead of people. PeriGenomics did charitable work, but it wasn't a charity. That was just a side arm of a corporation.

But I knew where his argument led and it wasn't pretty. Just like there should have been more repercussions after what the Academy and Dr. Mann tried to do. There should've been an investigation. We had practically been killed. But Kurt took these things as a sign that Heroes were the villains and we were within our right to fight back. To him, a preemptive strike wasn't just justified; it was a moral imperative. He was a bomb, ticking faster and faster, and I didn't want him to hurt my brother when he finally went off.

"Whatever," Alice said. "They didn't need those sell-outs. Right, Sarah?"

"Hell no, we didn't need them!" I said, boosted by Alice. "When that wind started picking up, Sam and I rocked it. We knocked the storm out of the way and kept the trailers and people stuck there safe from any harm. Not a single place was ruined. And then everything outside our little safety zone was decimated. Trees down, streams flooded, structures literally lifted off their foundations. But for the people near us, save some loose gutters and a few shattered windows, it was like a drizzly day. Sam and Sarah 1, Hurricane Randy 0." I put my milkshake on the table with a flourish. I went away this summer and I came back with a story. It felt good. It was like my friends knew that I did things, that I was different than I had been before.

But it wasn't the whole story.

There was a strange thing that happened when I fought the storm with Sam. It was as if our powers combined, like we were one. Like the time we made snow in that field before he had to fly away. But stronger, more powerful.

"So, wait, after you and Sam saved the day your other boyfriend Freedom Boy swooped in and got all the cats out of the trees," Hamilton said while dabbing paint from his glasses. He was wearing a shirt that had "Genius Child" printed on it.

"He is not my boyfriend," I protested. He was something, I guess. It was hard to be my boyfriend when he was always away and showing up everywhere with and armful of Danger.

"This summer was so weird," Butters said. "There was a distinct lack of Freedom Man defeating some major crime syndicate when the news cycle gets slow. Or at least a supervillain."

"Lady, La-deeeeee La-deeee Oblivion!" The Spectors sang.

"Coming for you!" My eyes went wide. Why would they sing about my mother?

"Ugh, god, ladies, stop it," Butters asked. "Please?"

"What's with that, Butters?" Johnny asked in a low voice. "You know my mother is not a supervillain."

"They saw the teaser trailer," Butters said.

"I'm soooo sorry!" Doris belted. "Lady is the catchiest backup word, you know."

"It's my fault," Butters blurted. "I shouldn't have let them see it."

Betty grabbed his arm and nuzzled up beside him. It was so sickeningly sweet I forgot about the Lady Oblivion reference. It felt nice to be back in Doolittle Falls with my friends. It seemed like the same, but I felt like a completely different collection of molecules in the same old booth at the diner. I wondered what this year would bring.

Just then a commercial came on in the TV in the corner for some Sentinel Alarm Company. The main robber trying to break into the house seemed to have powers, but Misshapey ones. Kurt and Johnny groaned in unison. When the robber phased through the window a red light blinked and a bunch of Heroes showed up, led by Freedom Man.

"When regular security isn't enough," he said to the viewers, "get the Sentinel. Endorsed by me, Freedom Man. Because Freedom isn't Free."

"He's got such a lame catchphrase," Hamilton chimed in.

"It took the team at the Kill Building six months to hone it, I heard," said Rosa. She had, to our relief, not been expelled. But since the incident on the Miskatonic she had been on thin ice at the Academy, and they were constantly threatening her with expulsion for associating with us.

"The Kill Building?" Betty asked.

"Yeah, it's this old company, been around since the Forties, that does 'Hero Management.' Basically they come up with catchphrases, theme songs, and scripts for Docs," Butters said. "The Spectors dream about going there."

"It's truuuuuuueeeeeee," they sang.

"Have you guys heard about Freedom Boy's doc?" Rosa asked.

Everyone rolled their eyes. I just kept my mouth shut.

But before I could get too morose, another commercial bleated throughout the restaurant. It was for the upcoming presidential election. Vice President Bergeron was shown walking around Doolittle Falls.

Rosa made a face at the screen. "That guy's the worst. My crazy aunt hates him.""Why?" Alice asked. "He's fine, right?" Kurt rolled his eyes.

"She was like an anarchist punk or something and hates all politicians," Rosa shrugged.

Alice's ears perked up. "A what? Really? Tell me more!"

"She was in a punk band in East L.A. in the Seventies. And did a lot of activist stuff in the Eighties and Nineties."

"What! What band?" Alice started tapping her fingers on the table. "Maybe she can give us some pointers."

"Yeah, like how to get some gigs," Johnny said.

"Or you know, how to write a song with more than two chords," Alice added.

"It had three!" my brother protested. He and Alice were so buddy-buddy.

"If you're interested you can ask her yourself. She's coming to my tio's moratorium party at our house tomorrow," Rosa offered.

"A party?" Johnny said. His eyes lit up. He was already there.

NINE

ROSA LIVED on the East Side of town near the hospital. Johnny drove and we got Alice and Hamilton on the way. Butters and Betty bailed last minute. According to Johnny, this summer Butters had been disappearing a lot to practice for Karaoke. Betty must have been really into him if she was willing to subject herself not only to Karaoke, but to Karaoke practice.

"So what exactly is a Moratorium party?" I asked. "Is it like, come to my party or else?"

"Wouldn't that be an Ultimatum Party?" Alice asked.

"True," I said. "Johnny, do you know?"

"Nope," said Johnny. "I was afraid to ask. She acted like it was something everyone had."

"I thought you would have spent all night researching it," Alice said sharply.

"Wiki your way to her corazon," I said giggling. Alice gave me a weird look. I was right though. Evidence at the house—including a Netflix queue that was all movies and docs by Alfonso Cuaron—showed that Johnny was still trying to learn Spanish.

"Shut up, man, she's just a friend," Johnny said.

Turned out that Hamilton actually knew what kind of party we were attending. He turned around from the front seat and told us all about it. "A moratorium was an important event in the Chicano Rights movement in Los Angeles. The Chicano Moratorium was a citywide march and protest inspired because of the poor treatment of Chicano citizens. A large number of them were dying in Vietnam, too, and they wanted everybody to know about it through their protest."

"Like the Misshape marches up in San Francisco in the Nineties," Johnny said. "Basically," Hamilton said, "until they shot some reporter for no reason. Then everything changed."

"Who shot him?" Alice asked.

"The cops. He was just sitting at a diner. And no one was ever held accountable."

"That's messed up," I said.

"Yup," said Hamilton. "Funny how when protests end violence, it's always those looking for change who get hurt, not those with power."

"Does this mean that Rosa's family are Latino revolutionaries?" I asked.

"Chicano," Alice corrected.

"What?" I asked.

"Chicanos are people whose families are from Mexico. Latino is anyone from South America. It was a Chicano Moratorium, not Latino. Latino is just something that politicians like Bergeron made up so they can say something in bad Spanish and hope to win an election."

"Well, yes and no," said Hamilton.

The two of them started arguing about Latino and Chicano identity and politics. Hamilton pulled up some Chicano Moratorium information on his phone and gave more details. Considering none of us was in either group, I figured it was probably best to get Rosa's thoughts and stay out of the discussion. I read over Hamilton's shoulder while Johnny pulled up to Rosa's house.

Her block was starkly different from most of Doolittle Falls. It wasn't as self-consciously quaint, with manicured trees lining the wide sidewalks. Rosa's block had small box houses with vinyl siding, no sidewalk, and small yards which ended in a gravely rut in the street. Fire hydrants were askew, placed at random in the middle of people's lawns. The cars were older models and looked weary.

We got out and knocked on the front door. The house looked empty. No one came to the door.

"Where's the party? Where's Rosa's aunt?" Alice asked.

"It's kind of quiet," Hamilton said. "Maybe we should check around back.""What if we have the wrong house?" I asked.

"No loss. It's not like we're breaking in," Johnny said.

I looked at Alice. Her face lit up. Her spidey-senses were tingling. "I think I smell BBQ," Alice said as she sprinted to the back. Hamilton and Johnny followed behind her. I followed along but they were all way ahead of me.

The minute we turned the corner I heard music and knew there was a party back there. Maybe not Rosa's party, but a party at the least. There were decorations strung along the trees, two men arguing over a large grill that was smoking, a bunch of middle-aged men and women sitting around a long wood tables, children running around chasing each other with water guns, and small groups on lawn chairs talking. Mostly people ignored us, except for one older woman whose eyes narrowed as she looked at us. Probably because we were strangers.

I felt shy and hid behind my brother. Alice, full of bravado, walked up to the grill. "Tremerato family?" she asked.

One of the men nodded. Alice put her hand out, like she was going to shake his hand, and he gave her a hot dog in return. More hot dogs and an enormous hunk of pork shoulder was sizzling up on the grill. I wanted to eat all of it. My stomach rumbled. I was starving. One of us stayed focused.

"Is Rosa here?" Johnny asked.

The man with the tongs handing out the hot dogs glared at him and pointed to a woman in sundress with a purple bob. She was talking to a few people, but we couldn't see them.

"Rosa!" he shouted. "Misshapes están aquí."

How did he know us? I wondered. And why the attitude?

Rosa popped her head out from the small crowd and gave the man a death stare. If she had laser eyes he would have been incinerated. She smiled at us and ushered us back to her seat. "Guys! I'm so glad you made it. Sorry about the cold shoulder from some of the family. I don't have many friends come over. My family's all super weird. Speaking of weird, meet my Tia Teresa."

We introduced ourselves to the women with the purple hair. She was in her fifties but seemed young for her age. She had on cat-eye makeup. On her dress was a small black button that said, "Ape Sex."

"Hi Tia," I said shaking her hand.

"You can just call me Teresa," she replied, shaking back.

Rosa was happy to see us, but I could sense that the way the man treated us bothered her. She said something in Spanish to Teresa. She sounded annoyed and Teresa answered back in a manner that sounded soothing. Rosa offered to get us some food and got up, leaving us alone with Teresa.

"I don't know Spanish but I do know drama. In any language," Alice said.

"I seriously doubt that squirrels have drama," Hamilton replied.

"What's with the vibe, though?" Alice asked. She was talking to the aunt.

"Well," Teresa started. I could hear a mental ellipses as she considered what these stranger kids could hear about their friend. "Rosa's Uncle Mike wasn't happy about what happened with her and the Academy. They've been threatening to throw her out because of the big fight last year, which would mean her dad and family might have to move back."

"That's ridiculous," Hamilton said. "She was fighting for us against a maniac.""I know. And they know," Teresa said, smiling. "I think you guys were so brave. And Rosa is the most brave! But Mike thinks she should have kept her head down and stayed out of it. There's never been a Hero in the family before, a Misshape or two, but she was the golden child since she got that letter from the Academy. Me, I think it would be good for her to stop going there."

"Why's that?" I asked.

"It's a school of violence. All they teach is fighting and warfare and how to resolve conflict with your fists. My sobrina's better than that. Did you know that's she's a beautiful musician? Better than I ever was."

Johnny had hearts coming out of his eyeballs. "For real?" he said. "What instrument?"

"Guitar mostly. Bass as well. Anything with strings really. It's the vibrations. But with her powers it's hard to control."

In the background we could hear Rosa whisper-fighting with her Uncle Mike. We tried to ignore it. Teresa could see our discomfort. "Don't worry. She can handle herself."

We stood in awkward silence. Alice broke it. "Rosa said you used to play yourself. A band in L.A. or something?"

Teresa smiled. "I've been in a few actually. Pretty obscure though."

Alice got excited. She was always talking about music and bands but other than practicing her drums and listening to music on the Internet, I don't know if she'd ever met a real musician before. She leaned in, like she wanted to interview Teresa on a TV show.

"Please," said Alice with a confidence that she normally had with me. "I know lots of bands."

"She does," I concurred.

"Ever hear of Banquet or The Jerks?" Teresa asked.

Alice wound up her face. I could tell the names didn't ring a bell but she wanted to think about it and try really, really hard before admitting it. Teresa jumped in before she could feel embarrassed.

"Don't worry. Each band only had a record apiece and they're pretty hard to come by. We were a dirty little punk band. Loud, fast, and angry."

"Like X and the Germs?" Johnny asked. Hamilton looked bored. He wasn't quite the wannabe punk that Johnny and Alice were at heart.

"A little like them but we were from East L.A. We played with them a few times and I knew Exene a little. But we were mostly playing at a place called The Vex with other Chicano punk bands."

"Still, I figured, I would have heard of them in passing somewhere," Alice said. "I thought I knew about every band ever that I should know about, right?"

Teresa's reply was philosophical. "Power exists everywhere. Even among outcasts. When history is written, they select the stories they want to hear. Most of the historians don't want to hear our stories." That was straight out of Howard Winn's line of thought, like what I read in *A Misshapes' History of the United States* last year.

"East L.A. punk rock is just written out of the history books?" Hamilton asked. Teresa nodded.

Rosa came back to our group, flustered. Strands of hair framed her face, her complicated updo wilted.

"You okay?" Teresa asked.

"Yeah, I'm fine. I heard you boring them to death with your punk rock war stories." She winked.

"We're not bored," Alice said.

"What did they think of your music?" Hamilton said pointing to a group of more conservatively dressed family members.

Teresa smiled. "Not fans. It was weird because we were outsiders among the other punks and outsider among our own people. It's like the Chicano moratorium. It was inclusive as long as you toed the line. They had trouble seeing I could be both part of their movement and do my own thing. It's like you. You're Misshapes but that's not all that you are."

"I feel like you're saying that we need to take our band to the next level," Johnny intoned.

Teresa laughed. We all joined in. Out of everything she said that that was his takeaway was funny.

But he persisted. He looked like he was going to explode with happiness. It was a rare look for him. "I mean, we have a band. But a better band."

"Although if you don't want to, you don't have to," Alice said.

"What are you talking about? You're always saying we need a lead guitarist," Johnny said.

"Your tia said you can play guitar," Hamilton said to Rosa. "Any they do need a better guitarist. Johnny kind of sucks."

"Hey," Johnny protested.

Alice looked annoyed by the exchange. I couldn't figure out what she had against Rosa.

"I'm not that good. And you know, with the powers, I can't play."

"Oh, nonsense," Teresa said to Rosa. "You should see her play," she said to us, then back to Rosa, "If you use the chair you're fine."

"What chair?" Hamilton asked. Rosa took us to the basement. It was your standard basement but in the center there was an elaborate chair made of wood and metal bars. It looked like one of those space ring rides you find at an amusement park. A chair in the center enmeshed in a web of wooden reeds that looked like a nest. The wooden reeds were suspended by taut metal cables that attached to three concentric solid metal rings. The rings were attached to a pivot that was held in place by a rigid square metal frame. It was a giant gyroscope with a chair in the center.

"It's called an aerotrim," Rosa said, shrugging. "My dad built it. He's really handy. It's modified to disperse any vibrations I cast off so I don't inadvertently start an earthquake. He built me one in Mexico before we moved up to here, when I had no way to control my powers and no one to teach me."

She sat down in the center and asked for us to hand her an

acoustic guitar hanging on the wall. Next to it was a refulgent green electric guitar that sparkled like dewy grass at sunrise.

"Sure you don't want the Gibson?" Johnny asked.

"This thing isn't that strong," Rosa said. "I haven't been able to play that in years."

Rosa strummed the strings on the guitar and the wooden reeds began to vibrate as well. The vibrations were dampened by the device and by the time they got to the metal frame were dead. But it gave the effect that Rosa was playing the chair and aerotrim as well, which gave off a low warbling hum.

After playing a few more chords and tuning the instrument—I guess creating tremors probably knocks guitars out of tune quickly— she started playing a song. I was expecting something quite and gentle, but it was fast and raucous. She sang along with it but looked down at the guitar, trying not to watch us as she played. Alice tapped her feet."El clavo de noche/Nos habla con bote/Nos hablan sus manos/Noche tras noche, noche tras noche," she sang.

The chair was shaking. The wheels started to spin, and by the time she finished I could swear she was going to knock the whole house down. But it worked, and the outside only vibrated mildly.

When she handed Alice back the guitar any annoyance or animosity was gone from Alice's face. She looked at Johnny in the eyes and said, "Okay. So when do we start practice? And where do we get one of those things?"

TEN

THE BAND had collected at my house, so I went into town. I wasn't really up for the early garage sessions of Nicholas Cage Fight. School was about to start up and I needed to stock up on supplies anyway.

"Sarah! What's up?" Hamilton said. He was walking down Main Street, probably en route to Boscoe's.

"Absolutely nothing," I replied. I wanted to get to the bookstore. But Hamilton pulled my hand, dragging me over to a telephone pole with a large poster on it.

"Did you see this?" he asked. I looked. It was a large poster stapled to the telephone pole, advertising an art show. It was a painting in a classic Saturday morning cartoon style of Freedom Man surrounded by adoring women, with the words "Another White Hero." Above the image was an announcement for a retrospective on the N.W.C. collective at Mass MoCa. Mass MoCa was a giant art museum an hour away in northwestern Massachusetts in an old industrial park.

"First I saw, man. Seems cool," I said, "but who are they?"

"It's a group of black artists. Musicians, writers, painters, and designers who focus on American hero culture," Hamilton said.

"And its limitations."

"What does NWC stand for? New White Capes?" I asked.

"Niggas With Capes," Hamilton said. "It's meant to be provocative."

Oh. The word stood in the air, uncomfortably. There weren't a lot of black people in Doolittle Falls. It was the first time I had heard someone say that word aloud. It should've been okay since Hamilton said it, but I didn't really know what to say in response.

Hamilton, not wanting to be distracted by my inability to navigate racial semiotics, got back to the point. "Stop thinking about the word. I'll play you A Tribe Called Quest song if you want to know more." He paused. "So we're going, right?"

I smiled. "Absolutely nothing is happening. The band is practicing. Let's get the troop together tomorrow or so."

Hamilton gave me a big smile, and I went onto the bookstore with a spring in my step.

The next day, a big group gathered for the road trip. We split up into two cars: Johnny, Butters, and Hamilton in one, Alice, Rosa, Betty, and me in the other. I was a little afraid whether Alice's car could handle the trip, but she assured me it was fine. Her car was not doing well. At sixteen it was almost as old as me and was held together with duct tape and bolted-on parts her brother had rigged up. The muffler, as it was, whinnied when the car was in neutral. She didn't like to drive it any farther than the next town over, and on the journey west, we had to hold our breath a few times when there were any hills.

Alice, having gotten over her lingering annoyance with Rosa, chatted with her about the band the whole times while Betty texted Butters on her phone and asked me about different karaoke-related performance questions he was sending her way. I felt left out. Shouldn't Alice have been trying to talk to me more than Rosa, anyways, as my best friend?

Betty interrupted Alice during one spiel. "Why can't Butters be in the band? Add Butters and you get a whole chorus."

"I'm not sure we're going for the big wall of sound thing," Alice said.

"Punk band," Rosa added. "But maybe." She didn't want to disappoint Betty.Not getting the hint, Betty kept going. "You should totally take him in. Besides, what classic album doesn't have good back-up singers? Stones, Bowie, all of them. 'You Can't Always Get What You Want,' 'Gimme Shelter,' 'Young Americans... '" She trailed off.

Alice said, "Let's see if we can write a few good songs before adding a big chorus."

Rosa grimaced. I think Betty was wearing them down. "We have to talk to Johnny, too, Betty. The band is a democracy."

Rosa turned around and looked at me trying to change the subject. "How's Freedom Boy, Sarah?" I was glad to be included, but I didn't want to talk about him."Making his Freedom documentary. I think he's in Malta. What have you heard?" I asked.

"Academy gossip. You know how it is," said Betty.

"I don't know how he is," I replied. "Flies in. Offers me a dream job. Flies off. I barely see him. And when I do, he's on T.V. arm-in-arm with Dangerous Chest."

"Stop reading the gossip rags," Alice told me. "And forget about that guy."

"Well, whatever. He's not my boyfriend and I could care less if I ever saw him again," I said, not even believing it myself.

"His dad's docs have a much better ring in Spanish. *Hombre Libre*," Rosa said. "That last one he did was the top grossing film in Mexican history."

"Well, if Freedom Boy's off limits, then what's up with Sam?" Alice asked.

"He is so hot." Betty and Rosa said in near-unison.

"Maybe. If he ever sticks around long enough. Doesn't anyone else in this car have a love life that's interesting besides me?" They all turned and glared at me.

"Sorry, I just don't want to talk about Sam or Freedom Boy," I said. I looked outside and the wind seemed kind of gusty. If there was one thing I didn't feel confident about, it was boys.

The car went silent. It seemed like Rosa and Alice wanted to say something but held their tongues. After a long minute, Alice said, "Hey, I think that's it up there."

We met the boys in the parking lot. I'd never been to the museum before and it was really cool. Large brick buildings sprawled out in every direction, some crumbling into the ground holding the remnants of rested iron machines, and others pristine and washed. Large signs directed us to the galleries.

Inside the main building there was a large spacious hall where children ran around while their parents looked at books and ordered food at a corner snack bar. They kept some of the old machines scattered around the main hall: a large metal seesaw, enormous cogs attached to axels in the walls, circuit boards with glass tubes and thick, unused cable spooling out like a flower.

Once we got inside the gallery, we circled the art like cats around a new toy, not sure about how we were supposed to interact with it. I got more interested in the way Hamilton looked at art. He walked right up to every piece and thrust his nose into it, like he was sniffing it out. He examined each brushstroke, plaster or stone statute, and hanging metal doodad like he wanted to get inside of it.

There were enormous paintings, elaborate graffiti murals on the walls, and sprawling sculptures made out of everything from used Coke bottles to gold leaf sculptures. An enormous mural that was one hundred feet long took up one large wall. It had a series of Misshapes of all sizes, shapes, and colors with their backs to viewer, their power labeled in a cloud over their head. I looked closer and realized that all the Misshapes were in handcuffs or pushed up against a wall, a stark juxtaposition with the smiling Heroes posing every ten feet or so, looking straight out of a 1950s advertisement. The piece was labeled Broken Windows = Broken Youth.

Hamilton spent an extra amount of time in front of this piece. There was a lot to take in. For him, there was meaning in every corner. "See the materials?" he said. "The Misshapes are in oil whereas a lot of the Hero pictures are literally 1950s advertisements, taken from *LIFE Magazine*. He melted some Freedom Man action figures for this piece."

He paused and glanced beyond me toward a shadowy figure at the end of the gallery. I saw his jaw go slack and his cheeks drop. The last time I saw such naked hero-worship was when Freedom Boy walked down Main Street.

"What is it, hambone?" Johnny said.

"It's him."

"Who?" Alice asked.

"NOYO."

"Who?" I said.

He pointed to the name. At the bottom right, in large letters, was the word NOYO in blue letters.

"He founded N.W.C. He was, like, one of the first graffiti artists."

"Your hero," Johnny mocked. "He's your hero!"

"Shut up, man," Hamilton said trying to hide in his embarrassment.

"Go talk to him," I said.

"I can't," Hamilton blushed.

"Of course you can," I replied. I pointed at a particularly destroyed Freedom Man figurine on the mural, whose entire lower half dripped off the canvas. "You shot a paintball at the kids of Doolittle Falls' most famous Heroes. You'll have tons to talk about."

He thought about it for a second, squared his shoulders, and said, "You're right." He walked down the gallery up to NOYO, and

Alice said, "Go get him!"

I could faintly hear Hamilton yell "Shut up."

I surreptitiously watched Hamilton out of the corner of my eyes. He sheepishly introduced himself to NOYO and started a conversation. It started out awkward, but once I moved on to another gallery, I saw Hamilton's posture improve, and he pulled out his phone to show NOYO pictures of his work, nodding eagerly while the artist talked. The next gallery was an enormous room the size of an airport hanger covered from floor-to-ceiling in multicolored fabric with fake Hero logos on them. It looked like a massive amount of capes just lined up like soldiers. Something whizzed past me. It was a sculpture of a Hero, made out of mirrored glass, attached to a track flying around the room. It was easy to get lost in all the capes, and I was soon separated from the group. I decided to cut out and head someplace a little less overwhelming. I walked through a few passageways and ended up in a smaller room with a bench in it. Hamilton was sitting on the bench. He looked deep in thought, though with his glasses on he could have also been deep into a nap.

"Hi Hamilton," I said quietly, in case he was asleep.

"Hey," he said.

"Enjoy the show?" I asked.

"Yeah, it's really cool." He seemed quiet. Lost in thought.

"So how'd it go? With NOYO I mean," I asked.

It took him a while to find the right words. "Weird. Good I guess. I don't know what to make of it." He looked out into the distance.

"Why, what happened?"

"Well, he was really nice. Like super nice. Though it took him a while to realize I was serious about wanting to be an artist. And when he did, he looked at my work, said it was all crap but I had some promise, and that I should stop with the graffiti nonsense." "Wait, but isn't he a graffiti artist?" I asked. That was the opposite of encouragement, I thought.

"That's what I said. And he said no. He was an artist first. That was just a medium he used." Hamilton's hand tapped on his thigh.

"What's so wrong with graffiti, though? He has this super cool show," I said. It kind of made no sense to me.

"Look, NOYO is the real thing. He apparently disavows all his former work. Says it only got big because when he was coming up, galleries wanted work not because it was good but because he seemed dangerous. It was authentic: street art from a black kid." He stopped. "Then when NOYO started selling, his friends were pulled off streets tagging, put in galleries, and the owners made millions off their work." His voice got quieter. "After the black graffiti trend passed, they were let go and went back to being punks. Some of them joined N.W.C., but most disappeared." Hamilton mentioned that he wanted to track some of them down. So many great graffiti artists had their moment, it passed, and then they were just spit back into the world. Maybe they'd have advice, too.

"That's screwed up," I said. "Did he give you any actual advice?"

"He was real. He was honest. He said get a studio. Or a closet. Or a shack. Something where I can focus on the work. Paint anything. Canvas if I can get my hands on it, discarded wood boards if I can't. And study. The greats and the hacks. That way, even if I get big, I'll still be tied to some crazy art market but at least it will be for the work and not the racist nonsense of my image. The work will be better."

"That's amazing," I said.

"I know. I still can't believe it. He also said, whenever I graduate, I have to move to NY, and when I do, I should look him up."

That was big. I knew that was big. Hamilton was going to get to leave Doolittle Falls. I could see it happening. "Are you going to do it?" I asked.

"Yeah. I have to." He paused. "Thanks."

"For what?"

"Making me talk to him."

"I just nudged you. You impressed him."

"I guess. But the support was nice," he said. "I mean it might seem like I'm fooling around, I do a lot of fooling around, but real support, well… it means a lot."

He took off his glasses. I had known Hamilton for a long time, years even, but I had never seen him without his glasses. I had wondered sometimes what it looked like under there, whether he was hiding something from the world, but mostly I just imagined Hamilton as a guy who was constantly wearing glasses.

To my surprise, he looked perfectly normal, except for his irises. I had never seen anything like them. They were multi-hued filled with swirling clouds and skeins of purple, pink, green, blue, yellow, orange, colors in brilliant hues and infinite variations circling each other around a dark black pupil. My brother's punk friend—a kid who was barely above a class clown to me—had very pretty eyes and was looking at me earnestly. It was enough to send a shudder down my spine. I smiled back and I got up to see another piece of art.

ELEVEN

HAMILTON AND Johnny had plans to go see some haunted mill or something so Alice drove the girls home from Mass MoCA. Once she got back to town, Alice went a weird, circular route. Instead of dropping me off first, she let off Betty, drove all the way to the edge of town to let off Rosa. After we said our goodbyes to Rosa, we were alone in the car, and she drove all the way south to Marston Heights, which was completely out of the way. It was, however, the first quality time I had with Alice, real quality time, since I had returned.

"Hi," I said. "How are you? It's been so busy since I've gotten back," I said.

The Germs played on the stereo. Alice's hands were tight on the wheel. "Look, Sarah, I wanted to drive you home last," she paused. Taking a breath, the next words came out in a rush. "I had something to say to you."

When people make sure to say out loud that they need to talk to you, it's not a good thing. It's a buffer for bad news, sad news, weird news. It was like that with Mom. I felt a hole in the pit of my stomach. I felt my body go tense. I looked outside at the sky and the town appearing below us as we descended from The Heights. The sunny, clear, blue color blinked at me, slowly moving toward purple.

"Just say it, I guess," I said. "Spit it out."

We drove past the Harpastball Field, and on to Main Street. "It sucked that you weren't here this summer. I didn't have anything to do." I nodded. "So I started hanging out with Johnny."

I felt a sharp pain in my back. Alice looked tense. Weird things started blowing in front of our car. A garden hose. A trash can. An upturned bag of garbage.

"So we're a thing," Alice said. "Me and Johnny. We're seeing each other. We started the band this summer as like, a thing to do, and we ended up making out after fighting. And we'll that's kind of how things went."

I felt like a record scratch. I felt awfully trapped in Alice's death trap. My best friend and my brother? This combination was wrong. How did this happen? Was it my fault? Did Alice use me to get to Johnny, or did my brother bother to hang out with me because of Alice? I couldn't imagine either situation with pleasure. It felt like an utter betrayal. The exact thing of a girl's nightmares. Neither my brother or my best friend liked me for me; they liked me for some other dumb reason. Alice had continued talking but I couldn't hear a word.

"… there was Freedom Boy, and Sam, and all this excitement and it was like you were the star of something and I was just the sidekick. And whatever, that's not true, but it was lame. Plus Johnny and I both missed you."

"Why would you tell me in the car?" I squeaked. "I just want to go home, Alice. Let me out." I pulled on the door handle but the door was locked and jammed.

Alice stopped short with a squeal. "Stop it, you insane girl!" she said. "It wasn't going to be easy to tell you, and I just wanted to be able to tell you without you running away. I knew you'd run away."

I curled up into a ball with my back to Alice. "Can you just take me home? I can't believe that my best friend is now with my brother. It's completely wrong."

We drove back in silence.

Alice slowed down in front of my house, unlocked the car, and I left without looking back. "I'm mad at both of you," I said, slamming the car door. I was a stew of emotions. I ran into the house, trying not to let Alice catch the tears coming down my face. The house was being pummeled by rain, snow, and blustery winds.

TWELVE

DAD WAS scheduled to return a couple of days later. I had spent most of those days in my room, chatting online with Sam and guiltily reading Freedom Boy gossip. I felt betrayed but didn't want to admit it. By him, by Alice, by my brother. I assume Alice told Johnny that she had told me, but I avoided Johnny, and he didn't seem like he wanted to broach the topic. I spent my time getting ready for school, speeding through summer reading and practicing my powers by the river.

When I was alone by the river I thought about my mother. How she swooped in, helped save the day, and flew off. I wondered where she could be. Just as that thought crossed my mind, I got a shiver. The clouds cleared for a moment, and a streak of sunlight twinkled on the crests of waves. It was as if a chorus of hosannas proclaimed what I actually should be focusing my energies: no more hanging out with The Misshapes.

No more trying to be a Hero or obsessing about the Hero Academy, or Hero movies, or Hero TV shows. No more obsessing over Freedom Boy and Freedom Boy-related gossip. There was only one person I wanted to save—my Mom. If I was stuck in Doolittle

Falls I was going to do something useful. I had to find out what happened to Lady Oblivion. I had to find out how my mother, the dean of Hero Academy, was framed and turned into Supervillain Most Wanted #1. I wasn't going to let some stupid movie define for the world who she is.

Maybe if I solved the mystery I'd see her again. Since the battle there hadn't been too much time for reflection, for confusion, for wondering why my mother came back to Doolittle Falls for one last battle. But my mother was out there. She was alive. And if I could find out what happened to her, maybe she could be my mother again.

The day Dad was coming home, Johnny knocked on my door. I was sitting at my computer looking at a Reddit thread on the Djed. It was hard to sort out the nuts with facts from the nuts who were being fed messages by the aliens.

"You're not going to find anything worth your time on there," he said.

"What would you know?" I asked. He had interrupted me.

"A lot. I spent months looking up the Djed," he replied.

"Uh, huh," I said, not looking up. I didn't think my brother would be able to help me.

"There's a good BBS on the dark web. Mostly legit. Crazy stuff, half mystical half deranges, but some evidence to back it up." Johnny leaned against the doorframe, pointing his fingers as he talked.

"Really. The Dark Web?"

"It just means you won't find it on a search engine."

"So I take it you stopped looking into mom when you found a new *project*. Something else to take up your time." I knew I was being a bitch, but this Johnny and Alice thing bugged the heck out of me. It was hard not to be a little passive aggressive.

"I heard she told you." Silence on my end. He sure could be captain obvious when he wanted to be. "I was hoping you'd be happy.

Or at least, not unhappy." He looked at me. I looked at the computer. "Look, she's your friend. You two can sort it out. I'm keeping out of it."

"Good idea," I muttered. I felt like Johnny had broken a code or something. Or maybe I broke the code. Or maybe Alice did it. I wasn't sure who deserved my enmity. All I knew was that I was mad. There was nothing more frustrating than your best friend dating your brother. Ominous fog leaked through my bedroom window.

Johnny looked at the fog and laughed. "Good luck, sis. So we're kinda square, let me tell you this: if you really want to find out more about Mom I can give you what I've found so far. You're smarter than me, maybe you'll dig something up."

He was buttering me up. This meant he was about to ask for something. "But if I give you this, I need one thing." He paused. "Please, please, please help me with the cleaning."

I smiled. The house was super messy. It had been gross since Dad went on vacation, and I wasn't going to raise a finger until I saw Johnny—who had caused most of it—start to pick up. Especially since he was the only guy who could get it clean, considering his power made everything antibacterial.

"Okay. But not for you, for Dad," I said. "I'm still mad at you for dating my best friend. You can't be mean to her, you know."

We spent the day scrubbing and cleaning the place to perfection. When Dad came in the door, the house was gleaming. Sparkling. You could eat a meal off the floor. It was a stark contrast to Dad, who looked woody and bearded in a big plaid jacket. He seemed different than when I'd seen him last, more ebullient and talkative. He told us about the woods and trees and birds and I told him about my summer as best I could. Things had seemed fine on the phone when I talked to him—once he stopped yelling at me—but now, in person, it seemed like something was up. He was too interested, too posed for us. It was like he was hiding something.

When he went upstairs to put down his things and shower

properly for the first time in a week, Johnny leaned over and whispered to me, "He saw Mom."

I nodded. That idea made a lot of sense. "Why? Don't you think he would tell us?"

"Remember how secretive and scared she was? I doubt it. It would be too dangerous."

It was odd that just as I was about to come home Dad went on vacation, springing it on me last minute. It sucked coming home to an empty house. I thought he would have at least waited for my return.

"You may be right," I said, playing dumb. "But why wouldn't he tell us? He could bring back a message or something."

"Too risky," Johnny said. "Not with Dad working at PeriGenomics and all that happened last year."

"Now he's happy, I guess, but what happens when the high wears off?" I asked. "Remember two years ago? When he came back from the conference all excited and then spent the next two months moping around, watching TV and eating ice cream," Johnny said.

"That was you," I corrected.

"No. Well, yeah, I did that a little too. I'd just gotten kicked out of the Academy. But you don't remember?"

I wracked my brain. I did remember. I just didn't want to admit it. "You know, yeah. I do. That was kind of scary."

We were silent. "Johnny, I don't want to go on like this. Seeing Dad zig and zag according to whether or not Mom's alive or meeting secretly with him."

"Agreed."

Again, another silence. Only the sound of Dad's shower running upstairs, a steady stream of water. "That's why I think I need to find out the truth about Mom. I helped clean, now get me up to speed."

A few minutes later Johnny came into my room with a bankers box filled with papers and an assortment of flash drives. He spent the night walking me through the materials, information on the Djed, on

PeriGenomics, on Innsmouth, on a series of people I'd never heard of. None of it made any sense. It was a series of leads that ended abruptly in dead ends, inchoate theories, incomplete images, and half-thunk thoughts. It made me even more confused than ever. The only thing that really stuck was from a tax filling Johnny had dug up, which showed that during the year of the Innsmouth disaster, Mom was on PeriGenomics board of directors along with Bergeron, J4, Freedom Man and with Dr. Mann. There was something to this that Johnny wasn't seeing. Over and over I thought about it, wondering what clue it revealed. I would have to use Johnny's information but start my own search. Fresh eyes, fresh mind, fresh ideas.

With the help of Teresa, Dad let The Red Shirts—their name du Jour—practice in the garage. I couldn't believe it. It was all Teresa's fault. She was maybe the strongest force in the universe I had ever encountered. I've seen people stop trains and wrestle an army of gorillas, but none of that paled in comparison to her powers. Her brothers moved the aerotrim to our garage despite their problem with Misshapes.

Dad was putty in Teresa's hands. I was impressed. After she was gone and the areotrim was taking up the space reserved for his car in the winter, he was still stunned as to why he said yes. And her only power seemed to be enthusiasm and the love of rock. "Would you rather have them making a racket in your garage or getting into real trouble?" she had said. Whenever Dad had a good counterpoint, she started speaking rapidly in Spanglish. The band was doing surprisingly well. Johnny had a crew. Even though some of the crew was my old crew.

As they practiced and the vibrations shook my room, I could hear them talk and joke with each other, try out new songs and riff on old ones as I sifted through information and began to build my own insane collage of leads on my wall, like a mood board for the mood of paranoia, a Pinterest for a bad detective. I was just starting to realize how alone I really was in the world.

PART II

THIRTEEN

I WAS ALMOST relieved when school started up. At least it would force me out of my room and get me to socialize. I expected everything to be different than last year. The battle changed everything. We fought the Heroes and won. Or, kind of won. We got them to concede at least. We took out a damn bridge. And now, not only was the world different, but I was different, too. I'd traveled the world in a jet, battled Hurricanes, helped indigenous people with their harvest season. I wondered if people would notice. But save a couple of weird glances from the Normals at Harris High, things felt fairly normal. Civic Responsibility even felt normal. Everyone was back except for Doodlebug—who I heard wasn't doing too well at the Academy—and a few graduates like Backslash. Dude was running from danger at Dartmouth, apparently.

There were a couple of new students. The most intriguing was a freshman who was tall, gawky, black, and had a puff of dark curls.

"Hi, I'm Tape Deck," she said to Kurt, not picking up on his anti-social vibe.

"That's not a name," Kurt replied.

"What's that mean, though?" Marcus asked. "To be a Tape Deck.

As a person."

"I can control machines," Tape Deck said. She smiled to herself, proud.

"That sounds like an awesome power. Like you could go up to an ATM and just make it give you cash?" Johnny asked.

"I heard of a guy with, what's it called, technopathy, who crashed the stock market day trading then disappeared on a military jet he hijacked," Alice added.

Tape Deck's smile fell. "Well, no. Nothing that cool. I can only control analog machines," she said. "Hence Tape Deck."

Our elation sunk with her. No shopping sprees at ATMs. She was a true Misshape, blessed with a useless power. Like Doodlebug, whose family became Misshapes when dowsers were no longer needed to find water, Tape Deck was born twenty years past her time.

There was one other new student in the class. Alessandra Fetti. Her mom was a big Hero in the Eighties named Discorella. Her power was mostly creating auras of light, which didn't really do much for fighting villains, but was a neat party trick. Also, she was a babe, so Hero teams clamored to put her in a miniskirt and have her light up the place.

"So are you also a one-man light show?" Marcus asked Alessandra. "Your mom was so hot. I always thought I could read her mind when I saw her on TV."

"Gross, Marcus!" Alice added.

"No," Alessandra said glumly, the weight of her Misshape-dom settling over her. "What can you do?" Marcus pressed.

"Nothing, really."

"Come on, you can tell us," Hamilton chimed in.

"Fine. I shoot brightly colored stuff out of my skin when I get really excited or angry." Alessandra shrugged. "My curse."

"Is it sticky?" Marcus asked.

"Is it deadly?" Kurt asked.

"Nope," Alessandra said. "Just bright. Like confetti. Hence,

Alessandra Fetti."All in all it sounded just as useless as her mom's power, but Alessandra was a gawky fourteen-year-old girl, with pimples, large glasses, sunken eyes and, unlike her mother, flat chested. Not the kind of item you would want trailing around for a fight, or for the party afterwards.

Ms. Frankl welcomed us back with a hello and made the class go around and introduce ourselves with how we spent our summers and who our heroes are in life. When it got to be my turn, I talked about Sam and storms, and my brain was still on the Hero channel, so I finished with "The Black Zephyr. He's my hero," I said with star-struck enthusiasm.

"Uncle Walter?" Tape Deck said.

"Wait, you're related to him? That's so cool," I replied

"Yeah," Tape Deck said. "He's cool, but loves to talk about the old days. He was like, the baddest brother on the Sentinels."

"*Only* brother, you mean," Hamilton added.

"Well he loves talking about it," Tape Deck finished.

With that, Mrs. Frankl changed the topic. "We have some work to do, kids." A groan. "We need to get releases signed for the debate." Another groan. Butters and the Spectors passed out papers. Even though the election was looming, it was exhausting seeing Vice President Bergeron parading around Doolittle Falls, national news entourage in tow. Our little town was considered part of his story, and he wanted to stay local in order to seem like a regular guy. That's why we were getting a presidential debate in the next week, like a real American town.

"What if we don't want to go?" Kurt asked.

"It's mandatory."

"What if we forget to get them signed and can't go on this mandatory trip?" Alice said.

"You should want to," Ms. Frankl replied. "It's historic. Even if you don't like his politics he's still important. If you can't go, you're going to spend the rest of the day in detention."

"Sign me up!" Johnny joked. The class laughed. Everything felt pretty similar to the way it was before. Save the fact that Butters had totally blown the first day of school. Where was he, anyways?

FOURTEEN

BUTTERS HAD been hiding in his room, preparing for the next competition. When I walked into his room, I heard him crying, "I'll never be able to beat Skylark. He's too good."

"You're just as good," Betty said, loyally. The Academy didn't start for another week. Rumor had it they were still looking for a new dean.

"Better, even," I added. "You can sing better than him. What's his power, magic birds? That's got nothing to do with singing." Betty had summoned everyone over with a text: *Butters is having a meltdown. Please help*. I had looked at it, reluctant to answer the summons, to spend time with the Misshapes and their various new permutations, until I heard another chirp from my phone: *You too, Sarah. I need you. Xoxo Betty*

"But that crowd ate out of his hand," Butters protested.

"Its all stage presence," Johnny said. "You got the chops, just bring it."

"But that's what the Spectors are for," Butters said, "people care about them. Not me."

"They're your back up. You're the main attraction. You got to be the showman and they're the side dish," Johnny concluded. "Try it out sometime."

"Hear that, Doris?" Butters asked. "It's about me, not you."

Doris came running over to Butters. She was pissed off. "Excuse me, little boy? I am not a side dish. If it wasn't for me this little dish of margarine would still be singing off key at the Doolittle dance hall on all-ages night."

"But aren't you just his projection?" Alice asked. "Like you don't exist without him, right?"

Butters jumped up, trying to shush Alice as she talked, but the damage was done. "Without him? Are you serious, rodent girl?"

Alice gave Butters a look that said, *How did she know my power and why is she mocking me for it?*

Butters shrugged. "Sorry, I can't control her."

"He can't control any of us," another Spector added.

Doris rolled her eyes. "I wasn't finished, Maybeline." She turned to Alice. "That's right, I'm talking to you, princess of squirrels. Maybe he doesn't exist without me, ever think of that? Maybe he's my, oh, what did you call it? My mental projection. Maybe I live a fabulous life and for some reason I have a stupid little boy pop out of my brain whenever I want to sing."

"But that can't be right?" Johnny said. "Or make sense?"

"Can't it? How could someone so lame create something as fabulous as Doris?" She was right. She was fabulous. She was in gold sequins today with the world's best cat-eye makeup. I was totally jealous of her style.

Butter scrunched his face and she disappeared. He was sweating and looked terrified.

"Are you okay?" Johnny asked.

"No. She's been doing that more and more. Just her, not the others."

"But she's your projection right?" I asked. "We're not all coming our of her imagination, right?" I shivered. Maybe reality wasn't what

I thought it was.

"Sarah, come on," Alice said.

"Sorry, it just made me nervous to think I was the product of someone else's imagination."

"Is there anything you can do?" Johnny asked.

"I've tried everything. It's like she's getting stronger. She keeps threatening to step out." Betty had her arm around Butters, patting him on the back.

"Let's focus on the show," Johnny said. "If you're relaxed about that maybe it will help. As we've established, they're your projections, so they come from you. If you can create someone like that you can tap into your own creative abilities. Starting with how you dress."

"What do you mean?" Butters asked.

"Well here are three women dressed to the nines and, um, excuse the insult, but a guy who looks like a dork," I added.

Butters looked crushed. Everyone kind of glared at me, even though I was right. Maybe being in the jungle for a month wasn't really helpful for my social skills.

"You're not a dork, you just dress like one. I blame Betty," I said quickly.

"Hey, what did I do?" Betty protested. She had been staying silent mostly, comforting Butters as the Spectors rebelled and we looked on in confusion. "You're his girlfriend, work on this," Johnny said.

"I think he looks dapper," Betty replied. Butters was in a polo shirt and khakis, with a navy belt that had little anchors on it. She had influenced his dressing so that he looked preppier by the minute. In comparison to Doris, he looked like a reed that would blow over in the wind.

"That's the problem. Dapper isn't show-stopping. Dapper is a ten-year-old at a wedding," Johnny said.

"Or a frat bro at the party," Alice added.

Johnny opened Butters' closet and started to go through his clothes. "Is this okay, Butters?" he asked. Butters and Alice went behind him to check out the scene. I pulled Betty aside to talk outside the room.

"Is he okay? What's going on with him?" I asked. I could hear the Spectors singing about a "brand new you!" in Butters' room.

Betty shrugged. She looked tired. "I don't know. This whole karaoke thing is getting to him. He's really nervous and he compensates with them and they get more cocky, and it's out of control sometimes."

"But this 'stepping out' thing. That sounds like some kind of mental break." "I know."

"Should he see someone?"

"Who? His parents sent him to a shrink when his powers first emerged and they just drugged him. There were no Spectors but there was barely any Butters as a result. Just a zombie."

"That's awful. Maybe if he's more confident it would help."

"It seems. The better he feels the less he needs them."

We went back inside and Johnny and Alice were dressing Butters up like a sparkling Martian. The Spectors looked on in disdain, especially Doris. She was getting to be a problem.

"Maybe they should be wearing something matching," I suggested.

"That's what I was saying," Johnny said.

"More androgynous!" Alice said. "It would look so good. Like Bowie."

"Hell no," said Doris. "That's way too Robert Palmer. I did not get into this to be a Robert Palmer girl!"

"You're so Eighties," Alice said in reply, some affection in her voice.

A moment later the Spectors were in matching tuxedos, all black and white, with skinny red bow ties.

"I look like a penguin," said Maybeline.

"You look great," said Alice.

"That's it. I'm done with this gig," Doris said. She disappeared.

The other two Spectors sang an, "OOOOOOH." It was a bit ominous, I thought.

FIFTEEN

"THIS IS BS," Johnny said. "They require us to come to this silly photo-op, then treat us like criminals when we show up."

"It's not that bad," said Marcus.

"Maybe not for you," said Hamilton. "I got everything short of a full cavity search."

"Hell no," a Spector, probably Doris, shouted to a security guard.

We all turned to look at Butters, who hadn't made it through the gauntlet yet.

Harris High had stuffed its students into the first forty yards of the Harpastball field. Vice President Bergeron was in the heat of his campaign and had decided to return to his home state in an effort to rally Hero support behind his run.

He was the mayor of Doolittle Falls when I was a kid, even though he was originally from Innsmouth. One of those mayor-for-life types, he was able to make a successful run for governor of the state with the help of his ties to all the Heroes and the bigwigs at PeriGenomics, both of whom adored him. He ended up with the vice presidential nomination after one term in office.

When the disaster at Innsmouth came he was on the scene immediately, every night, assisting with the rescue, speaking with reports, giving tear-filled pleas, talking about his love of Innsmouth. He was the face of the disaster, and it made him a national hero. I think it also gave him the political juice to be the front-runner in this presidential election. Nobody else running had the chance to be so sincere and heroic in front of the whole country.

The election was two months away. He had a commanding lead and an ironclad hold on our town. The Heroes had endorsed him; he had the support of everyone at the Academy and the top brass at PeriGenomics. Our whole school had to go to this event, and from the intense searches being pulled on every Misshape, it was pretty clear that they had some weird agenda.Bergeron was a big Academy cheerleader. He attended every Harpastball game, Academy graduation, and other special event they decided to hold. It helped that it gave him photo-ops with the most famous people in the country.Even Freedom Man — usually a political non-entity, "Freedom isn't red or blue," he'd say, "it's what pumps through your heart"—had come out big for Bergeron. There was a big endorsement and an announcement about PeriGenomics jobs or something. He was scheduled to speak to people at PeriGenomics the following day. But today they needed a teen rally in order to look good for the cameras. The children are the future, especially when they're being patted down by the Secret Service: Paladin Division.The Paladin Division was a mix of regular secret service members and members with powers. There were always a couple of them near any high-profile politicians, like the President and VP. They were rumored to be some of the most capable Heroes ever. Their powers remained secret mysteries, though, which was rare since most Heroes with any great powers were all over the news and documentaries. They also had some pretty serious anti-power weapons. When I was very young someone with a serious mental illness and a few minor powers involving energy balls tried to assassinate the President, and he was literally punched so hard by someone in the Paladin Division that he evaporated into a pile of dust. It was a favorite meme for troll sites like EarthStarHeroFight and Maximum Fighting Unlimited.

Butters came over to the Misshape seats, escorted by a man in a black suit with a white earpiece. We had to sit behind the rest of the students in a special place encircled with metal poles that cast a force field around us. Supposedly it was resistant to powers. The Academy students were in the front row with no protective shield. Half of them could kill Bergeron in a matter of seconds if the Secret Service Paladins didn't get to them first. It made no sense to me.

"Maybe he hates squirrels," Alice said.

"Profiling. Straight up profiling," Johnny grumbled.

Hamilton rolled his eyes at my brother. He got twice the crap Johnny got and was half the "bad boy" Johnny pretended to be. But he was black so he got more attention from the powers that be. "You would know, Robertson?" he asked, an edge to his voice.

Johnny stuttered a little. "You know if I don't shave I get mistaken for a terrorist, thanks to Mom."

"Sure, but you're also pretty white at the end of the day," Hamilton said. He had a point. Mom may have been Iranian but it never really read as anything between Johnny and me. We had less to deal with in comparison to Hamilton.

"They wouldn't even let Kurt come," Marcus said.

"Really?" I said. "I hadn't heard that."

"Do you blame them?" Tape Deck said.

"No. I wouldn't let him near a tree let alone a VP," Hamilton said. I smiled at him.

"I wish they banned us as well," Butters blurted. The Spectors looked on.

The Academy Band took the stage and played the pledge of allegiance. Then the new dean took the stage, introducing Bergeron. I tried not to fall asleep. She was very boring, and probably way less psychotic than Dr. Mann.

Bergeron took the stump in a wave of applause. Freedom Man and Freedom Boy sat behind him on the dais, next to another man who looked very familiar. That guy had a long narrow face, black hair and a deep widow's peak. He wore a slim gray suit and small round glasses, accessorized with a black collar around his neck. He was like Dracula if he rose to power. Super Goth. From the right angle he looked like a priest gone to seed.

"Who is that?" I asked Marcus.

"I don't know. But I feel like I should," he said.

I elbowed Johnny. "Any idea who that is?"

"His chief of staff and campaign manager, John Jay Glanton the Fourth," he said, unable to hide his disdain.

"As in, Chrissie and J5's dad?"

"Yup. J4 himself. Like son, like father."

I sat upright and started paying closer attention. This couldn't be good. When it came to powers that terrified me, the power of persuasion, as the J5 family practiced it, terrified me.

Bergeron continued, calling it a new day in America. He talked about our weakness. How we needed to be better. And the only way we could be better would be if we were all heroes. "Vote for me in November," he said, "and I will give you the *freedom* to solve your own problems. To believe in yourself. No more of this government butting into things." At the mention of freedom everybody clapped, Freedom Man leading the charge. Bergeron paused and told us to look up, onto the hill:

"There is a school upon that hill. That school is a symbol of all that is right with this country. It is a place where greatness has been achieved before the foundation of this country and continues to be a source of leaders to this day. It is a beacon of hope and promise. The Hero Academy is more than a school where the greatest Americans learn to defend this nation. The Hero Academy is the nation itself. *We are all Heroes.* We will throw off the shackles we have placed on our own wrists."

And necks, I added, muttering softly to myself, my eyes locked on J4's collar. Bergeron exited the stage to a roar of applause, David Bowie's "Heroes" blasting through the air. Alice seemed deeply offended by the song selection.

SIXTEEN

"**E**VERYONE'S A Hero in Bergeron's America!"

That was his slogan. It was everywhere.

Have you ever watched a town change in the span of a month? I thought I'd seen every face Doolittle Falls had to show—Harpastball Mania Doolittle, Post Apocalyptic Panic Doolittle, Doom Raid paranoia Doolittle, boring Doolittle, exciting Doolittle—but alas, it still held some surprises because I was unprepared for election fever Doolittle. Bergeron signs popped-up on every lawn, the local news followed his every word, interrupting my favorite TV shows—The Real Hero Wives of Gotham, and The Heroette—for meaningless election news, every billboard was plastered with his big grinning face, speeches were broadcast in the town square, rallies were held in the park, and the Academy became a surrogate for his campaign at every chance.

Dad was starting to get sick of it. PeriGenomics was one hundred and ten percent for Bergeron and they made it known to their staff. There was no distraction. Freedom Boy was away, but Freedom Man made frequent appearances shilling for Bergeron, causing a fuss anytime he was in Doolittle Falls.

Johnny, Alice, and Rosa were focusing on their band to distract them. They had a show scheduled in November and they'd gone from disorganized weekly practices to daily sessions, right after school, which were intense. Betty and Butters had disappeared into karaoke-land and I never saw them again. When I spoke to Betty she seems really nervous about things but never told me what was going on. And Butters had become kind of intense in a weird way I couldn't put my finger on. He mumbled to himself and nervously tapped his foot all the time.

I was no closer to finding out who framed Mom, but I was starting to suspect that Freedom Man wasn't the innocent do-gooder he'd like to present himself as. I read the entire BBS—all 2,325 printed pages—on the Djed. From what people had pieced together they were an ancient Hero guild. As old as recorded history, but rarely a part of that history. There'd been traces of their existence in every civilization that had left a trace uncovered on the earth. But often, the artifacts and records of them went missing shortly after there appearance. There were some translated scrolls in the BBS, from Sumaria, which, as to be expected, were stolen from a museum before they could all be scanned.

They were the slayers of Kings, the killers of killers, the hidden hand that policed Heroes. People had tried to wipe them out. People had tried to infiltrate them. People had even tried to hire them. No known members were reported, but there was a lot of speculation. Mom was briefly mentioned as a possible member but others on the bulletin board called that nonsense. Freedom Man was also suggested but most people agreed someone so eager for publicity would never be included. I clutched my necklace and kept my mouth shut and my hands of the keyboard. I was reminded of Freedom Boy's amazement when he saw my necklace. How much did he know about the Djed? I guess, unless he was a member, very little. Although who knows what gossip and legends Heroes know. Maybe officially being a Hero was like being a Freemason, loaded with the weight of history.

I turned on the TV to distract myself and The Heroette was preempted by election coverage. I was never going to know which Hero Andi would pick as her one true love. Instead of romance, we got poll numbers and recent events and the upcoming debate schedule.

At least there was one competition I could get excited about. Karaoke. Regionals were tomorrow night and I wanted to make an appearance, and cheer on Butters.

SEVENTEEN

I HITCHED A ride with Johnny and Alice, feeling kind of out-of-place the whole time. But when Butters saw us backstage, he looked momentarily relaxed. It felt worth it.

He then went back to his routine. He was pacing back and forth in front of the table. His starched white shirt looked tight around the collar. He was singing to himself, making tiny gestures with his hands like a magician, and generally looking unhinged.

We were at the House of Blues in Boston. The place was packed. Karaoke regionals were no joke. Well, at least to the thousand people in attendance and the fifty or so contestants hoping for a spot at nationals.

There were small tables around the perimeter and in the mezzanine and a large pit where people stood shoulder to shoulder and watched the performers sing and get judged. Butters had upped his sartorial game, donning dark jeans, a white shirt and a leather jacket. Combined with his high-strung loose-cannon vibe and an evolving sneer, if you didn't know him you might almost mistake him for cool. As he finished one lap in front of us, two of the Spectors appeared, in their standard sequin outfits. It was Maybeline and

Beverly.

Butters snapped his head to them and looked them up and down. He didn't need to speak, he just glowered.

"We just thought it would look better," Beverly said

"No. No. You don't think. I think," Butters snapped. "I'm the one who thinks. When I get on stage I slice like a hammer. The girls get shirts!" Suddenly they were back in their tuxedoes.

"Now where the hell is Doris?"

Someone tried to shoosh him from a table in front of us but he shot daggers at them with his face—not literally, he didn't develop any new powers, just a mean streak—and they turned back without saying a word. He turned his attention back to the two Spectors.

Something odd started to happen. Maybeline and Beverly's skin seemed to get tighter, like it was getting pulled across a drumhead. And then a crack appeared, the flesh parted across their face, and a dark red glow emanated from inside them. Butters, previously looking so serious, had a flash of concern on his face. He stopped pacing, closed his eyes, and murmured a countdown. The Spectors returned to normal.

Maybeline and Beverly looked at each other and shrugged. It was then that we noticed a woman in a floor length trench coat walking up to the sign in booth. There was an argument about whether she had qualified. She pointed at Butters and when she raised her hand we could see it was Doris. Everyone gasped. Butters looked stunned. "She stepped out. The bitch stepped out. I can't believe it."

When he spotted her, all of the Spectors got the instant facelifts. Their skin tightened, then split in half down the centers. Large dark shadows emerged from within, with a deep red glow pulsing at the eyes and mouth. They were terrifying. I lost my breath for a moment. Butters eyes grew wide. He was trembling. He balled his fists, closed his eyes, and just as quickly as the Spectors were, well, spectres, they were people again.

"I need a minute," he said. "Nerves."

"What the hell was that?" Johnny asked.

"I shouldn't say," said Betty.

"Betty, this seems serious," I said.

"Okay. But promise not to say anything. How much do you know about Butters' powers?" Betty asked.

"He can make Spectors appear," I said. "We know this."

"Well. Not exactly. Or rather, not entirely. He has mental projections. Which are like daydreams made real. Or day nightmares. There was a time before the Spectors, when he first got his powers, when they were out of control. He said it was like, one day someone hooked a projector up to his head and everyone could see his weird fantasies. Which made him isolated and depressed so pretty soon they reflected that. They grew dark.

"Soon he was plagued by visions of monsters and demons. But not just his visions, everyone could see them. So even more people stayed away. They frightened him and this fear fed on itself. Even his parents stayed away and mostly kept him locked in his room for his and their sake. He saw doctor after doctor until finally they got the right medication and they went away, but it just made him into a zombie. Finally he found a therapist who helped him channel his projections. He always liked singing as a kid, in choir and all that, and was a fan of girl groups, so that, after much trial and error, became his happy place."

Wow. We were all a bit dumbfounded. We hadn't known about any of that when Butters was the weird kid in school. Mostly we just knew him and the Spectors, always together, like a team. "And now?" I asked

"Well, with all the pressure and this thing with Doris. I'm afraid he's starting to crack," Betty said. She bit her nails. They were chewed down to the nub.

"We should get a closer look," Alice said.

"What do you mean? I thought he was confident and in control." I asked. "No. It's all false bravado. He's a nervous wreck. He kept pestering Johnny for a drink to calm his nerves. He's becoming a monster," Alice said.

"So this is like what, a psychotic break?" Johnny asked.

"I don't know. Oh god, I don't know. I'm afraid what's going to happen if she performs without him. And he breaks," Betty said. She was becoming incoherent.

We watched as Doris, a mental projection from the head of Butters, had a completes and coherent conversations with the judges, laying out an argument that she was part of a winning team, and was entitled to a spot on the roster even if her name wasn't on the list. Betty was stunned. So was I, but I was able to keep it together. I turned back to see Butters and he wasn't even watching her. He was staring at the mirror, yelling at the Spectors in his reflection.

He'd completely lost it.

"It will be fine," I said, still looking at Butters as he shouted at the remaining Spectors. "Fine."

We went back to the table and Butters was gulping down a large glass of water and joking with Johnny. I looked at Johnny. Was that really water? Johnny shrugged. He didn't. He wouldn't.

Butters got more and more belligerent after each song, and found a new reason to castigate the Spectors. Doris sat talking with Skylark at the bar and smirking at Butters whenever he caught her eye.

Based on a lucky draw the final three contenders, in order, were Skylark, Butters, and Doris. Betty explained the situation to the judges in order to get Doris pulled. She wasn't… real, just Butters' mental projection fighting his other mental projections. No matter what shape he was in, competing against his own mind couldn't be good. A pleasant but severe woman explained that, because of a quirk in the rule book, which Doris pointed out, since she competed and qualified with Butters, she technically could compete.

Then she whispered, "Your friend may need more help than I can give. I'm just a karaoke judge."

Skylark got on stage and did his usual bird tricks while singing

"Wind Beneath my Wings." It was a bad selection. His bird show was spectacular. But his booming voice and opulent display paired poorly with the song, which was low-key and maudlin. When he sang, "I can fly hiiiiiiii-gher than an eagle," he produced an enormous eagle that swooped over the crowd. Everyone was so impressed by the eagle they spent more time watching it than watching him sing.

"Okay. So Butters has a chance," Johnny said to me.

"At winning? Yes. But at what cost?" Betty asked. She was trying to cheer up Butters, but he was completely ignoring her, focusing on the judges. His intensity was terrifying.

The judges announced the scores for Skylark. He got straight 8.5 by all the judges, who noted that he should spend more time on singing and less time on the stage show. Butters pumped both fists in the air and shouted, "Yes!" Skylark glared at him, but Butters didn't care. He just stared right back. It was a Butters I'd never seen before. He strode up to the stage and just as his name was being called he grabbed the mic away from the announcer. The Spectors trailed behind him as opposed to spontaneously appearing on stage, and he made sure they were in the right position. He closed his eyes, the mic in one lowered hand, and his other hand in a fist raised to his head. He looked possessed.

A saxophone started and soon Butters burst into "Young Americans." It was powerful and the Spectors were perfect. He strutted around the stopping only to belt out a line so loud it hit the back of the room like a missile. By the time he sang, "Ain't no one damn song that can make me break down and cry," tears were streaming down his eyes, sweat was pouring out of him, and everyone was on their feet clapping and cheering.

The first judge scribbled something down. He raised it up. A 9.5. "Amazing performance. Just amazing. One of the best I've ever seen. But not *the* best." Butters looked disappointed but shook it off.

The second judge raised her placard. 10. "Perfect, just perfect," was all she said.

The last judge raised another 10. "Best rendition I've ever seen. You could teach Bowie a thing or two."

Butters jumped up. "Yeah! That's how you do it." He screamed. Everyone went crazy again. He was in the lead. The Spectors came over to hug him and wrapped him in their arms, which went right through him, being ghosts and all. They walked back to the group, making sure to pass Doris's table. Butters ignored her and the other Spectors "accidentally" checked her with their hips.

"Okay, and last but not least, Ms. Doris," he flipped over the card, looking for more.

Doris got up and took the mic. "Just Doris, honey. You can sit now. I'll be singing "The House That Jack Built" by Aretha."

She took off the trench and threw it on the floor. She was wearing the dress that she had on when she quit in Butters' room. Unlike the previous two songs she had no elaborate show, no magical birds or spectral back-up singers. Just a perfect voice and a charisma that oddly seemed like Butters. She didn't move or dance, just swayed slightly in place. But she sang it spectacularly, hitting every high note with such clarity it could shatter glass and make you want to weep openly. Also, oddly, she was sweating, which seemed unusual for a spectral being. Everyone gave her a huge applause at the end.

"What happens if she wins?" Alice asked.

"I guess they both go to nationals and knock out Skylark," Johnny said.

"So he could be competing against himself at nationals. What if she wins and he doesn't?" Alice said.

"I don't know. Can spectral beings win money and have a solo career?" I asked.

"This is getting too weird," Alice shrugged.

"If she's still around as a solo act after nationals," Betty said, "Butters will probably end up in an asylum. He can't maintain this that long. It will drive him insane." Betty had put a damper on our speculation.

The first two judges gave her 10's, which elicited even more clapping. We all stared at each other. This couldn't be good. The last judge waited for dramatic effect. Finally, he said, "Mrs. Doris, I must say, that was the best performance I have ever seen. You are going places. When this is all over, I'd like to manage you."

"Give me the score and we can talk about it," she said.

The judge was charmed. "Isn't it obvious?" he said, raising his 10.Butters' jaw clenched tightly and Maybeline's and Beverly's eyes turned completely black and their skin started to glow a crimson red. Doris, however, smiled widely, waved at the audience, and walked off the stage to thunderous claps.

EIGHTEEN

"COME CHECK this out," Sam said over the phone on a Saturday in September.

I hadn't heard from Sam since I'd gotten back. He had stayed in the Amazon to do more work while I helicoptered back, but I really had no idea what his plan was, generally. He was the kind of guy who could disappear for weeks on end and then pop up again like nothing had happened. "What are you talking about? School just started and I can't go running off again," I said. "I have homework," I added, lamely.

"No running. It's at the PeriGenomics building. You'll love it."

I was getting more and more curious about what he was selling but had other things on my mind.

"When did you get back in town? How long have you been here?"

"Six days. Maybe a week."

"Maybe a week? And you didn't think of calling me?"

"I've only got some time now. I meant to, it's just I've been training myself. I'll tell you about it, just come over."

"Okay," I said, unable to pass up a chance to practice at PeriGenomics or see Sam. The summer with Sam was intense. We lived together, trained together, and worked together. But the thing is, we never touched each other. Well once. When we were in the jungle.

It was the first few days there and people gave us this strange drink. It tasted absolutely awful, and it got me drunk or hallucinating or something.

Sam and I made out. It wasn't anything like when we created weather together, but it was fun and I had felt guilty about it afterward, thinking about Freedom Boy. But I forgave myself once I heard Alice's voice in my head, saying *Who cares? You know Freedom Boy's constantly fending off attention. Go for it. You deserve this.* Maybe I did. All I knew was that I really liked kissing Sam and I thought about it a lot.

I met Sam at our old haunt, Hanger X. He rolled up in a small golf cart with the PeriGenomics logo on the hood. Everytime I saw that logo a shudder ran up my back. I couldn't help it. It was the same logo that was on Dr. Mann's machine. I had some unanswered questions that the logo—and all it stood for—raised.

"Hop in," he said.

"Where are we going?" I asked.

"It's a surprise," he said.

"I hate surprises," I replied.

"Yeah? And I hate lame people who aren't excited by adventure." Sam laughed.

I jumped in the cart and he stepped on the pedal. The engine whirred to life and we took off at a lightning-fast fifteen miles an hour. It seemed like a turtle passed us. We drove through the back paths of PeriGenomics, zooming by large hangers that gave way to smaller storage buildings, large plastic tanks, and finally, on the edge of the property, maintenance equipment piled up in an unwieldy, Wicker Man-ish tower like lawnmowers and cans of paint.

"Are we leaving the property?" I asked.

"No. Not technically. But we're heading off the main campus. It's a secret place. It's a little dangerous." I thrilled to hear him describe whatever this was as dangerous. Yes. I was all for more danger in my life. Sort of. Within limits.

The path dead-ended at the Miskatonic and we took a right, following the river into the deeper woods on the outskirts of town. The small path cut a neat track through the trees, until the forest opened up to reveal an enormous building ten stories tall, made of corrugated steel. It was as long as the Harpastball field.

My mind was blown. How did this exist? So large and so close to my house? I hadn't seen any indication on Google Maps, either. As far as I remembered, there was just forest. Looking at the building, it felt magical in some ways. Or a tribute to the ability of industry to just build things in the span of a minute.

Sam parked the cart in front of a large steel door.

"We're here," he said with a sing-song ring.

After passing through the usual seven layer burrito of PeriGenomics security with card swipes, retina scans, full body MRIs, and stern glances from men with laser guns, we got to one final door. It opened with a simple key Sam had in his pocket.

When I stepped inside, I was so overwhelmed by the size of everything that it took a minute to get my bearings. I was in a room with giant black cylinders that looked like cellphone tower trees, the sort that look like real trees gone wrong on the highway and utterly plastic when you got close enough to see them. The trees had the range of a forest—some skinny, some fat, and some of them were monoliths, as wide as a small house and twenty feet high. There was a strange AstroTurf-like substance on the ground, but it was longer and felt more like silk than rubber. And the ground beneath the turf was squishy, like real dirt.

It was like being in a biodome, but an aggressively fake one. Like I was standing in front of a green screen with a forest behind me. I walked up to one of the black cylinders to get a closer look. The grass felt cool against my feet. When I looked at the cylinders, they showed a whole world. They had microscopic holes and small diamond shaped metal and glass pieces spaced in an elaborate harlequin pattern. From afar it all blended in, a virtual forest, but up close I could tell this was some kind of fancy equipment. Presumably not a cell phone tower.

"What's all this?" I asked.

"I'll show you," he said, "if you wouldn't mind stepping back to the safe zone.""The safe zone?" I gave my voice the proper note of confusion. I took a few steps back wondering what difference the safe zone made from the rest.

"Here goes nothing," he said, and flipped a switch.

I was blinded by a sudden burst of light. Reds and yellows swirled in my vision. I clutched my eyes and practically toppled over.

"Too much," he screamed, clutching his eyes as well and swinging wildly for the controller.

I placed my hand over my eyes but it did no good. It was so bright that the light poured through my eyelids like they were windows, making the light slightly pinkish. Finally he hit the right button and the world went dark again. But the after image still swirled before me.

He placed a hand on my shoulder. "Sorry about that. Still getting used to this."My vision slowly returned. "Get used to it quicker!" I snapped. "Sorry."

"Okay, take two," he said before I could protest.

This time the world remained the same. But in the distance I could see one of the black cylinders glowing yellow. When I squinted, I could see that it was on fire. A slow flame, at first, but it grew and grew until the entire cylinder was consumed. And then the one next to it caught the spark. And the next one. Pretty soon the trees in the center of the field were all aflame, flicking yellow, red, orange, and blue into the air. The chain of fire caught until a few trees in front of us were on fire. It wasn't as bright as the first time but was starting to get there ever so slowly. This time it was easier to adjust my eyes. The trees right in front of us burst into flames, and I stepped back when a single flame sprung out toward us, hitting some kind of shield. The fire flattened out in front of me.

"Safe zone," Sam said, and knocked on the shield. It made a hollow ringing noise. "Put this on."

He handed me a giant gray overcoat. It was heavy and said fire retardant on it. I slipped it over my shoulders and it hung over me like a sack. I noticed that, in spite of the flames, the room wasn't warming up. "What's with the temperature?" I asked.

"It's controlled. It's also why you can breathe. We're in a practice forest fire simulator. It's the only one of its kind. Colorado and California paid to build it after the last drought took out a few towns. It's pricey, but at the end of the day it'll be less than rebuilding a whole city from scratch."

"What are we going to do with this fire, then?" I asked.

"We step out of this cocoon, out of this shield and try to put it out," he said.

"Put it out? Cool!" I said.

"You got it." I swear I saw a twinkle in Sam's eye. Or the reflection from the fire and the glass. "There's a sensor that means it won't get too hot and cause too much damage. But be careful. Follow my lead. Okay?"

"Okay."

He grabbed my hand and we stepped through the shield. The room got hot. Face, meltingly so. I clutched my chest. It was hard to breathe, and each breath felt like fire. I felt woozy. I was having trouble seeing. I just wanted to get low to the ground, regroup. I was having trouble thinking. I just wanted to get low to the ground. I felt my knees give out and my body slowly fall.

Sam caught me. "You have to fight it," he said.

I tried but the fire was too strong. Every gust of wind we thought about paled at the wall of flames. Every attempt to cool the air was thwarted.

"Just a little at a time," he said. "Make it safe around you and then take on the fire."

I focused on the space in front of me. Just a small envelope of cool air. Just enough to catch my breath. I could feel it get cooler. I was able to channel my emotions, keep my head clear, and make some space.

"Good," he said. "Very good. Now, one section at a time. You can't fight it all at once. Not until you build momentum. We can do it together."

I followed him around the field, isolating fires with cool air, trying to cut off their oxygen supplies, and reducing the flames until they were burned out. We were able to stop most of them. It was exhausting. In a real fire, we'd work with other Heroes to build firebreaks—gaps in the trees and grass that deprived the fire of things to eat—to stop the spread of the fires.

We cut into the fake ground to build imaginary firebreaks, and create airflows around the trees to push the wind inward and blow the fire away from other sections. When we got to the center of the fire there wasn't much left to put out. The few remaining trees were just glowing a soft yellow. My shirt was soaked through with my sweat and every muscle in my body was sore. I'm not sure if it was my powers draining me or all the walking around with the shovel.

"One last section to go. But I'm going to make it hard for you," Sam said. He held up the controller and took a few steps back. "Sarah, all yours."

The last trees, which were embers a moment before, burst high with flame. It licked the sky and sent waves of heat back. I looked back at Sam. He smiled at me and stood still.

Here goes nothing, I thought.

I stepped toward them and tried to get a wind to circle around the trees to prevent the flames from spreading. Before the wind lasso had been mild, like a stream of air, and kept the flames confined. This time, something different happened. The wind was catching the fire and dragging it in a circle. I made the wind stronger, digging into my fear and terror, and instead of confining it, the wind it made a hot wall of circle flames. It felt like a furnace. I couldn't catch my breath. My controlled fear slipped away, and I felt my feelings slip into worry.

And that's when it happened.

The fire spun faster and faster, forming a heat point on the ground and spiraling up into an open mouth of flames. Heat waves circled faster and faster into a cyclone of reds and yellows and after a few seconds, the tip at the bottom turned a beautiful and terrifying blue. It was a tornado made out of fire, and I had no control over it. It spread across the field catching the fake trees instantly, until the whole room was ablaze. The fire was a menace, threating the walls. I could see my future go up in flames.

Behind me, Sam took a short breath.

"Oh crap," he said.

I heard a loud sound, like someone was puking. Nothing came out. Then I realized it was my own stupid body, protesting in fear.

NINETEEN

"TURN IT off! Turn it off!" I screamed.

"I am," he shouted back, "but it's doing no good."

"What?"

"The fire, it's no longer because of the system. It's not programmed for that. Nothing programmed for that," he said, pointing to the flame cyclone.

"What is that?" I asked.

"Fire tornado. They're illegal. And I don't know how to stop it. It's beyond the programming here."

"Let's make rain!" I said desperately. We held hands and tried to build up a massive cloud. Rain fell. I wanted to cheer. And then reality set in. It was too hot for rain. The cloud made the whole room steam up. White-hot steam sizzled in the air. "More," Sam said. "We can make this work. Focus on the tornado."

I tried to focus but it was no good. The tornado spun around the room, lighting every tree it hit until the whole room was blazing. Sam kept trying to turn the trees off but it was no good. It had overridden the system, and whatever was inside the big fake forest that made the cylinders burn was turned to the permanent on switch. Some of them were badly damaged, their once pristine black surface marred by ash and burn holes. Finally, the tornado veered to the right and hit the wall. Instead of slowing down, it seemed to spin faster and faster against the side of the building.

Sam focused his attention on the controller and was able to extinguish the trees, except for the ones in the vicinity of the tornado. I looked at the walls of the building. They were large white tiles that overlapped each other like the wooden clapboard siding on a house in a fishing village. The force of the twister had them vibrating, turning from bright white to a glowing yellow.

"Sam, are those things going to hold together?" I asked.

"The tiles are fireproof and heat-proof. They can withstand over a thousand degrees of heat and gale force winds," he yelled.

They vibrated faster and faster, making a loud banging noise and turning from red to yellow. "They don't look too anything proof to me," I said.

"Everything has its limits," he said peacefully. Or like he was faking it.

"And what happens when that limit is reached?" I asked.

"I don't know," he said, genuine fear creeping into his voice for the first time. We soon got the answer to my question. One of the tiles ripped off the wall, spun quickly around the tornado, and shot out in a small flaming ball. It went right through a tree and hit the opposite wall with a bang. The ball slid down the pristine tiles, melting them into thick white putty. In horror, I saw the wall disappear as the white stuff oozed down to the ground, leaving a metal latticework of structure underneath it. It blocked out access to the exit beyond the wall, a basic white hallway that beckoned like it was heaven.

Sam came out of nowhere and pulled me to the ground, yelling "Duck!" Another flaming tile flew right over our heads. Then another right in front of us. Fireballs were shooting off in all directions, going pop pop pop like fireworks. Soon a barrage of fireballs shot out in all directions. Tiles fell, the walls were oozing, and the metal beams started melting into a firewall of heat and crackle. The tornado grew strength in its corner of the wall, spinning against the side as if it was trying to escape.

We rolled out of the way of the shooting flames and took refuge behind a large tree. We took a second's break and three loud electronic beeps echoed through the room. A voice, calm and feminine, sort of British, began to speak. "Our systems have detected and emergency situation and our fire suppression system had been activated," she said.

I saw Sam's Adam apple jump up and down. He looked nervous. "In thirty seconds we will begin release of fire suppression measures including Halon 1301. Please be advised to exit the building immediately. The room will no longer have oxygen once the measures begin, which will make survival for organic life difficult. Exit can be found at both ends of the building. Please exit the room in thirty seconds... twenty-nine seconds... twenty-eight seconds..." She continued the countdown.

Having stopped, dropped, and rolled, we crawled toward the exit, through what felt like a wall of flames. When we were a few feet away, a large creaking noise sung through the air, and I felt Sam pluck me away as a crash-landed right in the spot where my body had been. Dust filled the room. My eyes watered, but as they cleared, I saw that our exit—our salvation—was blocked by a tree with numerous fire holes cut through its center. Long black metal strands jutted out of the bottom, which were matched by similar strands on the stump still in the ground. I looked up at the door, or where the door should have been. Nothing but tree.

The nice lady announcing our deaths continued to count: "Twenty-one seconds... twenty seconds... nineteen seconds..."

"We have to get to the other door," Sam said.

"It's too far!" I yelled.

"Sure," he said. "If we crawl."

"Do we have other options? Is there another way?" I asked.

"We can fly!" A look of glee passed over his face. Then he was serious once again.

"How?" I made a face.

"Stop fretting," he said. "It's easy. Yes, you can. See, we have a strong tail wind right now. If you put your arms in front to block the landing and position your body just so, you'll take off." He pointed to the tornado. "Sarah, if you can make a tornado, you can fly. Trust me."

He grabbed my hand and put the other in front of his face. "Follow my lead," he said.

"Fifteen seconds... fourteen seconds... thirteen seconds... " the woman bleated.

We locked eyes and did our own countdown. I had a sudden thought. "Won't the fire follow the—"

I couldn't get the word out. We whooshed forward with a powerful wind behind us. The fire followed, trailing us by inches, biting at our toes with wisps of flame. We had to keep going. I couldn't get scared and I couldn't flinch, or we'd end up slamming down into this deathtrap. It was terrifying but after a couple seconds in the air it felt weirdly exhilarating. I was in control. My life was in my own hands.

"Ten seconds... nine seconds... eight seconds... " The countdown went on.

We sped past the trees. Fireballs flew left and right and we dodged fallen branches and hot metal spittle from the melted beams.

"Six seconds... five seconds... four seconds... " she said.

The door was in sight.

"Three seconds... two seconds... please exit immediately." The announcer's voice got louder. It was time for detonation.

We put our hands up. The wind and fire was behind us. Safety beyond.

I could see a metal slab dangling, ready to fall in front of the door.

"1 second. Beginning fire suppression sequence." There was a moment of pure silence as the forest raged around us.

I covered my face.

We hit the door at full force, pushing it open with the weight of our bodies. Just as we made it past the doorway, the metal slab slammed down. Some claws of the fire escaped, trailing after us into the hallway. The sprinkler system snapped on but one still singed my arm. I could feel it burning, and I took off the coat and saw a long red line up my arm.

We could see into the practice room through a porthole window. Sam got up to take a peek, still wearing his protective gear. My hands and shoulders felt bruised and I had trouble pulling myself upright. I took a space next to him and watched the room fill with a gray mist. The fires quickly consumed the remnants of oxygen and greedily lapped it up. The fire extinguished like a light turning off when the inert gas poured in through the vents. The tornado was the last to go out. It spun slower and slower and the flame became a dull green before disappearing in a cloud of smoke and ash. It disappeared, and we could see hardened pools of metal, massive white balls of former tiles, and very expensive fake trees burnt to dust. On the ground was a blackened path tracing its course from the center to the wall, which was in bad shape, but still standing.

I was alive. It felt amazing. Sam and I were sitting on the ground, breathing heavy. I tackled Sam, so excited just to be alive. But then a thought crossed my mind. I had just destroyed the most expensive—and secret—thing in all Doolittle Falls. "So," I started. "Are we in trouble?" I got up, wiping the dust off the suit.

"Don't worry. They won't find out," Sam said.

"Won't find out? The place is ruined." There wasn't really anything we could do about it.

"Oh, you mean about the sim room? That's nothing. This thing gets wrecked all the time. They'll fix it. Wouldn't be the first time.

Fire is dangerous and hard to control. Though I've never seen it that bad," he said.

"What do you mean they won't find out?" I didn't necessarily have faith in Sam's ability to hide what we did.

"The fire tornado. It's illegal to make one of them. If the Bureau of Superhero Affairs finds out we'd get in big trouble. But like I said, they won't."

We got our things together and walked outside the building. I had some questions. He just made me feel a little like an interloper. "Illegal why? I thought I could work under your Hero card."

"Doesn't matter. Hero card, approval, or anything. Some things are just forbidden. Too dangerous. Like those mind control collars they give telepaths. We have limits, too." He had pulled out the Hero card on me, literally and figuratively.

"Nobody is allowed to do a fire tornado. Not even the Black Zephyr," I said.

"Even your hero," Sam answered. "It's powerful stuff. The Bureau, because of people's fears, prevents Heroes from doing what comes naturally to them. When someone, if allowed, could figure out how to control something like the fire tornado and use it for good. But instead we can't touch it because someone decided it's dangerous." He looked petulant. He wanted to do it again.

"That was scary," I added. My heart was still thumping.

"Well, yeah, because we didn't know what we were doing. But if we practiced it wouldn't be, like anything else. That's why all the Heroes are behind Bergeron. He wants to revamp the Bureau, put someone in charge who knows what it means to be a Hero, and stop this silly bureaucracy."

"But isn't Glanton 4 supporting him?" I asked.

"He's the best," Sam replied. I raised my eyebrows. "He'll totally fix the bureau. Now Normals get to set the standards, and it's silly if they do that for Heroes. If Glanton's in charge he'll fix it." For a moment, he sounded like Dr. Mann.

"Really?" I didn't agree with him. Unchecked powers didn't sound like an empirically good thing for the human race. "Well I can't vote and right now, I'm just happy to be alive and hope to never see another one of those for as long as I live."

"Oh, so you're not up for a second round?" he said.

"Sure, are you?"

He laughed. "Called my bluff. Let's get out of here," he said, and he walked me back to the golf cart. A clunker on the way in, I looked at it with new, grateful eyes after having narrowly escaped death. After the day we had, it seemed like a majestic steed, ready to take me home.

TWENTY

FALL RUSHED by in a blur. Instead of leaves changing and apple picking, my days were taken up with time on the doc, and going to campaign events for Vice President Bergeron. It was like they kept us on file as stock images of happy teenagers whose lives were going to be improved by this guy running the government. Instead of celebrating Halloween properly this year, we were forced to attend another stupid campaign event. I felt like we were being used as props, local school children to pan the camera to when they needed to make a point about the youth. I also secretly suspected they wanted to make sure the Harris High Misshapes were included to quell the rumors that there had been Hero/Misshape fighting in Doolittle Falls. Sure, the story was nonexistent in the eyes of the media, but that seemed to me like a big conspiracy. But even the tightest container has leaks. Having us there, smiling, was probably more evidence that all the stories were fake.

The event was at the Miskatonik University auditorium, where they normally had basketball games. We walked in, passing an enormous white tent for the media, and Ms. Frankl led us through three layers of security along with a few other government classes filled with Normals. The Normals had no trouble getting through, but they had to call over the Paladin Division for us. Every Misshape had to wait while enormous men with powers galumphed toward us to wave special wands over our bodies. This time they didn't accost Butters for nearly as long, but he was also able to keep the Spectors at bay until we got through.

The basketball court had been transformed into an enormous amphitheater. There were rows of bright red chairs lined up in all directions. In the center of the court were two podiums, an enormous presidential seal, and a heavily decorated table with microphones on it. Men and women were scurrying around fixing the lights, checking wires, moving chairs around, directing the audience. It felt a lot like the movie set for Annihilation Day.

After we were seated, the ushers led groups into the various sections. They carefully selected people off the chart to make the room look as diverse as possible in every way; white next to black; fat next to thin; rich looking next to working class; Hero next to nobody; and Misshape next to Normal, albeit only Misshapes who were clearly Misshapes, like a man with large yellow plumage around his neck.

Once the auditorium was filled the moderators from the major stations came in and sat at the long table. There was Fox Tackler from RNN, Ken Beck from HOUND News, and Ann Glanton from WXBS. I was amazed that HERO BIBLE was there, considering that her husband, J4 worked on the Vice President Bergeron team. She had on her distinctive scarf.

Fox stood up with his microphone and explained the rules of the debate. The usher would give everyone two cards, and they would write their name and their question on both cards, then hand one card back. The ushers would review them and then give the best ones to the moderators, who would review them further, and then select twenty questions. The ushers would then return to the person that wrote it down, inform them of their selection, and tell them to be prepared to ask the question they wrote down. This whole process took an hour. I could tell by the quickness that our usher looked at our cards that we weren't getting picked. A few minutes after our cards were summarily dismissed, she whispered something into the ear of a freckle-faced junior at Harris High, whose face lit up as she clutched her card to her chest.

The candidates came in to polite, but loud, applause. They were given a few minutes for opening remarks, which were unremarkable, and then the audience started peppering them with questions. They trotted out canned answers, sometimes in response to the question, and other times, they changed the question to fit their response. The moderators held them to the fire when they avoided the questions and asked follow-ups. There were questions on tax policy, jobs, the economy, education, the cost of rent, healthcare, natural disasters (and whether Heros could do more), high college tuition, gay marriage, marijuana policy, and the penal system.

And Bergeron made sure to trot out his Hero bonafides whenever possible, including answering every foreign policy question with a call for more Hero involvement in combatting terrorism and small asides about his Hero friends like Freedom Man and The Red Ghost. Once, on a question about healthcare, he even started by saying, "As my good friend Freedom Man once said, who, mind you, has never needed a doctor in his life, the best medicine is an active life and a healthy home-cooked meal like his mom used to make." He answered any question about the enormous prison population and the fact that it's exploded with seven hundred percent more inmates over the last thirty years with a reference to the effectiveness and efficiency of the supervillain prison, The Luther. It was hard to hear The Luther being thrown around so casually. Even though I knew my mom wasn't there in my heart, I knew, also, that she spent some time there. I didn't want to think of my mom being tortured when she was innocent.

Behind the curtain, I could see the team of candidate advisors. J4 was there, paying particularly close attention.

Ever since learning Mom was on the PeriGenomics board, something that would have been meaningless to me a year ago, I'd been fixated about the other board members. In fact, I'd become the family conspiracy theorist.

"What do you know about J4?" I asked my brother.

"Hero pedigree. Went to prep school all the way through the academy then Hero College. He's the fifth generation of his family to go to the Academy. All mind readers. All total jerks," Johnny said.

"His great-great-grandfather's super power was massacring Native Americans for fun," Hamilton added.

"Then what?" Alice asked. "After graduating was he on a Hero team?"

"Nope. Straight to the military," Johnny said.

"Was he in the blue brigade?" Alice asked.

"What's that?"

"It's the all Hero brigade. Mostly they're for entertainment. They go to parades and show up in commercials, since the Rittenbaum treaty bans Heroes in combat treaty," Hamilton said.

"Well officially, but no one follows it," Johnny said. "They are allowed in non-combat, which means they end up in fights all the time. Anyway, he was not in blues. He was in the hero units you don't know about."

"Ohh!" Alice and Hamilton exclaimed quietly.

"Ohh, what? What are you talking about?" They were getting way too into Hero minutia and Hero politics. I just wanted the straight gossip.

"Secret military groups, black ops, no public record," Johnny said.

Johnny had a deep wellspring of knowledge about crazy Hero theories. I think he spent time on Paladit, the website, and he did consider himself a quasi-expert on this kind of thing. Ever since he'd been in the band, though, he didn't seem to spend any time at home or nearby his computer.

"Like the ones fought all shadow wars during cold war in south America and Cambodia?" Hamilton asked.

"Yeah. Also the ones that hunt down US enemies, assassinate them or torture them in black op sites," Johnny said.

"Crap, that's serious!" I said a little too loudly. The usher gave me some serious stink eye and we all whispered. But mine was the Irish whisper.

"Bunch of fascists," Alice said, not whispering.

The usher gave us a death stare then walked up to the junior, who stood up and was handed a microphone. The girl said, "Hello, my name is Natalie Baker, I'm sixteen years old and I go to Harris High School in Doolittle Falls, Massachusetts. I'm too young to vote but I am still concerned for the future of the country. Vice President Bergeron, you have said that you support using our Hero resources in more productive ways to spur our economy and fight crime. But Governor Mather has said you are just going to lift the restrictions on Heroes and allow vigilante law in the land. Are people with powers capable of helping us? Or is it too risky?"

Bergeron's face lit up. He prattled on for a while longer than started in on his plan to deregulate the Bureau of Superhero Affairs. I could see that J4 was particularly focused during this question. It sounded like he was going to let every Hero go totally Batman on crime, and I didn't like the sound of that future. After all, Batman was a lone loony who only had his money to keep him warm. Other Heroes who fought with teams actually changed the world. Batman just changed his own world.

Johnny got real quiet. "Sarah, this guy is bananas." He continued, "I never believed who he was. After ten years in the army, but no record to show for it, he makes national headlines by saving a bunch of marines pinned down in the mountains. He gets medals, press, and a Hero's welcome."

"What's wrong with that, though?" I remembered when Bergeron was a national hero, even though he was a Normal.

"It was so perfect it seemed staged. Like, he's got no record of service because he's been doing black-ops for years, then out of the blue, he does something amazing right as he's about to end his secret black-ops career, the perfect thing to help his transition to a new life. He comes home, does some talk shows, and starts his political career. Meanwhile people accuse him of all sorts of heinous crap, including torturing people in the most terrible ways imaginable with mind control, but he's a hero, people owe their lives to him, so they get no traction."

I watched Bergeron on stage. People whispered in his ear. Bergeron's replies were perfect, right timing, no missteps. He had the rhythm of the debate nailed. Started, stopped, excused.

"He's also on the PeriGenomics board," I noted. I just found that out the other day. It was why I was a little bit more interested in politics than I wanted to be at the moment.One of the large fans cooling a light fell over and pointed directly at the moderators. For a second, Ann Glantons' scarf was blown from her neck. She quickly grabbed it and wrapped it back around, but I saw what her neck looked like. Just like Christie or J5, I would've guessed. Underneath the scarf there wasn't a distinctive metal color, but plain pink flesh. I looked at Johnny immediately and could see that he saw it too. Ann didn't have a collar. She was broadcasting the news without any inhibitions on her power.If she had done this for her whole news career, this changed everything. Innsmouth. She was there at Innsmouth. She told the whole world that my mother was a supervillain who ruined Innsmouth. If she was on the scene at Innsmouth without a collar or anything, who knows what she was sending out through the airwaves?

I whispered to Johnny, "Can she control minds through the television?"

His eyes widened. "I have no idea."

Bergeron droned on, but Ann's lack of a collar was all I could think about. I had plenty of time to do so, anyways, as the usher chided us, once again, with a "Be quiet!" She was staring. It was time to pay attention to the debate. I heard a small noise two seats over from me. I looked. Alice was half-asleep, snoring.

TWENTY-ONE

THE DEBATE had taken all of the energy out of Halloween. There was no time to plan any costumes, to do trick-or-treating or anything. We just wanted to stay inside. Besides, Butters seemingly had some PTSD considering that Halloween was the one-year anniversary of his defeat at the hands of Admiral Doom's goons. Hamilton was hosting the party in the garage that his parents let him use as a studio.

He had installed some black lights and splattered the walls with Day-Glo paintings. "How the hell did you get the paint to look like that?" I asked.

Actually I had no idea how any of his powers worked but the Day-Glo was so fascinating and out of the ordinary.

"Well, most of it is just paint I bought and used brushes, except that one," he said, and pointed to a small, five-inch-by-five-inch painting of a white skull that had a hazy blue glow. "I had to eat this strange squid from Japan for a week. It was disgusting and when I was finished the seventh day of slurping it down I was all set to paint, and all I got out was that much. That's when I bought some paint and threw out the other three tins of squid."

Hamilton was a genius. I was starting to get it now. I was one of the first to arrive, like a total dork, but soon everyone showed up. Johnny and Alice arrived together, hand in hand. I guess they were officially out as a couple. Next was Marcus, then Tape Deck, Hocho, Wendy Slothtrop, who had been practicing flying based on her landing in front of the place as opposed to walking up, Butters and Betty, who were not holding hands but were leading a procession of Spectors in pumpkin dresses, Kirk slunk in and stood in a corner, and finally, Rosa came too, and even the new girl, Alessandra.

Hamilton put on some music, lowered the lights, and soon the party was in full swing. Hamilton and Johnny goaded Tape Deck into remixing some of the songs blasting out of the small corner boombox, and for a few minutes it played weird robot music until we all broke into hysterics and Tape Deck took leave of the machine.

"Turn it up, turn it up!" Alessandra shrieked when a song I didn't recognize came on. It was dancey and electronic.

"What is this?" I asked Alice. She shrugged.

"Dr. Snake remix," Hamilton said looking at the boombox.

Alessandra danced wildly, all arms and gawky limbs, pausing only briefly to push up her glasses, which kept slipping down her nose. The rhythm increased and she kept pace until, during a crescendo, bright fluid shot out of her skin and flew around the room. We stopped and looked at her in shock and a wave of embarrassment crashed over her face. Alice ran out, grabbed her hand, and started dancing with her. Johnny ran out and followed suit, and soon everyone was surrounding her as the music blasted and lights blinked against the Day-Glo paint.

And then a knock came. A loud thump, thump on the garage door.

Hamilton ran over and turned off the boombox.

"Probably just my parents," he said.

He opened the door and a stone-faced man stood there with his arms across his chest.

"Hi, Hamilton."

"Hi, Mr. Crispin."

"You know why I'm here."

"Sorry. We can turn it down."

"I can hear it all the way in my basement."

"I'm really sorry. We'll lower the music."

"No. Turn it off. It's getting late. If your parents don't care about the rules I can call the cops on their behalf to teach them to you."

"Okay. No more music." Hamilton nodded vigorously. "We're done here, okay?"

The neighbor clenched his jaw. It was like he was looking for a fight. Hamilton was doing nothing but being pleasant and the guy was a total jerk. I was pissed off for him, but he kept calm.

"If I hear another sound…"

"I promise."

He turned abruptly and walked off. Hamilton apologized but said we'd have to go. "He'll call them in an instant. Even if we talk loud. He does it all the time."

"So that's it?" Tape Deck said.

"Hardly. It's all hallows eve. Let's take this party to the streets," my brother said. God, he could be such a jerk sometimes, but when it came down to it, he was the coolest guy I knew. And Alice was the coolest girl. Maybe it wasn't so bad they were dating. They were two of my favorite people in the world.

Within minutes we were outside roaming the streets taking in the fall air and looking at the decorations around town. I was a little traumatized from last Halloween—I sure as heck wasn't going to let my eyes off Butters or leave the group—but being surrounded by all my friends felt good.

The houses were decked out in jack-o-lanterns and ghouls

hanging from trees. A few places had signs on their roofs that read, "FREEDOM MAN LANDING ZONE." I wasn't worried about running into Heroes again, since they were all on full time Bergeron campaign duty. Speaking of which, we walked by a lot of campaign-themed costumes. Little Bergerons and little Porters ran around in tiny suits. It was kind of adorable.

When we got to downtown the stores were all closed for the night. Along one boarded-up lot were a series of Bergeron posters with him standing in front of an American flag next to a cadre of Heroes. It was right next to the Bergeron campaign headquarters, which was closed for the night.

"In Bergeron's America," it said. "We're All Heroes!"

Hamilton and Marcus gave each other a look and broke off from the group. Marcus pulled a metal can out of his bag. Hamilton took off his sunglasses.

"I thought you weren't doing that anymore," I said to Hamilton.

He turned to me and I got another glimpse of his eyes. Oceans of blue and green were circling around his irises like oil slicks.

"This isn't art. It's public service," he said with a smile, then turned back to the poster.

Other than his closeness with J4, I couldn't see the big deal about why Bergeron was the worst. Sure his speeches were cheesy and he seemed way too pro-Hero, but who wasn't in Doolittle Falls? Johnny and his Rock against Bergeron group were adamant that he was the devil incarnate.

Just as they were finishing adding moustaches and beards to all the Heroes on the poster, a group of men came up behind Hamilton and Marcus. Considering their size and thick black boots, it was amazing we didn't notice them coming. It was a group of five men, all a head taller then us, and as thick as freighter trains.

"What do you think you're doing?" the one in front, presumably the leader, said.

They were all in black, from head to toe, with no indication of who they were or worked for. Based on their annoyance, we guessed they were Bergeron's people.

Hamilton slipped on his glasses and put on his serious face. The same one he had when dealing with Mr. Crispin. He must have had to deal with this a lot.

"We were just being kids," he said.

The one in front took several sharp steps and was in his face. "Funny, you don't look like kids. You look like criminals to me."

I slipped my hand into my pocket and hit the 911 button. Or I hoped it was the 911 button. While I was wary of the cops—especially in light of the graffiti—I would prefer them any day to these guys. I didn't trust them.

A man behind them held up a smartphone and pointed it at Hamilton and Marcus. He studied the screen while the leader studied Hamilton's face. He was managing to keep his composure, though his whole body was tense.

The one with the phone shouted, a little too excited, "And Misshapes. All of them. That's Hamilton Collins and Marcus Wilson. Students at Doolittle Falls High School. Big eyes has had a few run-ins with the law, all expunged. The other one can fly. But Misshape-level fly. And won a minor lawsuit against a petting zoo. And it looks like we also have the illustrious Robertson Family," he said turning to us.

"How did he know?" I whispered to Johnny.

"I'm afraid to ask," he whispered back, then pointed up to a small black box with a lens on top of the Bergeron headquarters.

They must have been Bergeron's men. Why would someone with the Secret Service need petty goons to do his bidding? I guess maybe it was to do things like this, intimidate kids. And the fact they had so much information on us at their fingertips was unnerving. I was starting to see why everyone hated the guy so much.

"What should we do about this?" the leader said in Hamilton's face.

Hamilton finally cracked and took a step back "Do? What are you talking about G.I. Jerk Off? This is public space. The posters have no right to be there, so we can do whatever we want to them. It's not a billboard, he doesn't own the building, so we have the same rights as the person who put up the poster."

The man stepped up and shoved him in the chest. Hamilton sprawled back and hit the poster, making a wet thud as he hit the paint.

"Is that how you see things?" he said.

Marcus went up to defend him but another thug grabbed him and held him back.

Just then a police siren wailed in the distance and blue and red lights flickered down the block.

"I guess tonight's your lucky night," the leader said, and with a swift move of his arm, punched Hamilton in the stomach. Hamilton hit the wall and slumped down. "Happy Halloween," he said as he winced and we ran to his help.

By the time the police arrived they were gone, disappearing into the blackness of the night, while we tended to Hamilton. The police proceeded to interrogate us like we had done something wrong. They called us liars when we tried to explain what Bergeron's men did and threatened to arrest us if we didn't go straight home. I was starting to understand what the problem would be, in Bergeron's America. As known not-Heroes, we were basically criminals-to-be, the minute we were deemed Misshapes.

TWENTY-TWO

ELECTION DAY rolled around soon after. We had the day off school, and our gym was a polling station. When I was younger my dad would take me in the booth with him and we would pull the lever together, but I was getting a little too old for that. As he left the house to go vote—all PeriGenomics employees got the morning off, and the company pushed their employees to vote for Bergeron—Johnny yelled after him, "Vote for the other guy. Screw the company."

Dad smiled back and said, "Glad to see you taking an interest in democracy." Johnny was going to practice with his band after they all protested Bergeron down at Harris High. Rosa stayed home because her family was worried that someone from the Academy would see it, record it, and she'd get in more trouble with the powers-that-be.

Johnny was obsessed with this concert series, Rock Against Bergeron, which had been touring the country. He drove hours to check out the show when it hit Boston and Troy, NY. I think he had been emailing back and forth with that group because he was going full Rock Against Bergeron for Election Day. He had helped out with the Doolittle Falls show, booking the venue and getting a slew of bands to play. I wasn't too sure what name the band was going with for tonight, but I heard rumblings of something like ACLU Benefit. It felt okay to tag along in this case. I still felt weird tensions with nearly every Misshape that wasn't Hamilton when I walked into a room, but really, the air was filled with Bergeron-related tension these days. It was nearly refreshing.

As soon as we were certain Dad's car was a safe distance away, Johnny went up to the attic, came down with a box of picket signs, and we got in his car. He picked up Alice on the way. Her car was currently up on blocks in the front yard.

"My brothers claim to be fixing it," she said. "But with about twenty minutes of work a week, and four hours of drinking tall boys and arguing about what they should be doing, my guess is it will be done by the time I graduate college."

"I could take a look at it," Johnny offered.

We both stared at him in disbelief.

"What. I can fix things. How hard can it be?" he said.

"Johnny, you couldn't hang a poster without putting three holes in the wall," I said. "Maybe Tape Deck can take a look. She keeps it analog."

Johnny pouted and shrugged his shoulder. "Not a bad idea," Alice said. Advantage, me.

When we got to the high school Hamilton was already there getting set up. We had to protest in a select "protest zone" just outside the fence that surrounded the school. It was a federal law that we couldn't be too close to the polling station. The protest zone extended around the perimeter of the school, but mostly people were standing by the main entrance, the part people had to drive through to get to the gym where the voting machines were. There were five people on one side of the street with official Bergeron posters that said, simply enough "Vote Bergeron" and a few with placards for other local elections. On the other side of the street were Porter supporters, with signs for their campaign. While we weren't the biggest fans of "Pick

Porter" either, he wasn't Bergeron, so we stuck by that side.

Hamilton had an easel setup and Johnny handed him blank signs to paint. The first one said, "No Powers for Bergeron" in black letters and was decorated with cartoon action balloons like "POW!" and "BLAMO!" He handed it to me and I held it up sheepishly. The Bergeron crowd glared at me and I sunk down, mentally willing myself to disappear, a fog spinning around me like cotton candy until Alice popped up next to me with a sign that said, "BERGER-WRONG FOR AMERICA!" The fog cleared and I felt strong again. When Hamilton finished painting, he put the easel away and stood next to me on the other side. His sign had no words, just an elaborate picture of Bergeron's face, done up like a vampire version of Bergeron's face.

"Hamilton, you are straight-up good at protesting. Tell me why you do it. I want to know," I said. "I'm not super up on the dude's policies. Do they even affect us? We're so young. Isn't the government for old people?"

Hamilton became very animated. "That's the thing, Sarah. Government's for everybody, and Bergeron's a really bad example of it. He's got no policies. It's all empty rhetoric. He clearly wants to give the Heroes all the power they want. And his ties to J4." He shuddered. "That guy will ruin this country. He'll ruin it."

There was a pause. I wanted to fill it with a question. "How's the painting going?"

"Great. I'm working on a large piece. You should come by and see it. Although with band practice and whatever Butters craziness is happening, I don't get as much time to paint as I'd like."

"Wait, what's up with Butters?" I asked.

"What hole have you been in, Sarah?" Alice snapped. "He's over there anyways," she said, signaling down the street. Butters was heading to the school, three of his Spectors following behind him, and one gesturing wildly alongside his loping stride. It looked like they were arguing. "It's been like this since he broke up with Betty."

"No. No, no, no. You can have three songs. Any more and you

might as well get you own album," Butters said.

"Well maybe I should have my own album," the Spector said.

"Not this again. You can't have your own album."

"Yes. I. Can. Doris is stepping out."

"You can't step out. You're a mental projection. You are me," Butters insisted, sputtering.

"I sure as hell ain't you," she replied. "I'd be better looking, for one."

"But you are. I control you. You're my Spectors. You do what I say."

"Oh, Butters the Big man. When I was..."

"Ugh, it doesn't stop," Hamilton griped.

"This has nothing to do with her!" Butters shouted at Maybeline, before she, and the rest of the Spectors, disappeared.

He joined us in the protest line, clearly upset, but trying to hide it under his usual cheerful mien. I felt very out of the loop. I hadn't heard about the breakup or anything. We stood for a few hours, holding our signs and talking about school and bands and concerts and the big documentary and my training with Sam. After the post-work rush to the polls, we called it a day, and headed home to get ready.

The concert was held in the VFW hall in downtown Doolittle Falls. An enormous man sat next to the door in a folding metal door and checked IDs. He looked us over and handed us all green bracelets, then stamped both our hands with a giant UNDER 21 stamp. I didn't want to drink—and even if I ever did, there was Johnny—but the stamp seemed a bit excessive.

I relaxed a bit more once I got inside the hall. A dirty, cramped rock show was kind of the only place I wanted to be on Election Day, or night, as it was. I could barely see in front of me, and the darkness reeked of cigars and stale beer. Most of the light bounced off the

Ballentine mirror in the back, behind the small bar filled with a row of bottles, labels peeling. A mix of Misshapes and Normals, a variety of ages, sat at the bar, talking, drinking, and watching a small TV that hung from the ceiling. A newscaster was on, standing in front of a polling station, reporting on results across the country.

Posters from the VFW members were hung along with walls, damaged, with peeling corners and yellowed paper. Perhaps the good ones were stored away somewhere. The walls also had deer heads, American flags, and pictures of motorcycles. There was one enormous bear head, sticking out of the wall totally staring down a deer on the other side of the room with enormous antlers. The antlers must have been three feet long and were poised above a group of kids in black t-shirts sipping from red solo cups.

The room focused on a small stage, not much higher than the ground, covered in amps, guitars, drum kits, mic stands, and wires. The stage looked more like wires than a stage. The band that was playing was losing out to the election results, as people were watching the TV or looking at their phones. The vibe was weird.

When I saw Hamilton, he was talking to some Harrison High Normals who all had shirts on with Bergeron as a vampire on the front in red and black. I guess it was a meme that was going around. They spoke animatedly about how terrible he'd be for the country, that he was a war hawk that was just interested in showing might and playing Hero from the Whitehouse. Most people echoed what Johnny had been saying, which was he was a mediocre mayor who abused the memory of Innsmouth for political ends.

"Do you notice that he can't go for more than a sentence without mentioning Innsmouth?" one of the kids said.

"It's his *Raison d'être*," Hamilton said.

The needle, it scratched.

"Sorry, it was in an article I just read. But, like, it's all he had going for him." "And he might win on it," Johnny said, dejected, breaking into the group.

A skinny boy in black jeans and a white t-shirt got on the stage. He staggered up to the mic, picked it up, and tapped it with an unsteady finger. A loud crackle and hiss boomed over the crowd, and we covered our ears. He ignored the noise and our unhappy response. Someone shouted something about feedback and he flipped the kid off.

"Good Evening, meine Kinder! Mein Name ist General O'Duffey! Welcomen to the end of day. The latest results are in. Bergeron has won our very own state of Massachussets. New York is still too close to call. Carolinas and Georgia went for Porter. Florida for Bergeron. And the rest are still being counted. I'll be back later with more updates. "Next we have a band called," he pulled out an index card and studied it, squinted, and said, "How I Broke Elastic Man."

Three boys with greasy black hair with guitars larger then their torsos got up on stage. The one in front lifted a flop of black hair from his eyes, muttered "hey," stepped on a distortion peddle, and windmilled his arm once and played a loud fuzzy chord. He did this three times and on the third the band joined in. He started yelling something into the mic, but the guitar noise was so loud I couldn't make out a single word. The chorus was either "strawberry monkey party crime," or "raw ferry making art rhyme." Neither made sense.

I went off with Hamilton to another room, which had red walls and a pool table in the center. Rosa was standing in the corner, picking the label off a bottle of Crypto Cola. "Hey, when do you get here?" I asked.

"Just now," Rosa said.

"Nervous?" Hamilton said.

"A little. I mean, not the kind of place the Academy would like to find me out. But how would they know? Right?" Rosa looked worried. I felt terrible for her. The Academy wasn't the place for her, but it was her only chance for a better life for her family.

"It'll be fine, Rosa," I said. "It's just a concert. People are so busy tonight. Where's the Academy?"

"A bunch of them are in Boston at the reception for the anticipated Bergeron victory. There's also a viewing party at the school," Rosa sniffed.

"Not a Bergeron fan?" Hamilton asked.

Rosa rolled her eyes and we all cracked up.

"My Tia is back in LA for one of the big Rock Against Bergeron concerts."

"That's awesome," I said. "You should play with your band. Aren't you guys ACLU Benefit right now?"

Rosa smirked. "Actually, it's Laika's Space Cadets now. And I don't quite think we're ready."

"It looks like Alice and Johnny might disagree," Hamilton said.

He pointed to the stage and another band was pulling the duo on stage, handing Johnny a guitar and Alice some drum sticks. They seemed bashful. I'd never seen either one of them so embarrassed. Alice's cheeks were bright red and Johnny's shoulders were at his ears.

"I'm not sure about this," he said.

"Come on man. You got this," a boy in an oversized army jacket and a guitar over his shoulder said. "Don't you want to hear my boy Johnny?" he asked the crowd.

They cheered.

"Okay," he said.

Johnny played a few strings and listed to the response in the monitors. Alice hit the drums lightly. He turned around and said something to her. No one could hear it. Her pallor returned to normal and her posture relaxed. She whispered something back, again inaudible. They nodded at each other. "This is, uh, ACLU Benefit," Johnny said.

Alice counted off four with the sticks and they started playing.

It was a slow song. Johnny sounded nervous. The music was too loud to hear the lyrics, but it sounded like it was about our fight down at the river. But it was a triumphant we will overcome tune gussied up in a sad wistful song. It seemed wrong that they were playing without Rosa, though.

"Why aren't you up there?" Hamilton asked Rosa. "I mean, I've been playing with them sometimes but you're the soul of the band, right?"

"Didn't know they were playing. But even still, I can't play in public. It's too dangerous." Rosa looked a little depressed. I sort of got it.

Johnny and Alice finished to a burst of applause. We made the biggest noise possible from the pool room. Even though things have been all over the place with my brother and my best friend, there was still something sweet about seeing them perform for a crowd. A flush of pride overwhelmed me and I felt like it was a perfect moment, just for a moment. I had no idea what the weather looked like overhead.

After they stepped down, bands continued to play. Alice and Johnny were swallowed up by the crowd, surrounded by groupies. When they spotted Rosa, they ran over to her and sort of jumped on her in sheer puppyish excitement.

"Can you believe it?" Johnny asked. Alice also looked flushed with excitement. "It was good, guys," she replied.

"Yeah, but we didn't have you. We need you, Rosa, and then we're going to be the best band in the world!" Alice nearly squealed. Hamilton and I shared a look. He mimed something at me. I thought he was saying something like *What am I, chopped liver?* While we were talking, one of the bands finished and announcer boy came up again. Things were looking grim for Porter. Bergeron had taken a clear lead.

More bands played, each one louder and angrier. The kids toward the front of the stage were jumping around and thrashing. After each set the boy got up with more and more bad news about the election. At around eleven o'clock he got on stage to announce the last band. He looked tired.

"WXBN has just called the election for Bergeron," he said. A large booo errupted from the crowd. "The other stations are not calling it. They say certain states are still up in the air. Sorry for the wonderful introduction, but now, our last band of the night, Wayne Enterprises!"

Hamilton tugged on my sleeve. "We need to get out of here. And fast." I followed his lead, going to a corner with a high window covered in thick fabric. He pulled the fabric aside and looked outside, where there was a row of police cars. Cops in riot gear were assembling. I saw the large bouncer from earlier handcuffed and sitting on the sidewalk. A couple kids walked outside to smoke and were grabbed by a few officers, who threw them in the back of a paddy wagon.

"We can't get out that way," I said.

"I know," said Hamilton. But where could we go?

"There's an entrance in the back through the kitchen," said Johnny. "It leads to a small fenced in BBQ area. We can hop the fence. But I need to warn everyone."

"We should go," Alice said.

"You start. I have a responsibility," Johnny said.

As he said this, the boy got back on stage. The other two stations had called the election for Bergeron. The crowd was moving toward the stage, angry. Johnny tried to make his way through but the sea stopped him. There was a loud BANG and smoke filled the room.

Alice grabbed his wrist. "We need to go *now*," she said.

"No! I have to tell them," Johnny protested.

"They can figure it out!" I yelled.

We headed toward the kitchen at the right time. As we got to the door the police stormed the room. "Time to shut it down, kids," we heard, through the mechanical whine of a megaphone. The kids weren't going to stand for that. It took a minute and the night became violence. A bottle flew by us, shattering on the wall. Glass flew everywhere. The room was covered in smoke and my eyes were tearing up.

We kept pushing forward like Lot and his wife, trying not to look back at the previously placid punk rock show. The cops were grabbing kids violently and dragging them out of the building. Those that resisted, or even looked hesitant, were being tasered or hit with batons. I saw one kid with powers try to give up, but as soon as they saw sparks run down his body there was a scrum of police on him swinging clubs and fists. Hamilton grabbed me and pulled me through the door.

We rushed through the kitchen and exited through a rickety wooden door, which hung loosely on its hinges. In the dark, we saw a small square patio surrounded by a wooden picket fence, a few rotting benches, and an enormous BBQ. We ran to the back corner and Johnny and Hamilton helped boost Alice, Rosa, and me over the fence. We landed in someone's backyard with a thump, and a few moments later Hamilton came over and then Johnny, who fell to the ground. We started to creep through the backyard toward the street when we heard a loud "Hey!"

Two cops came running toward us from the street. We couldn't make out their faces and, since we were in the dark, we hoped they couldn't make out ours. I was about to start running when Rosa took her hand, balled it into a fist, and punched at the ground. It started to shake and the officers toppled over each other and hit the ground. They tried to get back up but when they did, the earth shook again and they fell again.

"Run! Now!" said Rosa, and we sprinted through backyards as fast as we could until we stopped a block later, panting and out of breath. There were no more cops around. We were in the clear. But we could see and hear the sirens in the distance and smell the tear gas rising into the air.

When I got home, shaken to my core, I went to my computer. I wanted to know whether this was a thing happening everywhere. Sites like Twitter and the official Rock Against Bergeron message board were abuzz with reports of police presence at all of these shows.

It wasn't just the Doolittle Falls concert—all across the country, police came in with great force to shut down the punk rockers. It was a symphony of cruelty: videos of people being hit by police with truncheons, people being tear gassed, people carted off in paddy wagons by the dozen. It was a trending topic for a while, popping up on websites thanks to its relation to the presidential election.

But there was a shift.

The narrative of injustice changed. Rock Against Bergeron shows were classified as just riots, people getting out of hand who needed to be shut down. Next, the videos were coming down. YouTube replaced each home video with a note that it was "A National Security Threat." I watched as one by one, the people who were talking, publicly, about what happened at these shows were disappeared. Twitter accounts shut down. Other avenues silenced. I stayed up all night, watching the story change before my eyes. It felt like a cruel magic trick.

Johnny walked into my room at 4 a.m. "They suspended my account," he said.

"Which account?" I asked.

"All of them. I was posting stuff about tonight…" he trailed off.

"I saw. It was good," I said.

"Thanks. About a minute ago I got a message from all these sites informing me that my account is being temporarily suspended because of suspicious activity. I sent some very angry emails to them and they said they couldn't tell me more, just that it was at the request of the government's Palladin anti-supervillain division."

That was a big deal. "What?" Computers were a thing that worked. They're not a thing that shuts down because the content is wrong.

"I can't even get on the websites anymore. They blocked my IP. And when I tried to use my phone, they blocked the IP there, too."

I motioned to my brother. "Sit next to me. Mine's up. Join here."

He sat next to me on my bed. We watched as the voices of protest were silenced and the narrative became about the election results, ignoring the revolution in the streets.

The morning paper was full of articles we had already read about the election. Porter had a concession speech, Bergeron promised "a new way" for America. On page 15 of section B—the local news section—there was a small blurb about a noise complaint at the VFW hall that the police responded to and the arrest of several local youths that were responsible. It was one paragraph long, dwarfed by a piece about Sugar Shacks.

TWENTY-THREE

"**H**OW COULD they do that?" Johnny asked.

"Technically or morally?" Tape Deck replied.

"Well, morally, I know. They have none. They're evil," Johnny said with a flourish. "Johnny, what did we say about calling people one of two things? People aren't just evil or villains," Ms. Frankl said. She was trying to control the class. It wasn't going very well. She'd given up on the day's lesson once Johnny's hand shot up and he started in on last night.

Johnny pointed one long finger at her and said, evenly, "Chamberlain!" "Johnny!" Ms. Frankl admonished.

He muttered a sorry.

Ever since Johnny's Social Studies class covered WWII and he'd become obsessed with appeasement and the early English response. In his evolving worldview everyone who wasn't on his side was either a Chamberlain, an Eichmann, a Good German, or a Hitler. Ms. Frankl was not a fan of his new classification scheme for the world, though it did seem to align with her favorite book, *A Misshape's History of the United States.* Johnny took on a more controlled tone and asked Tape Deck deeper questions. "So, technically, the Internet is free.

It's everywhere. But how can they just close down every source of information and silence every voice? Isn't that censorship?"

Tape Deck had a reply. "You're wrong, Johnny. Check out my phone." She pulled the black mirror out of her pocket and pulled up Facebook. "The Internet isn't free. It isn't everywhere. It costs billions of dollars to maintain."

She paused. The class was silent for a second, and it looked like Ms. Frankl was about to continue with the discussion. But then Hamilton sprung up and sat on his desk, ready to speak. "She's right, dude. The Internet is a big giant forest, a rainforest where everything is so interconnected that if a butterfly flaps its wings everything goes wrong. Large multi-national companies pay billions of dollars to keep servers alive so they can profit off of the Internet. Because of that, they have an interest in keeping certain people happy, like the governments that allow them to operate."

I loved watching Hamilton talk. I could listen to him all day. He actually talked in a way that made heady ideas seem approachable, down to earth. Lately I felt like he'd be a better teacher than Ms. Frankl. While I was daydreaming, Tape Deck was in a heated conversation with Butters. He was sputtering about scary groups online, and how they were proof that the Internet was a free market.

"Entire nations have blacked out their Internet during periods of unrest, and other places have controlled what people can and can't see. It could happen here. You're a fool if you think otherwise. The Internet is not above the power structures of the world. It's beholden to them."

Having just smoked Butters verbally, the Spectors joined in. "FOOOOOOOOL!" Butters blushed.

TWENTY-FOUR

I**T WAS** a dull gray day when Alice picked me up for the doc shoot. Things were weird between us. It was like whatever magic lasso that linked us together snapped in some way over the summer once she told me about her and Johnny. I didn't hate her, but I didn't want to be alone with her. But we were the only ones who had something to do, a one-day internship that was way more prestigious than it should've been, once Freedom Boy's doc was in town. Alice offered me a ride and I couldn't say no. It didn't mean that I felt super weird being in her car.

A snowflake hit the windshield and got swept up by Alice's wiper as she drove to the shoot. A few more snowflakes hit the window and then a barrage of white poured out of the sky. By the time we got to the trailers the world was white and we couldn't see more than a few feet in front of us. It was hard seeing the movie set.

"I didn't know it was supposed to be this bad," Alice said.

"Me neither. They said it was headed out to sea."

"Kind of early."

"Nah. There's plenty of storms in early December. They always catch us by surprise."

We got out of the car. We were first to set, which was surprising since it was a big shoot. Just a few trailers and one pink Escalade with the CA license plate DNGRGRL."Ah, I guess we should go meet this chick. She drives an Escalade," Alice said, looking at the plate.

"She's probably paying for everything, I bet," I said. "Let's go find her." I was desperate to hang out with someone who wasn't necessarily Alice. Hopefully this girl could help.

We went into the nearest trailer, hoping to find some craft services and someone to tell us where everyone was. Instead it was filled with lighting equipment. Alice and I pulled out our phones and held them up only to find there was no reception.

The set was in the woods on the north side of the Miskatonic. Central Massachussets had a lot of mid-sized towns like Doolittle Falls, and some small cities, but there were large patches of woods with nothing but lakes, trees, and mountains. Alice was on set to wrangle the wildlife, which had proven to be difficult. A family of squirrels gathering the last of their winter provisions had been ruining their shots for weeks, apparently. The director insisted that they needed rare songbirds to flutter behind Freedom Boy's love interest, Dangerous Girl in her epic speech about fighting against the impossible and the power of love.

I was supposed to help with the weather that day. I was going to control the lighting while the team worked on the possible clouds passing over from the nor'easter that was just about to miss us. But then again, it seemed like the nor'easter didn't really miss us.Alice and I tried to see if our phones would work outside but had no luck. It was starting to get cold and wet and Alice's car was piling up with snow. If there was a ton of snow, we were going to be stuck, I bet. We had no shovels, just a small window scraper. My powers—whatever weather came out when I was heated—weren't strong enough to melt this snow. It was coming down hard.

We visited more trailers, but they were all empty. No pink Escalade girl. The only trailer left was the one for the actors. I felt nervous, even though it was pretty clear Freedom Boy hadn't gotten there yet.

"Maybe we should just head home," I suggested.

"Why?" Alice asked. "We came all they way out here. And I don't want to leave only to learn they docked us for not showing. I drove here, I'm getting paid." She looked at me. "The car will live, Sarah."

I groaned and followed her into a trailer named Lucy. The other one was labeled Desi. Inside was a medium sized room with a sleeper sofa, mirror, chair, some books, and pages from the script scattered around. Dangerous Girl sat in a large blue armchair. She had big green eyes and her hair was pulled back in a tight ponytail. It was hard to recognize her, at first, since she wasn't wearing makeup—and any picture I'd seen of Dangerous Girl had her in full armor, red lips popping, eyebrows sharp, lashes so lush you could draw them from memory. She was wearing blue leggings and a top with a giant circle cut in the center, which revealed her upper abdomen and lower breasts. It was hard not to stare. I looked at the enormous plaid blanket draped over her shoulders.

"And you are?" she said, as imperious as a queen.

"Crew. Looking to see where everyone is," Alice said.

"Oh crap. It's weather girl and rat girl," Dangerous Girl said. "The wonder interns. I heard about you. Freedom Boy is excited."

I was so surprised she knew what we did that I ignored the insult. "Where is he, anyways?"

"I don't know. Not one told me and I get no reception out here. I've been waiting for makeup for three hours."

I looked out the window. The world was pure white. I couldn't even see our cars ten feet away. Alice's car must already be a foot deep.

"Why don't you go back to the hotel?" Alice asked.

"I'm here to work," she said. "And if I'm not here, everyone can show up and get angry and call me a diva for ruining a day of shooting. It's not my style. I come to work, do my job, smile, and don't pull any of that crap that gets you a bad rep. Why do you think I'm the first one here, always? Spectacula was cut from the film because they couldn't insure her after missing shooting during Dreadnought 3: The Dreadening because she kept getting [air quotes] laryngitis."

"It's so easy for people to think you're a diva," Alice said, appreciatively.

"I don't think anyone's coming," I said. "The snow won't stop."

"Fine. You're probably right. Ugh, today. If I could get reception I'd fire my manager right now. This is just the worst."

She got up, grabbed a large leopard-print bag, and sashayed out the door. When she opened it, a gust of wind blew in, leaving a pile of snow on the linoleum. She paid no mind, slammed the door behind her and just kept walking to her car.

"Think she'll make it?" Alice asked.

I shrugged.

A minute later she came in, threw her bag on the ground and slumped back in the chair, caked in snow.

"I told you it was bad out there," I said.

"Whatever, weather genius," she snapped. A defeated look ran across her face, then suddenly a light flicked on. "Wait, weather girl. Make it stop. Can't you stop the snow?" I took another look outside. "Not with this weather. This is a hundred mile system. Anything I do will last seconds before collapsing, and we'd still have to dig out the cars.""Useless," she said. "No wonder you're an intern."

"Don't you have powers?" Alice asked. "Can't you fly away or lift the car up or melt it with lasers?"

"No," said Dangerous Girl, quickly. "I tried everything."

"I guess we're stuck here," Alice said, walking over to her fridge and pulling out two cans of Diet Solar Cola and handing me one.

Dangerous Girl stood up and grabbed a Solar Cola while we sat down on a small red couch. She opened it with a quiet "Pop" and looked out the window. "I guess you're right," she said, then opened the door in the back which led to another smaller room lined with clothes. She emerged a couple minutes later in blue sweatpants and a baggy blue Academy West sweatshirt, rubbing a cloth across her face.

I took a closer look. She really looked different without makeup. She looked like a teenager. And less like a cartoon.

"Don't take photos," she said. "The paps love photos of me without my Hero drag on."

"I didn't even think of it," Alice said sardonically.

"What?" Danger Girl said defensively. "Look, I don't know who I can trust. You two seem cool, but it's so hard and tiring," she said, collapsing back in her chair.

"I. We. Didn't even think of it," I said, trying to cut some of the tension in the room. Being caught in a trailer during a snowstorm between America's prom queen and Alice seemed like the most dangerous situation Dangerous Girl or me had ever been in. "You never know," Dangerous Girl said. "But thanks."

"So why do you do it?" Alice asked.

"What?" Dangerous Girl replied.

"Wear all the Hero Drag. The makeup, the tight costumes, the—excuse the expression—boob windows?"

Dangerous Girl laughed. She looked ready to spring. She and Alice had some weird chemistry. It was like they were going to fight or fall in love.

Alice apologized. "It's not an attack. I've seen your films. All of them. And your crossovers like this one."

I looked at Alice, shocked. She shifted on the red sofa. She had never admitted to liking or even hate-watching any Hero docs. I always thought that she was too cool for it. "You're pretty damn impressive," Alice said. Dangerous Girl smiled like a queen. "You can fly, fight, tie most villains in knots, lift a tank with a demure smile, backwards in high heels and all. I don't get it. Why do it? Aren't you beautiful enough without the revealing outfits and hyped-up sex stuff?"

The trailer was quiet for a moment, and then Dangerous Girl asked a question. "Have you ever heard of Princess Bellona?"

We thought for a moment and then said, "No."

"Exactly. Bellona is a boss bitch. Real bad-ass. I once got in a scuffle with her. Just roughhousing at school, and she juked me on the chin. It was a light tap with her fist, and I flew through three walls and woke up in the school infirmary three days later. She broke every strength and speed record our school ever had, and helped us with the Harpastball cup three years running almost singlehandedly. Even knocked a freshman Freedom Boy on his ass freshman year."

"Damn," Alice said. "So where is she now?"

"Nowhere. Well, no, that's not true. She's been doing some work in the Northwest on their ShWAT teams and will probably be in the Secret Service Paladins if she wants to. Though she's not too keen on authority figures. These days I heard she's in Portland with her girlfriend, coaching young Heroes that don't make it to the Academy."

"If she's so amazing how come I've never heard of her?" I asked. I did have my Hero obsession-stage. I had, at one point, the bulk of the Heroes to watch memorized. "Well, she's not pretty, for one. And two, she won't play the game. Won't even try to dress the part or femme herself up," said Dangerous Girl.

"That's super bad-ass of her," Alice said.

"Sure. But bad-ass doesn't pay the bills. She can't get sponsors. Sure, some places want to sponsor her, but not major brands. And you can't have a career without sponsorship. She once saved Brooklyn from a nuclear strike and it got a mention on the evening news. I save a cat from a tree and Hero gossip blogs talk about it for months on end." Dangerous Girl put on a funny voice. "What was she wearing? Did she look good? Who's she dating? Is that a baby bump? By saving a cat, is Dangerous Girl playing a dangerous game? That stuff gets eyes, and eyes get sponsors. Saving millions of lives, on the other hand—irrelevant if you're not playing the game. I know perfectly well that my meal ticket is a pair of double Ds while my waist is still slim. It won't last, but if I work hard, I have fifteen years."

"That's you, though," Alice said. "Other female Heroes aren't showing off their chest like you and they do fine."

"It was a trademark by the time I was barely out of puberty. Once you get an image and a look it's hard to change it."

The hours passed while we waited in Dangerous Girl's trailer. The vibe never got less weird. Dangerous Girl was both weirdly hostile and desperately lonely, Alice was alternately making fun of her and acting like her new best friend, in a way that alienated me, and, well, I was just there until I got a ride home. Which, if the snow had its way, wasn't happening anytime soon. I wished I had enough power to dismantle a system of this strength, but as much as I wished for it, it wasn't happening today. Meanwhile, Dangerous Girl was bored enough to give us loads of gossip on just what Hero life was like. It sounded exhausting.

"Wait," I said. "So you're saying that the Dangerous Girl persona is something you fell into. Who gave you the look?" I asked.

"My first manager, a total sketchball, and my mom put a costume together. My boobs came along right about when I got my powers. The manager promised get me into the Wonder Teens Academy West as long as I wore the boob window costume," she said. "That's screwed up!" I blurted.

Dangerous Girl sighed. "Way of the world, little one. And speaking of the way of the world, we should probably start talking about the elephant in the room. You and Freedom Boy." She reclined in her chair and sipped her Solar Cola. She seemed like a cat playing with a mouse, lazily toying with us for her own amusement. "As his official girlfriend of the moment I know that, no matter what he tells you, he's not your boyfriend and, if his million dollar sponsorship deals have anything to say, probably never will be. Now you're the townie that he talks about all the time, and I bet your all-too-infrequent conversations follow a similar pattern. Let me guess. He keeps telling you that once something's over or once something has happened, your love can be on again. It can be real."

I thought about all the times Freedom Boy changed the subject immediately to all the pressures that he had on him and in his life the minute he I tried to bring up our relationship. Or when he disappeared for a summer. Or the way I didn't feel like I could tell him anything, even though I wanted to tell him everything. My silence spoke volumes.

Dangerous Girl continued, "Sad to say, it's not unique. They all do it. All the Hero Boys. They all have one true love, someone they can tell their secrets to and they give a promise ring to and someday, they swear, it's all going to be real. Sometimes it's someone they knew before they got their powers, other times it's someone they met on set. Usually someone paid to spend time with them, like a makeup person or costumer or a young PA. It's always true love with these girls and everything else is for show. Funny thing is that true love lasts a year, tops."

Her know-it-all attitude was starting to get to me. "What do you know?" I asked, defensively. "We've been… a thing," I said, lamely, "and it's been for over a year now. He's been in public with me."

The trailer grew quiet. Dangerous Girl raised one perfectly arched eyebrow. Alice was watching our détente like it was a tennis match. Just when the silence was more than I could take, Dangerous Girl muttered, "You seem like a nice girl. But you should watch out. You're either gunning for a broken heart and an 8x10 signed glossy or a screaming bastard in nine months."

She was bitter. So bitter. It turned the air thin. "I would never date someone just for the sake of an 8x10," I responded. "I would at least want a poster."

This last sentence got lost in the air, as Alice replied, "Freedom Boy wouldn't do that. He's decent."

"That's what my mom said about SilverMan," Dangerous Girl

replied. "But look at me."

"You're Silver's daughter?" I asked. SilverMan was known for his facility with the world's coinage. He could make the US nickel bend to his will, and the results were usually torturous. There were too many nickels, for one.

"You tell anyone I'll kill you. Though it's a widely known secret," Dangerous Girl said, with an air of boredom.

Alice's jaw dropped. She was disappointed. She really had a secret thing for Dangerous Girl's work, I guess.

"What, you believed the race of Superwomen from the planet Saphon delivered me? I'm from Pensacola, Florida. Born and raised. Saphon's made up. It's where all the bastard girls of Heroes come from in our mythology."

This was shocking news. True behind-the-scenes stuff. Maybe I was naïve all of my favorite female Heroes, strong women, all of them, were from the planet Saphon. "But wait," I asked. "If everyone knows SilverMan's your dad, why hasn't he been taken into account? You could get a ton of money…"

Dangerous Girl nearly got lost inside her sweatshirt. "He had good lawyers and refused any blood tests. In exchange he helped get me on the Wonder Kids and probably got me the manager with the connections to Academy West. I didn't ask too many questions. We were poor but when things got bad my mom played some cards I didn't know about and then things got better."

She took a swig of her Solar and got up and walked around the room, checking her phone again for reception. "Sorry, I'm not usually so chatty. It's just rare to be stranded in a trailer with nothing to do and no Wi-Fi. Sucks, right?"

Alice rolled her eyes in solidarity. "I had band practice," she said. "Totally missing it."

"Band practice," Dangerous girl laughed. "I thought that was the case. What's your deal, bird girl? Talking to animals, hipster, playing in some silly band."

"You got me," Alice said, not taking the bait. Dangerous Girl seemed like she was up for a fight.

She lit on me. "So when it comes to you, you can control the weather enough to be on set as an apprentice. Yet you're not in the Academy."

"Two words for you," I replied. "Lady Oblivion." Dangerous Girl screwed up her face, totally confused and drawing a blank. "The Bane of Innsmouth?"

Her eyes lit up and she giggled. "Dude, that was your mom? And you're Freedom Boy's townie? That's amazing. Total Romeo and Juliet story right there. Freedom Man's whole raison d'etre is to destroy your mom. Can't wait for that doc!" She broke down in laughter. "Wow... just, wow." When she finally stopped, she said, "But why did that keep you out of the Academy? I knew kids at Academy West whose parents were real villains and that never hurt them."

"My powers aren't great. I control them with my emotions and they're not that strong."

Really?" Dangerous Girl replied. "Weather Girl, that's some patriarchal BS. Your emotions matter. I mean, when I act, I'm just calibrating my emotions on various levels. Maybe you're just not a great actress, man. If you're a better actress, then you'll have full power."

Alice nodded. "That's a really good idea. Sarah should just do some acting classes."

"Most of them aren't that good, though," Dangerous Girl said. "Dirty little secret is that half of what they teach is showmanship so we can be on teams and in docs. You can read books, I guess, or move to Los Angeles or New York and take a real class."

It sounded magical. But I was stuck in stupid Doolittle Falls. "Can you teach me?" I asked.

"Really?" Dangerous Girl said. "That's cute, but I can't. I'm super busy, have an image to maintain, commercials, events to go to. I can't just teach you how to act."I was losing her. But, at the least, I had one thing in my pocket. "Look, that makes sense. But I have something I can barter your way if you want to take, like, ten minutes to tell me what books to read and how I can study real acting techniques."

Dangerous Girl looked at me, dubious. I continued, "I can give you light."

"Huh."

"This is a big doc. Huge. From what I know, it's the biggest budget film you've done. And you need it to succeed as much as Freedom Boy, but unlike Freedom Boy, you don't have your own franchise. So you not only need it to do well, you need to look good doing it. So, what better way to look good then to have one of the weather people specifically focus on making sure the sunlight is properly diffused and hits you at the right angle?" I was bluffing, a bit, but it was the only thing I had.

"You can do that," Dangerous Girl said slowly. She seemed dubious.

"I mean, I can't stop the snow, but I can move the clouds around to make you look beatific." I paused. "And I can get the other weather people on your side. A friend to the crew is a friend to all, right?"

She chewed on the thought for a moment. "The lessons will be short. When we finally get out I'll suggest some books and do some exercises with you when I practice my lines."

I thrust out my hand so we could shake on it. She grabbed it, a slippery, limp fish. "I think I got some DVDs in here," she said. "Want to watch The New Wonder Teens?""Yes," Alice said, loudly. She looked bored to death, as if her spirit left her body during the second hour of snow.

As we settled in to watch the DVDs, I had absolutely no idea whether I'd ever see Dangerous Girl in person again. She was a busy young Hero, and we had a limited amount of time working on the film. To get the kind of access that we had to her life, if only for a snow day, was the result of a gigantic snow system that covered half the country, dumping a foot-plus in Doolittle Falls and requiring weeks of digging out. But sometimes the weather had a weird knack for putting the right people in your path, if you let it happen.

TWENTY-FIVE

A COUPLE OF weeks later, I got a big package in the mail. The yellow envelope had a message scrawled on the outside: "Good luck, sucker!" I had a feeling it was Dangerous Girl making good on her end of the deal. She had sent me an old copy of *The Drama of the Modern Hero*, yellowed pages and all. It looked well loved, with a creaking spine. The book was published in 1996, but the original edition came from the Sixties. As I flipped through the first few pages I could tell that it was a book from another time with its antiquated prose and casual racism.

"There's so many things to worry about, from the Red Menace at home and abroad…"

"Russian missiles bearing down on us and only you can stop them…""Women starting to become Heroes, the eye candy is almost to much to stay focused on real crime…"

"Secret Nazi scientists still lurking in mountains working on nuclear monsters…""The "urban element" taking over the streets…"

The book was useless. Just some old man bloviating about how hard it was being a white male Hero in the 1960s and how working on Docs was so much more difficult than people knew. I was about to throw it away and then one line caught my attention: "Controlling your emotions are the key to being successful as a Hero, both in fighting a supervillain and filming a super documentary. Most people don't realize this but a lot of being a Hero is acting, and many powers are controlled by their emotions. Female Heroes coming on the scene may have an advantage, though it is likely lost on their distractibility and inferior strength.

But your ability to control your powers is only as strong as your ability to control your emotions. Take, for example, the Stupendous Monster. Scientists and America's laboratories have tested the strength of his punch. When in a good mood it's about four times the strength of Cassius Clay. But when he's angry, it's as powerful as a jet engine hitting a brick wall. And he's not alone. Some Heroes even control their powers with their emotions."

The charmer ended with, "I know, it sounds crazy, but it's true."

I underlined the sentence, circled it, and put seven asterisks around it. It was the first time I'd heard anyone mention the connection between powers and emotions. I gritted my teeth and read on.

The key to acting, as this guy put it, was sense memory. If you thought about memories with strong emotions attached to them, you could add them to your arsenal of weapons, like a laser gun or energy shield, and pull them out as needed. As you got better, you didn't even need to recall them, you could just go to the emotion.

I thought about the time when Johnny dared me to jump off the roof of the house. I was terrified and I thought I'd hurt myself, but I screwed up my courage and did it anyways. I think that day was linked to something like courage, and as I felt that memory in my body, I could see a shaft of sunlight come through the window.

Little did I know that getting the acting book in the mail would be just the beginning. I was trying some sense memory experiments in my room, writing down what memory yielded what feeling, and what weather was emerging in response, when I heard Johnny yelling up the stairs. "Hey, Sarah, come watch the T.V."

There was a breaking story in Chicago. Someone was holding a nursing home hostage. But while the police had surrounded the building and were busy trying to negotiate with the bad guy, The Red Ghost had burst onto the scene. Technically.

The Red Ghost wore a light red costume and he could vanish in quick blurs of motion. He had showed up and rushed into the building, ignoring the police. Apparently The Red Ghost killed the villain, and some residents of the facility were seriously injured in the melee.

As a black body bag was rolled out of the building on a stretcher, The Red Ghost came striding out of the building, as proud as a peacock. A rush of reporters pushed their way toward him with their mics thrust forward. In unison, they barked the usual questions: "What happened?" "What was it like in there?" "Who was this deranged madman?" "How ever can the city thank you?" "Where you scared?"

Before he could answer, a man in a black suit came to his side, probably his PR guy or agent. The Red Ghost deflected all the questions. "I was just doing what anyone gifted with my powers and talents would have done. It was hectic in there but I wasn't scared. I just thought of the good citizens, people's grandmothers and grandfathers, important people, and how tough it was for them. They needed to be saved."

Johnny muttered something and I shushed him.

The conference continued, and The Red Ghost gave the usual spiel. "The citizens of Chicago need to feel safe from terrorists and maniacs. I will not sleep until this town is rid of such scourges and…" Before he could finish an elderly woman cut him off, screaming.

"You bastard!" she screeched, in a howl of pain. "You evil lunatic. You killed my son! You killed my baby!" She was crying and swinging her arms, trying to attack him. The reporters held her back.

The Red Ghost looked a little shocked but quickly regained his stiff-jawed composure. "I'm sorry, ma'am, but your son was threatening the lives of the good people being treated at this facility. Having fought him, I can tell you he had powers but was no Hero. He was a supervillain, bent on destruction."

"That's the media code for Misshapes," Johnny said. "You know it. That's how they blame all crime on Misshapes. People with powers who are 'no Heroes.'"

The woman persisted. "He wasn't a supervillain. *You're* the villain!"

The cameras pointed back toward The Red Ghost. His face went white. "I'm sorry but you must be mistaken. The man I killed was dressed in a ridiculous outfit, was making outrageous threats against the people in there, which is why the police where called."

"My son was visiting me!" she sobbed. "He's not well but he's no villain. How dare you, you…"

We watched as the press conference lost total control. The cameras turned to The Red Ghost, his composure shaken to the soundtrack of a bereaved woman's tears. The man in the suit was trying to control the situation and directing the police to take her away. Take her anywhere off camera.

"I empathize with your pain," said The Red Ghost. He paused, his face a mask of sincerity. "But that's no excuse to threaten people's lives. I saved the people in there.""All of them except one," my dad grumbled. "It would've been different if he was…"

The camera turned back on the woman. The police took her away as she shouted, "He did nothing wrong. He has a condition. He's a good boy," she cried out "He's not well but he's a good boy. He's a good boy."

The woman disappeared, and The Red Ghost refused to take any more questions. The press conference was over, but the damage had been done.

The next morning every channel was covering the story. The press conference had gone viral, a slow-motion car crash. Bit by bit, we got more details. The "villain" was a Misshape who had the ability to make small sparks with his fingers. He had a history of mental illness but never anything violent. He was, in fact, visiting his grandmother. Something had made him agitated, or he got in a fight, it wasn't clear, but some residents got nervous and the police were called.

Speculation flew back and forth. Talking heads bloviated about the story, whether he was a threat, if The Red Ghost had overstepped his bounds. On WXBS, pundits, all in the pro-Hero camp, about the dangers of Misshapes—though they called them The Unregistered, as in people with powers that don't have a Hero Card—and how this incident was clearly not Heroes going wild, but a reason to put greater controls on Misshapes.

The Police Commissioner and the mayor were on another channel telling people not to rush to conclusions and think of all The Red Ghost's good work. The man who stood next to The Red Ghost at the event was defending him at his very own press conference, with a row of citizens behind him whose lives had been saved by the Hero. On another channel, a woman with a shock of red hair was demanding he be prosecuted for his crimes while a man with Botoxed cheeks told her that the old women should be arrested for assisting terrorists like her son.

But while the twenty-four hour news speculation had begun, there was no real movement on the story. It was just a case of Hero-said/she-said, with just enough information that every channel could devour it, minute by minute. I couldn't tear myself away from the T.V. The case was unsettling, messy, and it seemed like it was a cover-up happening in real time. Johnny was outraged, and I was too. I wanted this Misshape's name to be cleared. I didn't think he was a murderer, a crazy guy keeping a nursing home hostage. I had a suspicion that it was really The Red Ghost who caused this mess.

The non-stop television coverage was stopped with an official report from the Bureau of Superhero Affairs. Every channel featured J4 behind a podium with the Bureau of Superhero Affairs logo. The Red Ghost stood next to him. J4 made an announcement that "the case has been looked at thoroughly, and there was no wrongdoing." He continued, "While it is unfortunate that the man did not get the treatment he so needed, this is an indictment of our mental health system, and the need for more care in the community. Who know how many lives may have been lost if not for The Red Ghost's heroics? As I said when I took office, Heroes are the protectors of our great nation. We need to allow them to do their jobs without the intervention of Bureaus like my own, or all of us are at risk. I want to thank The Red Ghost and apologize to him on behalf of the country. It's time for us all to move on. Justice has been served today."

My brother snapped. He threw the remote across the room, and it hit the window with a clatter. "Justice? He's a murderer. They're congratulating a murderer! And this 'exhaustive investigation' took an hour or two. Justice went out the window with The Red Ghost."

I didn't know what to say. There really wasn't anything that I could've said. I felt sick.

TWENTY-SIX

THE CASE of The Red Ghost wasn't just an isolated event of Heroes abusing their powers. It was the first in a wave. Day by day, the news had some story, about a heroic Hero helping justice occur but they all seemed shady around the edges. There were never enough interviews with witnesses. All the press conferences sounded like party lines. Perhaps Johnny's paranoia was getting to me, but I didn't buy it. The media felt like a propaganda machine. There was a story behind the story they were telling us.

We kept talking about all these cases in Civic Responsibility. The Division of Palladin Affairs was suspending new Hero Laws everyday so that Heroes could correct any wrong in society the way that they saw fit, and when some dudes loitering are confronted with a guy who has the strength of a Blue Whale, the guy with crazy animal strength may not use if for good. With each new incident there was initially a cry for justice, followed by a counter-report from government officials and Hero advocates that the incidents were in response to rising crime rates. "This is the price of defending freedom," was a common refrain after a bystander was killed during an operation or an innocent person was mistaken for a supervillain.

There was a Hero team in Detroit called the Motor City Marauders that was accused by community leaders of harassing people who did nothing wrong or of disproportionally injuring people for minor crimes. The mayor and several business groups defended the Heroes as the only ones capable of cleaning up the city, and they had safe neighborhoods for the first time in decades. The public echoed it, at least in the papers and on TV, with people coming forward to thank the Motor City Marauders for saving their lives from gangs and junkies.

The narrative was too simple. Someone who was born evil with nothing but malfeasance in their heart was stopped from wreaking the havoc that was born to them, across our fallen cities, by a noble Hero. The newspapers and T.V. stations would show the spectacular footage of someone flying in and stopping a villain in their tracks, over and over again so that it was the only story. In class, Ms. Frankl tried to lead us in conversations on the balance of liberty and safety in society, the need for Heroes and the equal need for limits on their powers. We didn't listen, though. There was so much awful news, and we started complaining about Heroes who already screwed up our lives. I have to admit, I was really enjoying this new, freeform version of Civic Responsibility. It was my favorite class.

When Hamilton walked into the classroom, he made a beeline for the teacher's desk and held up a small red thumb drive high enough for everyone to see. Ms. Frankl looked utterly confused.

"I've got it," he said to Ms. Frankl.

"Got what?"

"The segment. The one they pulled." Hamilton was beaming with pride. "Guys, we could blow this case up. We could make it go viral."

"How did you do that, dear student?" Ms. Frankl asked.

"I'd prefer not to say." He clicked his glasses shut.

"Hamilton, you didn't..." Ms. Frankl blurted. "We won't get in trouble, will we? I'm on thin enough ice."

"Look, the less you know the better. I got it off the Internet, isn't that enough?"

"But they've been threatening every site and getting it pulled down left and right," her voice dipped to a whisper. We all leaned in to hear what she'd say next. "Even all the torrent sites. They shut down Bandits Ally for a week just for someone's errant post.""Yes, but, I did it," Hamilton said. "So we should watch it!" He handed the thumb drive to his teacher and she clutched it tightly in her hand. Hamilton walked to his seat."Are you in the dark net?" Backslash said.

"What's the dark net?" Hocho asked.

"It's like, the super-secret part of the..." Marcus said, and Hamilton shushed them with a gleam in his eye. Ms. Frankl was running around in the front of the class, taping pieces of black construction paper over the window in the door, and shutting the blinds tightly. She signaled for Wendy's help, and together they moved a computer from the back of the classroom to her desk, facing the class.

"Sweet, video time," Kurt said.

"Ms. Frankl, why can't we watch it on a TV?" Alice asked. "I don't have my glasses."

The teacher turned, sharply. "You have to check out the TVs from the A.V. room. And we don't..."

"Want to leave a record," Hamilton finished.

Ms. Frankl turned off the lights, put the drive in the computer, and clicked on a file. It was an unedited clip from Real Time With Bob Dine on EBC.

Bob sat in a large black chair. Across from him was a teenager in a wheelchair, probably about my age, black. He got oxygen from a tube and his body was immobile from the neck down. There was a small tube in front of one of his eyes. The boom mic, cameras, and crew were still visible. They were setting up, and the set hummed with a busybody industriousness. The clip looked weird. The color was off, it was overexposed, and there were numbers at the top and bottom of the screen.

The sound crew was checking the microphones. Donny, was able to speak but not move his body. He had to take deep wet breaths every minute, which caused a loud mechanical sucking noise from a machine attached to the wheelchair, which looked like an accordion. There was a tube coming out of his mouth, siphoning of spit.

Bob Dine said, "Check, one, two. Okay, we're good."

A producer stepped in, talked to him briefly, and yelled action with a click of the clapboard slate. The cameras pulled in so the frame held Bob and Donny. The color was still weird. Bob leaned in. "I'm here with Donald Peterson. Donald, it is a pleasure to have you with us."

"Thank you, Bob. You can call me Donny," he said. It was hard for Donny to talk. Each work took effort, and his face looked pained.

"Okay, Donny. Now can you tell us what happened to you?"

"It was a stupid prank. My friend Kevin and I had a silly competition where we tagged abandoned buildings around town."

"Tagged?" Bob needed that word explained to him.

"Marked them with graffiti. Drew stupid pictures. It was childish."

"And illegal." Bob seemed like a schoolmarm.

"Yes, illegal. We trespassed. But most the places had no owners. It was victimless."Bob had a look of glee on his face. "Except the last one. It did have an owner."Donny replied, slowly, "Yes, yes it did. I didn't know that at the time." There was a pause, and the two men just stared at each other. Donny broke the silence. "Kevin had really stepped up his game with the water tower. Everyone in town could see it. I had the SATs coming up and really needed to spend nights studying, not slinking around trying to get the more impressive tag. But I was obsessed with topping Kevin…" he trailed off. "It was going to be my last."

Bob interjected, "Bill, can we get a cut to Kevin's water tower tag at this point?" A yes came over the loudspeaker. "Go on, son," Bob said, motioning to Donny.

"I'd always dreamed about doing it. Two round mounds, on the edge of town. So big everyone could see them from downtown, which was miles away. Two old gas storage towers, painted in a faded pink. One red circle and a large concentric circle around each would be all it took and the town would be mine. I'd have the best tag around. Easy job, an hour max. I'd sign my name and retire."

"How did you get in?"

"The gate was easy enough to get over. Ever since I got my powers, gates and fences weren't a problem."

"So you're Empowered," Bob said, and another bleat over the loudspeaker said, "Good job, Bob. The people don't like the term Misshape." Donny cringed.

"Sure."

"How long?"

"It was two years before the accident."

"What did you get?"

"I could, stick to metal. My hands. Not so much these days," he said, looking down at his curled up fingers. "Fences, as long as they weren't wooden, were easy."

We watched as he launched into his story. His power sounded cool. Kind of Spiderman-ish. You could climb a whole city in metal. I felt awful for Donny. "The first oil tank was easy enough. It was larger in person. The width of this entire school. It was night so I was unable to see the dull pink paint, and instead just a large black shadow. There were some pipes jutting out of the bottom at various angles. I put a foot on one and pushed myself up the smooth surface of the tower. I placed one hand on the large wall, spreading my fingers wide. It was cool to the touch. I tensed up my hand and felt the pads of my fingers find purchase on the wall. With all my strength I hoisted myself and my backpack upward."

Bob motioned to the crew. "Now we have some shots of the towers. They're about what, fifty feet high?"

The screen went black with the words *insert footage from reel 4A*.

" I climbed the one on the left first. It was hard. Even with my powers I still had to pull myself up with one arm, pushing from my legs. When I was at the top I was sweating so much that my grip got slippery. If I touched sweat instead of metal my hand would slide right off. Smaller movements made it easier, but they made the trip take twice as long. I reached the part of the building where it started to curve upward. I looked down and my eyes went wide. I was so, so high. I wanted a third hand so I could've taken a picture but my phone was in my bag. Besides, I had better things to do. Like tag. I scrambled to the very top of the mound and pulled my can out of my backpack. In under a minute I had done it; I made a large red circle around the tower. Hilarious. The perfect tag."

Bob was unamused. "What where you thinking?"

"It was stupid. Like I said, just a prank. I imagined the entire town looking up and laughing, including Kevin. So after that I climbed down a little to where the tower started to curve and worked on the large line that would become the outer circle. I had to cling to the wall while I did it, and it was a much harder job. I finished in five minutes by painting with one arm and swinging along with the other. When I was finished, I climbed down and went up to the other tower."

"That sounds exhausting. You were exhausted, right? That's what the press said." "Sure. You would be too. But did they also explain the missing security footage? Or that Hero's lame-ass alibi?" Donny paused, serious. "I don't know how many times I have to explain this to people, but I. Didn't. Slip."

"Whoa," Bob said. "You seem pretty angry."

Donny didn't seem angry, just tired. Tired of explaining himself. Tired of having to justify his existence. "Please don't put words in my mouth, sir. I'm not angry. Let me tell you the rest of the story." He continued, "The next tower was easier. I scrambled to the top and I knew what was happening so I knew how to tag it with ease. When I finished the large circle I sensed something odd. I couldn't quite place it. At first I thought it was the wind or some kind of bird. But it felt larger. More ominous. And close."

"I turned slowly to look. Was there something out there? Didn't think so. All I could see was the dark town and the farms in the distance. When I turned my head back to the work, I saw a man. An enormous man, in a silver and blue uniform, his arms across his chest, hovering slightly above the tower. He had a stern face, high cheekbones, pale gray eyes, and thin pink lips. His muscles bulged out from under the suit. I could feel his breath tickle the top of my head. My hands startled and I nearly lost my grip."

"And that was Cryo-Man. What did he say to you?"

"I'll never forget it. He had this stupidly deep voice, like one of those kids trying to pretend to be adult things. And he bellowed. 'I am CryoMan. Defender of the right. Punisher of evil,' and I just stared at him."

"Was that the first time you'd seen CryoMan?"

"Yes. Well, no, actually. Once before, at a Mall signing before the Dallas premiere of his documentary. I was eight maybe, and I went with my dad. I remembered, I know this is weird, I remembered those hands signing my ticket stub at the moment they grabbed me by the shirt and lifted me into the sky."

"And in that moment CryoMan wasn't thinking about an innocent eight-year-old waiting in line for his movie, was he?"

"No."

"What do you think CryoMan was thinking?"

"To CryoMan, I was a black Misshape trespassing and defacing property. I had to be punished."

"Not stopped?"

"If he wanted to stop me he could have said so. I wasn't putting up a fight. I couldn't outrun him."

"He says you did."

"It's a lie."

"You didn't try to spray him in the face and run away."

"Run where? I was fifty feet up. The guy faces down laser tanks in his documentaries. Even if I did spray him, it was a reflex. He scared the crap out of me." "And what did he do next?"

Donny stared at Bob, deadpan. "Can't you see? He pulled me by the collar off the tower and held me above the ground, just floating there. I looked down and screamed. I was so scared. And he got up in my face; he was red with anger. Not like you see in documentaries, where he has that stern but fatherly look. He seemed deranged. And he said to me, "What do you have to say for yourself?' and I said something like I'm sorry. I'm sorry. *Don't tell my parents, Please don't tell my parents.* I know, after all that happened, that there were worse things then my parents finding out. But I kept thinking I would be paraded in front of TV cameras, and they would be called down to the police station and I might be sent to juvie and I'd never go to college."

"Why did you think that?"

"Because things are different for me. As you can plainly see. My buddy Kevin is a Normal. He has the background and the money to get in trouble and his parents take care of it. And he still got a car for his birthday. You call me Empowered, but I'm a Misshape, sir. I was attacked by a Hero. When I was a kid I thought Heroes were supposed to be the good guys. I'd heard stories, on the news, from friends, of Heroes getting more audacious. The nightly news keeps showing a regular stream of villains bested by local and national heroes. Always some plan foiled, someone on their way to the Luther. There was the occasion mention of an accidental death. Someone being seriously injured who was at the wrong place at the wrong time. But those were just stories. Stories are things that happen to other people."

Bob looked bored. He was the worst. "I know this is hard, but can you please tell me what happened next?"

"CryoMan lifted me high into the night sky. It was freezing. A hard wind blew against me and I was shivering with cold and fear. CryoMan held me firmly in his hands. I looked down. The ground seemed miles below. It was so scary. He kept rambling on about justice and liberty and rightness and vandals destroying the sanctity of the community. All in the third person, like a crazy politician. Stuff like, 'You have committed a dastardly act. Betrayed your town. Violated its laws,' which sounds great in a doc, but deranged when someone is threatening your life."

"I tried to reason with him. 'It's just a prank,' I said. 'Disorder is no prank. Every crime, no matter how small, rips the fabric of our great society. Little holes can do as much damage as big holes.' 'I didn't mean to rip anything. Please. Take me to the ground. Take me to the police. Anywhere but up here.' 'The ground you say,' CryoMan said with a smirk. And then, with a flourish, he dropped me. I shrieked and plummeted to the earth."

"CryoMan flew down and grabbed me. We were still high above the ground, as high as the towers. I kept pleading with him. Telling him I was sorry. CryoMan kept a stern look on his face, then, the last thing he said to me was, "I think you've learned your lesson.""

"Last thing before what?" Bob asked.

"He dropped me," Donny said. "For real this time. I felt his hands start to slip. For some reason his grip had loosened. Maybe it was my shivering. Or it was another attempt to scare me. But this time it was different. His face changed. He scrambled downward but I knew he wouldn't reach me in time. The ground was too close."

The bell rang but we all remained in our seats. The tape cut out and a message that read, "Ripped by XGremlinX" came across the screen.

"And then what happened?" Marcus asked.

"He ended up a paraplegic from the fall. And CryoMan denied everything. And the bureau closed all news from coming out," Hamilton said.

"How could they prevent the news from coming out?" I asked.

"New laws they passed," said Ms. Frankl. "Under the cover of night as a rider on a budget bill. They now have control over news as it relates to Hero incidents."

"But that's unconstitutional," said Alice.

"Maybe. But for the time being it hasn't been challenged. They claim it under their oversight of Heroes. It's claimed to be public safety related.

"Did he go to prison for that?" I asked.

"Heroes don't go to prison," Hamilton said. "They don't even apologize. That would undermine the hero ethic. Instead their press people apologize for the 'misunderstanding.' In the rare case the Palladin Division does a huge investigation, says mistakes were made on all sides, and issues a report for minor corrections. No one holds them accountable, and, by the end, they are the victims for getting caught up in everything. Meanwhile mistakes on all sides and one side dead."

"It's so wrong," Johnny interjected. "A justice system where the right person can kill for minor crimes or no crimes at all. Only criminals go to prison. And if they are Misshapes they go to the Luther. Heroes are never criminals, even when they are."Ms. Frankl added, "But, Heroes do, on occasion, go to prison. It might not seem like it, but there have been a number of incidents where people with powers were prosecuted for their crimes. The system is built against it, but it's not impossible. Like Mr. Atom."

"Who?" Butters asked.

"Mr. Atom. Though you may know him as Dr. Radion."

"Wasn't he some Cold War villain?" Hamilton asked.

"Yes. That's how people know him now. But he worked for the government for most of the Forties and Fifties before they found out he was responsible for all those deaths.

"That's the thing though," Johnny said. "The only story they tell is of a villain who tricked people. It's never a Hero, doing what people expect Heroes to do, that did something wrong. It was always someone who wasn't a real Hero, or was a spy or something. So we don't question the fundamental lie that is the Palladin Division's whole program."

"So," said Ms. Frankl with a grin. "Question it then."

TWENTY-SEVEN

H AMILTON HAD set up a TV in his studio so we could all watch the competition together. We gathered around the television to watch the competition, which was being broadcast live on the Real Network—one of those high digit channels that people with deluxe cable packages get—but Hamilton had found a live stream. It was being held at a Casino in New Jersey.

"How'd he get there?" I asked Betty.

"Bus."

"Are his parents there?"

"They don't know about it. Well, they don't know it's today. Things haven't been great lately."

A large "National Karaoke Challenge" logo popped up on the screen and the camera zoomed over the crowd. It was being held in a large theatre, although the attendance wasn't that high. Lots of empty seats. Finally the camera settled on a view of the judges' table and the stage, which was light up in white, red, and blue lights. There was a solitary mic in the center and a small T.V. on a tripod to the left of it.

The competition was good. People had elaborately choreographed dance routines to go with their song—one guy even did a split during a crescendo—everyone could sing, and powers abounded. Light shows, hovering, double, triple, and quadruple jointed movements, and even some strange vocal powers where people sang their own choruses, time looped their voice somehow. One girl who got up was able to turn the mic into a sort of Theremin—or at least that's what Tape Deck called it—and warbled her own voice by moving her hands around in elaborate gestures. I wouldn't call it pleasant sounding, but it sure as heck was cool.

When Butters got up we started to hoot and cheer. He had his two Spectors with him. No Doris. According to the schedule, she was going after two more people. He looked nervous but composed. Based on the competition he would have to be better than we'd ever seen him, but we had faith. Butters had been practicing relentlessly. The Judge announced Matt Butters would be performing an "Old Fashioned Love Song."

"Which old song?" I asked.

"No silly," Alice said. "It's a song by Three Dog Night."

"Who?"

"No, not Pete Townsend. Three Dog Night."

I gave her a blank stare.

"It's a band. They wrote a song. Called Old Fashioned Love Song."

"Well that's confusing," I said. "And not old?"

Butters stepped up to the mic and Johnny shushed me. He thanked the judge and the lights dimmed. The music started and he sung the word "Just" before the backing instrumental stopped suddenly and the lights went on.

"I'm sorry, there seems to be some issue," the judge said. He was speaking to a producer offstage.

Just then Admiral Skylark appeared on the stage, flanked by men in white coats, and a nice older couple.

"What the heck is going on?" Hamilton said.

"Are those…?" Betty asked, between her hands.

"Who?"

"His parents."

"There seems to be a violation in the rules. The contestant has split his entry," the judge announced.

"That wasn't me. That was Doris," Butters said.

"Yes, but she isn't real. She's a projection," the judge noted.

"They said it was okay!" Butters cried. "She was the one who started it!"

The men in the coats approached him. He caught them out of the corner of his eye and then the screen went black. We heard a bulb burst and a woman's scream. And then a face appeared on the screen. Terrifying, its skin partly melted, its mouth a maw of flame. It shrieked. And we all shrieked back at it, terrified from beyond the screen.

"What the hell was that?" Johnny asked.

"Oh no," said Betty. "Oh no, Oh no, Oh no…"

She kept repeating it. I wrapped my arm around her as she looked on between her hands in horror.

It was too confusing to make sense of through our stream. Floating apparitions, screaming harpies, flashbulbs reflecting off of lab coats, Skylark grinning as birds flew around him in whirls of gray and brown, Butters trying to run, more creatures popping up on screen. It seemed like a massacre. Like hell unleashed on earth. But when the lights went back on everything was fine—no one was hurt, just some scared looking karaoke fans—except Butters.

The men in coats were leading him out while his parents, faces covered in tears, trailed behind trying to comfort him. He wasn't resisting, he marched with them, but he looked empty. Skylark was shouting empty sentimental comforts to the Butters family about how they would get through this, but after they exited the building, he lingered, and spoke to the judge.

There was another conference among officials with Skylark pointing out in the rulebook that, as the runner-up, he was allowed to take the place of Butters and Doris in their absence. He was granted permission after a commercial break, and before he started singing. He dedicated the song to Butters and wished him well.

We turned off the TV instead of watching his smug performance, and tried to call Butters but got nothing. We each spent the next two hours trying to figure out what happened and calling and texting every number we could think off. All the mental hospitals we tried said they couldn't say anything because of confidentiality. The best we could figure was that Skylark, as a concerned adult, had told Mr. and Mrs. Butters what had happened and convinced them their son needed help. Given Betty's story they were probably expecting something like this and didn't need too much convincing.

Our theory was partially concerned when Johnny finally got through on Butters' cell phone. His father picked up. Johnny held out the phone so we could all hear.

"Our son in getting treatment right now and needs time away from such stressful situations and people who are unhealthy for him. Please stop calling or I will tell the police you are harassing my family and our sick child." Johnny gave him a series of "yes, sirs" and was as polite as apple pie, and then he got off the phone quickly.

"That was a bust," he said. "Should we go to the diner?"

TWENTY-EIGHT

BETTY WAS a wreck. Watching Butters carted off like that and not knowing where he was started to drive her crazy. She would drive by his house for any signs of him, check obsessively online for any messages or hints of his location. It was on TV so there was a chance some gossip rag would cover it. But nothing. I tried to intervene when I found out that she had been driving by nearby mental hospitals, learning when they let their patients outdoors, and seeing if Butters was among them.

The rest of us weren't much better, but we had things to distract us. Johnny and his band. Hamilton and his art. And me and my... well, I was splitting my time between researching Mom and improving my powers. I'd decided the best course of actions was to take a break from my normal training regime and start on a new one.

I'd been reading Dangerous Girls' books on acting like they were SAT prep work. Every night I would open one up, read the chapter once, read it again with a highlighter, and then spend an hour or two doing the various proscribed exercises in the mirror. One week I spent every night crying on command for no reason. Well it started with reasons, but after a few days the book explained how to tap into the raw emotion. After eight hours of crying over nothing I checked off sadness and depression.

Unfortunately, not only did this mean I cried constantly for a week, it also meant Doolittle Falls got record rainfall and the weatherman was confounded as to why. "Aberrant system" was the best he could come up with for why we had seven sunny days with deluges from 7:30-9:30 each night, which ended precisely when my favorite show (there was a Hero Housewives of Gotham marathon that week) came on. When the Bureau of Palladin Affairs was called in to investigate, I decided to switch to another emotion. Had I had one of the power dampeners they keep at the Academy I could have cried to my hearts content without a single drop falling on the precious Doolittle ground.

I was slowly becoming a master of my own emotions, which was having some pretty strange side effects. Gale force winds hitting our house on a calm day, enormous balls of hail terrifying the neighbors dogs, snow, sleet, slain, sun showers, humidity on cold days, any and every form of terrestrial excretion. There were a million types of winds and precipitations and I was learning the precise emotions to make them happen.

Though the emotion itself wasn't enough. It just created the raw nature. To build something bigger, like a system, required knowing how the weather worked. And for that I needed Sam and his toys at PeriGenomics. I could will myself to anger at the drop of a pin, but I needed to practice directing lightning or it would just strike anywhere and everywhere. Which it did. Dad, after losing cable because of a downed power line during a particularly exciting Maximum Fighting match, had a talk with me about my practice. Also, between researching Mom, my practice with Dangerous Girl's books, and my practice with Sam, my schoolwork was starting to suffer.

Sam and I spent several weeks on what he referred to as supersonic winds. They were winds so strong that they were rare in nature. One gust could knock down a skyscraper and a sustained wind could level a town. But such forces were outside the hands of anyone because they required so much energy to create. The best most people could do was small, localized winds that could move objects at fast speeds. They could make simple objects into projectiles. The better (weather control people) could lift cars and send them flying with them, but even Sam didn't have that level of power yet.

After honing my skills for the better part of November, he told me to meet him at the Richman State Forest in Asher Falls for the "next step" as he called it.

TWENTY-NINE

ALICE VOLUNTEERED to give me a ride to the park. She was weirdly supportive of any time that I could spend with Sam. I didn't understand why she cared.

"I don't even know what this 'next step' is," I said.

"Sounds dirty," Alice said.

I blushed. "Shut up, Alice."

"What. All this time with Sam, whose main attribute seems to be shirtlessness and you haven't even thought about it." She took a break. "I really don't believe it."

"Well," I said, and got lost in my thoughts.

The car was silent for a minute.

"There's something I need to tell you," she said, suddenly sounding serious.

"What is it?" I asked. This statement portended doom. I was not prepared for the next thing out of her mouth.

"Your brother and I hooked up."

"Yeah, I know that," I replied. "You said that."

"No, we hooked up," she said, slowly. "It was my first time."

It was a small statement but it felt like she hit me in chest with a laser beam. I don't know why. I thought I should be happy for her, right? This was a big deal. But for some reason it felt like a blow against me. "What? Who?" I asked.

"I've been meaning to tell you. I wanted to for a while now."

I wanted to undo my seatbelt and jump out of the passenger seat. I knew what her answer was going to be, and I dreaded it.

"It was after the show. Election night. When we played together and escaped the cops."

"I can't believe that, Alice," I said. "Hang out with him, whatever. But the next level? With my brother? That is so weird."

"I know!" Alice said. "I was kind of unsure about how to tell you. It just sort of happened. We've spent so much time together in Rex Manning Day. And that night was so crazy. And scary. And after we played together and escaped he took me home..."

The implication hung in the air. I was grossed out and weirded out and I didn't know how I felt. We were silent in the car. She was waiting for me to say something. But I wasn't going to say anything. Congratulations seemed like the wrong thing. I guess I was supposed to be happy for her but it felt like she was just leaving me in the dust. And making it even worse, it involved my brother. Alice frowned, muttering, "What the hell, Sarah?" When I got out of the car without saying a word. I walked up to the trailhead where I was supposed to meet Sam, taking big, bold steps on the dirt. I didn't know what weather went with this feeling. There were a lot of things stewing in my brain and my body, but most of all there was a feeling of complete and utter betrayal.

It was as if Alice and I just had a fight. A really big fight, the kind where planets collide. But we hadn't said anything at all.

THIRTY

WE WALKED up the trail, which cut its way up through the forest to the top of a small mountain, Mt. Madness, the highest point in the range. By the time we got to the top I was panting. Sam asked me a question, and I changed the subject to his upcoming plans. I didn't want to talk about my life.

"I'm going to Africa again," he said. "I'm working with a team from Heroes Without Borders which is trying to redirect the migration patterns of a certain bat population which has been spreading a really nasty disease."

"You can change the flight patterns of animals. That's crazy," I said.

"That's the theory. There's someone on the team with supersonic powers, The Chiropterror Man. They think if I can shift the wind patterns and he can control them with sound waves, we might be able to get them to a less populated region." He was nearly bounding over the rocks. I envied his fitness.

"Won't that screw with the ecosystem?" I asked.

"Maybe. But it can't be worse than the spread of the Morsburg virus."

I thought about his plan as we created the trail. There was a lot of controversy about these interventions. You change one thing and the whole world shifts. Like the butterfly effect he had taught me. Maybe those bats ate bugs with a worse disease. But who was I to question whatever Sam was doing? He was always so excited about it. It sounded right.

The trail ended at a clearing that should've had a view of the valley, but you couldn't see it with all the trees. In the center of the clearing there was a metal fire tower, forty stories high, old and rickety. At the base of the tower was a sign that read, *climb at your own risk*. I felt like I was risking something by climbing. My lunch, maybe. My stomach jumped into my throat and I felt a gust of wind push at my back.

"What's the next step?" I asked him, looking up at the platform fifty feet above me. "You're being vague like usual." It didn't bother me, though. I liked hanging out with Sam because he was the only person in town who wanted to improve his powers lately.

"You have to get to the top, Sarah," Sam said. He bounded past me, rushing up the steps like a golden retriever.

The tower seemed to sway under our weight. The stairs were made out of grated metal, so I could look straight down and see the ground beneath me getting farther and farther away. My hands were starting to sweat and felt slick and the railing was perilously low. Sam mocked me with his relative ease. I was all nerves. Thoughts of Alice were miles away.

When I met Sam at the top, we walked to the edge and took a peek over the side. It was a far drop and an easy one to slip and make. I was nervous just thinking about it and I could hear the rumble of thunderclouds forming overhead. Sam grabbed my hand, trying to calm me down. "Today, we're going to learn how to fly," he said.

"Shut the front door," I blurted, stepping away from the edge to the relative safety of the center of the platform.

"Sarah, you already have the skills to do it. You even did it in the fire room. You just need to put it into practice."

He had such faith. It was something to see. But I didn't believe him. I felt very small as he looked at me with wet eyes. "I can't," I said, feeling myself grow small. "What if I screw up? Clearly death is the solution there."

"I got you. Now we'll start small," he said. He pulled a baseball out of his pocket. "I want you to catch this with a supersonic wind and keep it aloft, okay? It's simple." He lobbed the ball off the tower and I created a wind to push it upward. It hovered in the air at eye level for a moment, and then shot off into the distance.

As it flew into the forest I hoped there were no people in its way. Like it could hit Alice and — Oh no, Alice! The thought of her sent me reeling. She was out there somewhere, walking through town, mad at me. Or maybe I was mad at her. We were feeling emotions together. My mind just kept thinking about my conversation with her. Was she right? Had I been selfish? I just didn't know how to feel.

I needed to get a grip or this would turn out terribly.

"Okay," Sam said. "Not bad. It was light so it was hard to control. Someone your size shouldn't fly so far. Are you ready?" He grabbed my hand.

"No," I said, glumly. I would never be ready. Not with a brain that kept thinking thoughts that tried to kill me. He took my hand and led me forward. I dug my heels into the platform and had to be dragged the last foot. My toes were at the edge. I leaned my weight on the back of my feet so I wouldn't topple by accident. I looked over at Sam. He was as cool as a cucumber, his head high, hair blowing in the wind, a smile on his face. I, on the other hand, was a wreck. My shoulders were up to my ears, my hands were sweating and my entire body was tensed up.

He reached into his pocket and pulled something else out. Marbles.

"What else do you have in there?"

"Some granola and a good luck charm a shaman in Mozambique

gave me."

I just shook my head at him and snortled.

"Okay," he said, holding the marble-filled hand over the edge. "Now try again. Control the force of the wind. We've been doing this all week, now we're just a little higher up."

I tried to relax and focus on the marbles but that didn't help. I watched them slip out of his hand. They dropped fast toward the ground. I remembered my mirror at home. The hours with Danger Girl exercises and pictured her in my head shouting, "Joy, dammit, Joy!" Suddenly the marbles flew upward into the sky, but I was able to temper my feelings in time and they stopped launching upward when they got to eye level. I watched as five black and blue marbles levitated before my eyes, held aloft by a gust of wind I had created.

"Impressive, Sarah," Sam said. "Now the tricky part. Try raising one of them two feet higher then the others."

I creased my brow and looked at him. "Seriously?"

"Precise control is essential."

"Fine," I said, then created a fast stream of air to raise one of the marbles above the others, and then snuck the other four into the slipstream. They lined up nicely with one at my head and the others lines up in a row at my knees.

"Very good. I think you're ready," he said. When he did, all five marbles dropped immediately to the ground below and landed with a barely audible plink.

"To fly? But I'm not a marble."

"Sarah Robertson you certainly are not. And neither am I," he said, before stepping off the ledge.

THIRTY-ONE

I SHRIEKED AT first but before the sound exited my lips I was already responding, as if on impulse. Fear had to give way to joy, to wind that was under control. Danger Girl had trained me well. Sam plummeted for a second before flying upward, hoisted by my air. As he started to pass me he thrust out his arms and slowed to a stop.

"You're ready," said Sam. As calm as Yoda. "It was you, Sarah. All you. I just created the force that kept me from flying off the planet. You don't know your own strength," he said, then held out a hand. I grabbed it and placed one foot off the platform before stopping and rocking back on my other foot. Sam jerked down for an instant than regained his space.

"Woah," he said, still unsteady. "Don't lose me now."

"I'm scared," I said.

"If I can trust you, you can trust yourself."

I thought about it for a second. I closed my eyes tight and stepped off the ledge.Like standing on a cushion at first. My feet sank down into it but eventually it held firm. It was solid, like a rock. It was strange to feel something as flimsy as air formed into a force that could keep two people floating through the atmosphere. I continued to maintain my emotional state, but a little part of me wanted to take it to another level, jumping up and down out of excitement. It was like I had two brains at once.

Sam looked at me with a proud smile. "See, I told you. But that's not it just yet. Right now we're floating. And I said I was going to teach you how to fly."

"What do you mean?" I asked.

He grabbed my hand again and without any other words we shot upward, traced an arc until we were just above the trees, and began to fly above them like two birds. The wind rushed past me and pushed me from behind. We dipped below the trees for moments and weaved through branches and trunks. It was exhilarating. My heart was pounding out of my chest.

"Now you take over. Be careful of the vectors. Your wind interacts with the others. Also, the terrain shapes the flow so don't get too low. And watch out for eddies behind large objects."

"Shouldn't I be writing this down?" I asked. I usually wrote everything down when I learned it. Even when I figured out how to do makeup through a YouTube tutorial. "No, you'll get the hang of it," he said, and suddenly the wind that projected us forward dropped out. We fell for a moment before I caught us from below and we hovered above the trees. I looked at Sam, he nodded at me, and with a few mental twitches, a gust of wind burst behind us and we were sailing above the trees and down the mountain. We hit the base and went up the next hill. It was harder, there were forces coming from all sides. We slipped a few times and Sam had to catch me. I couldn't believe it. I was flying, and it was due to my power. I wanted to whoop and yell, but I figured that would tip my emotional equilibrium to the other side. I couldn't stop smiling.

As we got to the top of the next peak, we hit a plateau and dipped behind a boulder. My wind suddenly cut out and we fell down to the earth. I landed hard on my butt. Sam did, too. It was only a few feet so it wasn't too bad. He stood up, stretched out, and massaged his butt where he had landed.

"What happened?" I asked.

"Eddy," he said. "That wind slowed and got caught behind the rock, so we lost it.""Can we do this again?" I asked, dusting myself off. I wanted to tackle Sam to hug and kiss him to thank him for this gift, but I figured it was time for the next best thing, which was more flying.

We flew for an hour, through the mountains over towns, along highways, until we were back in sight of Doolittle. I was getting exhausted. Concentrating on one emotion that long is enervating. When we flew over the high school I looked down and laughed at the students practicing football. But when I looked over toward the Academy I could see a sky teeming with other kids my age, practicing drills for Harpastball and maneuvers for class. I may have been able to fly, but that still didn't make me that special in Doolittle.When I saw my house, Sam and I veered toward it. When we landed I almost fell over. It was really hard maintaining the correct body position in the sky, like staying in plank position for ten-minute chunks of time, and walking on solid ground again felt weird. Like coming ashore after months at sea.

He gave me a huge high five and hugged me. Then he flew home and left me standing in the street, the sun slowly setting at my back and the stars rising over my little town. As I walked back to my house I pulled out my phone and sent a text to Alice."Flew home. No need for a ride."

She sent me back a very unpleasant emoji.

THIRTY-TWO

"**Y**OU BUILT all these?" Hamilton asked.

"Yup," said Tape Deck, admiring her handiwork.

"They're amazing," Alice said.

"Well, let's hold off on that until we hear them," Johnny said.

"Always the skeptic," said Alice. "Well, they look amazing."

There were five enormous speakers standing in our backyard, ready for our party. Dad was away over the weekend and we had one night to throw a party and a solid twenty-four hours to make it look like the party never happened. It was Johnny's idea. Things were weird between us. I made a lot of demands, and he promised me quite a bit if we pulled this off. Cooking. Cleaning. General good brothering. I would have him in my pocket for a year, which felt like a fine price to pay, considering he stole my best friend and everything.

"Well let's give it a shot," Johnny said, slapping one of the speakers. It was as tall as him, painted lustrous silver and had five circles with grates over them. They were sitting on a stage made out of cinder blocks and wooden sheets Hamilton and Johnny had built. The sheets were buckled slightly under the weight of the speakers.

Tape Deck held up an iPod. "I thought you'd never ask."

She pressed a button and a wall of sound burst out of the speakers in unison. They were loud, but the sound was crisp and pure. A cello hit me in the face, then a horn, then a series of trombones. It was some classical piece. I felt like my face was in the middle of an orchestra. She could have picked any song, but she choose classical, not out of love of the music but out of love of the speakers—and she was right. I had never felt so in the center of a world of sound. It was magical.

"Turn it down!" Johnny screamed. He had a look of genuine fear in his eyes. It was the first time I'd ever heard him complain about noise. In sixteen years. Johnny pointed to our neighbor's backyard. Ms. Slovinsky was glaring at us through the slates in our wooden fence. Her blue eyes pierced us like arrows.

"Oh boy," I said. "I guess the concerts off."

"What?"

"No way," said Alice.

"Well, it wouldn't be terrible," said Rosa. Johnny and Alice shot her a death stare. "Fine," she muttered.

"Okay, so what do we do so this thing doesn't get shut down before it starts?" Hamilton asked.

Just then Kurt and Backslash sauntered around the side of our house and took a good look at the speakers.

"Nice," said Backslash. "Noiiiiiiice."

"I've got an idea," said Tape Deck.

One trip to Home Depot, later the backyard was littered with blue tarps and wooden two-by-fours, piles of drills and circular saws. Just looking at a circular saw made me cringe, so I was pretty useless. There sharp jagged teeth just made me think of lost bleeding fingers and the safety lecture Mr. Dumont had given us in seventh grade shop class, which he punctured by holding up his stump of a left pinkie.

Rosa and I were in charge of stapling the blue tarps to two-by-fours, which Alice, Johnny and Tape Deck cut to size. Tape Deck was the real mastermind behind the whole thing and turned out, in addition to being a mad genius with inventions, was also quite handy. She was kind of the coolest chick. Alice was smiling like a demon as sawdust kicked up in her face. She chopped board after board, laying them down between my dad's old metal saw horses and slicing them with loud whirrs and hoots. Johnny wasn't picking it up as quickly, and after a piece of wood flew up and hit him in the face, he threw his hands up in exasperation and started just feeding boards to Alice to cut.

I laughed at him while Johnny said, "Come on! I have to protect my hands. For the music."

Two hours later, the blue monster—as Marcus had named it—was finished. It was a series of large gates, each one consisting of two support beams and one top beam. A large blue plastic tarp hung from the top beam. We had to work together to hoist them up. When upright they were about fourteen feet high, and we stuck them in the ground along the fence, so the entire backyard was covered in blue plastic. They blocked the sun and gave the backyard a cool bluish glow.

"It's like Christo's gates, except, you know, blue. An ecstatic accident produced by void and fire," said Hamilton. He muttered "Maggie Nelson" after that last thing, walking around, inspecting the strength of the beams. He pretended to drunkenly attack them, seeing if they would fall, and he pulled out a small camera from his pocket and started taking pictures of the shapes they cast on the ground.

"So this will block the noise," I asked Tape Deck.

"No, but the next thing will," she said.

Johnny schlepped a ladder out of the basement and they coiled a long black hose across the top of the gates, so it ran the length of the whole mass. Plastic ties kept it in place. Johnny plugged it into our spigot. Water leaked down the blue tarps and onto the ground. I wasn't sure what the point was, other than an elaborate way to water our lawn. Or maybe a really steep slip and slide.

Tape Deck signaled to Kurt, who walked up to the first gate, stuck his finger in the cascading water, and walked the length of the gates, letting water splash over his outstretched finger. As he touched it, the water slowed down to a barely perceptible drip, until finally it all stopped. The surface looked like a clear, pebbly glass. It reflected light in small twinkling bits like a diamond. I reached out to touch it and Tape Deck grabbed my hand.

"I wouldn't do that," she said. "Not yet." Johnny and Tape Deck picked up handfuls of sawdust and began tossing it at the glass wall. We all joined in and soon the surface was covered in yellow sawdust. When we threw it at the wall crystals would form around it and spread out. When we were finished we had walls of dust-covered ice, which strained the gates, though they didn't fall.

"Okay, time to try this again. Sarah, you know the neighbors. Mind sneaking on the other side of the fence?" asked Tape Deck

I said yes. Alice followed me and we made our way to the back of the fence, through the backyards of the Codys and the Gellers. We waited around but nothing happened. No noise. No anything. Alice talked about the show, but the excitement she had when she spoke to the others was gone. "What's wrong?" I asked.

"Wrong? What's wrong?" she snapped. "I can't believe you, Sarah. You mean, uh, besides abandoning me in the forest while you went flying around town with Sam? Or ditching me every time Freedom Boy comes by? Way to have no reaction to anything I tell you. What's up with you? You're more frozen than Elsa these days. I tell you things and you ignore me and go off to something else. It's so selfish."

This rant came out of nowhere. It felt deeply unfair. Hadn't Alice made the first cut, hooking up with Johnny? I tried to respond. "How was I supposed to react? You and my brother, Alice. That's so weird."

"So what?" she asked. "It took a lot for me to tell you and you just ran away. You'd rather risk killing yourself playing Hero than have a single conversation with your best friend. I'm just a convenient foil for your adventures. Maybe I should apply to the Sidekicks Alliance as the occasional companion of world-renowned Hero Sarah Robertson."

I rolled my eyes at her. "Look, you liked this last year. That I wanted to be a Hero. Now you have your band and stuff and what am I supposed to do, twiddle my thumbs?"

Alice mumbled something. I asked her to speak up, and she repeated herself. "You have the attitude down. All you need is the card and a few accidental kills, and you could be a national celebrity!"

Before I could respond, my phone rang. It was Johnny, asking where we were. "We've been screaming your names," he said. "Come back."

We walked in silence. When we opened the back gate and walked through a break in the blue, we heard it. The classical music. It was blasting.

"Did you have this on the whole time?" Alice asked, spacing herself away from me as soon as possible. "We couldn't hear a thing."

"I guess that means the party, as it is, is on." Tape Deck grinned.

THIRTY-THREE

THE MISSHAPES were the first to show up. There were kids that we didn't even know showing up. I was uncomfortable with all the strangers but Johnny or Marcus or Hamilton seemed to know them, and if I was around they introduced me. When some old guy came in, probably in his twenties, Johnny nearly tackled him with the strength of his hug. I didn't know why that was.

"Bobby!" Johnny burbled. "This is my sister. He's awesome. She's fine."

We both laughed. I asked him how he knew Johnny. Bobby said they met on the Misshape message board. "First time we've met in person," Johnny said.

It was as if a light clicked on in my head. "That's where all these people have heard about this, huh?" I asked, a little nervous, eyeing the growing crowd bathed in blue ice light.

"Most of them," Bobby said. "But don't worry, they're a good crew. Won't wreck the place or anything."

"Sarah," Johnny said, "take care of my man over here. I have to get some provisions for the partygoers." He was making drinks. I knew it. I gave him the dirtiest look I could. We had made a deal: the party would be okay if there were no drinks. I was fine with having people over but having drunk people over was another thing entirely. I felt like a nagging wife on a sitcom.

Johnny disappeared into the crowd, making his way toward the stage. Bobby told me all about the message board and his work in Boston's Misshape community in Boston. He helped provided free legal services to Misshapes around the country who were being unfairly prosecuted. They were petitioning the government so that they'd prosecute The Red Ghost for violating the civil rights of the man he killed. It hadn't happened. The city and the state had already refused to press charges, and when that was announced, protests broke out. But the papers all claimed it was hooligans and riots. "I mean, Sarah, you gotta read Henry David Thoreau," Bobby said. "That dude knew what was up. It's important for the people to unite, to stand up and say that they're not taking this anymore."

I listened to Bobby and met some of his friends as the last light of the day gave way to the night. I wondered when the band would play. The stage lit up when Tape Deck plugged in some lights. Everyone cheered and then returned to their conversations. People walked by with drinks, stumbling and talking loudly. Johnny was a generous bartender.

When I went to the bathroom, there was a girl draped over the toilet, puking her guts out. She had greenish-blue hair, plaid skin, and was clutching the side of the white bowl with white knuckles. Sometimes I really hated having only one bathroom.

"Are you okay?" I asked.

"Ughh," she moaned. "I need some air."

"The air is outside. Do you want to go outside?"

"Yeah. Outside. Air." She made a move as if to get up then slumped down and started puking again. It smelled vile. Her hair undulated when she puked, moving like a wave up toward her head and crashing at her scalp. A very Misshape power.

I didn't know what to do. I had tried to cajole and lure her out of the toilet, and I needed to pee. At this point, I went on a mission to find my brother. I didn't want to have people over for a party in the first place, and then super-drunk people? This was my brother's responsibility. I was just trying to keep things relatively tame.

The band was practicing in Johnny's room. When I knocked on the door, I heard groans, as if they were expecting to get in trouble. I opened the door and Alice's surprise quickly turned to a glare. I hated to be on the opposite side of it. She was my best friend. But she didn't seem like she wanted to make up any time soon.

"Johnny, there's a girl puking in our toilet."

"So?"

"She's drunk. Very drunk."

"Well it wasn't me, if that's what you're asking."

"Why would I be asking, Johnny? It's pretty obvious. I didn't even want this party here and I have to pee, and can you at least get her out of the bathroom?"

"We need to practice now," Alice said, her back to me, ignoring my request. "Give me a minute," he said, getting up.

When we got to the bathroom, it smelled even worse. The girl was just slumped on the toilet, drool dripping down her mouth.

Johnny walked up beside her. "Hey, are you okay?" he asked, nudging her. "Nuhuh," she mumbled.

"Are you drunk? Can you tell my sister here that I was not the person who got you drunk?" Johnny looked at me. "I know you think it's all my fault, Sarah, but I was in my room practicing, so..."

"I'm not drunk, you're drunk," the girl blurted. She made like she was going to push Johnny over.

He lowered his voice and talked to her slowly, like they were conspiring on something together. "Look, I need to know if you've had anything to drink. I can make you better, but if you're not drunk and just sick, it could be dangerous." A large tide rose up her hair and crashed at her bangs. "So, what have you had to drink?"

"That nice girl with the singing ladies gave me two, no, wait, five, glasses of something and Coke. Berta. Her name was Berta."

" Betty?" I asked.

She pointed at me, shaking her finger like a schoolmarm. "Yeah! Betty. And those singing ladies. So nice. They're soooo nice."

Johnny glared at me. So he was innocent. Strike one for my brother. The drunk girl wailed, "I love those ladies and they're soooooo talented and they're going to be the best singers ever." The last word came out in a burp.

The girl nearly toppled over. Johnny put his hands on her shoulders. "Stay still," he said. "This will feel strange, but it will make you feel better." She began to sweat profusely. It glistened on her skin, dripped down her face, and soaked through her clothes. The waves on her head grew more intense, the color of her hair went from greenish-blue to black, her breath grew quick and tight and her mouth pinched together, like she wanted to puke all over Johnny. But after a moment of true fear, her skin started to regain its color. The sweating stopped, and the dazed look in her eyes ceased. She shook her head and the waves subsided. The color of her hair normalized itself as a vibrant green. Johnny let go of her and she wobbled, slowly righting herself into a real person.

"What just happened?" she asked.

"You were really drunk," Johnny said. "And now you're not. You okay?" He looked tired. Whatever he did was exhausting.

I jabbed his arm and he winced. "Cool trick, bro."

"I turned the alcohol in her body back to water so she feels all better, right?" The girl nodded. "Your ph and everything might still be a little messed up, but the drunk part is over."

"Thanks," she said and pecked him on the cheek. She waltzed out of the bathroom like a brand new person. I shooed my brother away and finally had a moment of privacy.

THIRTY-FOUR

W HEN I got out, I was on a mission to put a stop to Betty
before she did any more damage. I found her by the
fence with some people I didn't know. Her alco-meter
was blinking bright red. "Saaaaarah!" she cheered, and gave me a
big hug. She grabbed at my hair and stuck one finger through a curl.
"You, you, you're just so great. Did you know that?"

I took a step back and said, "Do you see your alco-meter?"

She shushed me and put a finger to my lips. "No problem. I'll just
take a few of these," she popped a pill in her mouth, "and I'll be better
in no time!" She stood up straight, feigning properness of some kind.
She was wearing a shirt that said, "Don't Kill My" on it. She never
wore anything with any kind of graphics on them. She was usually
such a boring preppy. "So have you met my new friends?" I started to
say no but she cut me off. "Meet them. They're wonderful."

I grabbed Betty by the arm. "We need to talk." If I could get her
alone at least I could stop her from ruining the party.

"Okay, Mrs. Robertson," she said, loudly for her audience. "Ha,
Mrs. Robertson. Don't try to seduce me."

I yanked her away toward a quieter corner. "What's wrong with you? You'll get yourself sick. And everyone else."

"I'm just being friendly. Making friends. Johnny does it all the time. It's a party," she said, waving her arms to show me the party in case I forgot.

"Is this about Butters?"

"What? No. I'm just trying to have a good time. Can't I have a good time while he's out there, somewhere, alone, with no one to..." at that point she started crying so hard I couldn't understand her. I pulled her to my shoulder and she leaked like a faucet. There was nothing I could do for her. All efforts to find Butters had turned up nothing. "Let's talk about it later, okay. For now, stop handing out drinks or we'll get in trouble. If not for me and Johnny, then do it for our dad. Your uncle. We all know Johnny's the bad one in the family, right?"

"Okay," she said, sullenly.

"And none for you either. It doesn't seem to be helping any."

She looked at me, blotted away some tears, and gave me another okay. Suddenly, the lights dimmed. Alessandra got on stage and Tape Deck manned a makeshift control booth to the right of the stage. The band started to set up their instruments. Rosa plugged in her amp and put on her bracelets. The rest of the band plugged in their guitars and Alice practiced hitting the drums. I knew I was mad at her because she just seemed so pleased with herself and it drove me crazy. Johnny smiled at her and she smiled back. They were so in love. It was disgusting.

After a couple of notes and some back-and-forth with Tape Deck about the monitors and vocals, the band was ready to play. Alessandra got behind the microphone. "Thank you all for coming out tonight to Doolittle Falls," she said. The crowd cheered. "Tonight we have the first-ever live performance of Doolittle's own, The Paulines!"

Johnny tapped Alessandra on the shoulder and whispered something into her ear. She adjusted her glasses and tapped the mic. "I'm sorry, the first ever performance of Explosive Framing

Device!" The crowd cheered again, this time a little less steadily. Alessandra made a face. She was doing the breathing that I taught her, from Dangerous Girl's drama book. Her skin flashed red, then orange, then blue and she shouted, "Let's go!"

She burst like a human firework. Bright colors popped out of her skin and flew up into the sky. The streamers floated down over the audience and the crowd went crazy. Johnny stepped on a pedal, strummed his guitar once, and the band launched into a song that was loud and fast. Surrounded by stripes of blue, green, red, pink, and yellow, people started whooping and dancing and pushing up against each other. The sound was raucous and loud. The speakers blasted out against the crowd, hitting us in the face, and bouncing off the walls of ice. Alice, her hair flying, pounded on the drums so hard that she looked like the coolest girl in the world. Even if I was still mad at her.

The song ended with a loud clash of cymbals and a distorted guitar cord, and Johnny took the mic. "Thank you. We're The Paulines and," someone tapped him on the shoulder, "I mean we're the Exploding Framing… Ah, screw it. We're the Misshapes, you're The Misshapes, and this is *our* music!"

They all looked pleased with the impromptu name change and the next song started out with a barrage of loud chords and drums like a Gatling gun. When they got to the first chorus, something strange happened. The music was so loud that it took me a moment to realize that it wasn't just the vibrations of sound that I was feeling. It was the earth, too. But the earth was shaking in time with the music.

When it clicked, I tried to get Rosa's attention. She saw me in the crowd and nodded at me, making a rock on sign with her hand. She thought I was dancing. Her bracelets were still on, blinking red. The stage wobbled and threatened to collapse. Once Rosa realized it, she dropped her guitar like a hot plate. But it was too late.

The cinder blocks went first. A large crack spread from her feet and spider-webbed outward until the whole stage was cut up by large lines. In an instant the blocks turned to dust and they to the ground. People screamed and ran for the exit. The cracks cut into the ground and spread across our backyard. When they hit the fence, the ice shattered and blew out over the crowd. People covered their eyes and heads. I ducked and watched as a large rivulet sliced through the earth below me. Our backyard was becoming quicksand, trying to pull the crowd down into the earth.

"Run," I screamed. The earth below us was sinking and we all rushed away from the hole. I looked at our house and prayed it wouldn't get swallowed up, which in hindsight, was selfish. I should have been praying that no partygoers were swallowed. When we got to the front of the house, all the neighbors were in the street. Most of them were on their cell phones. I could hear the police and fire sirens wailing in the distance. The rumbling stopped. Rosa was walking around, pacing back and forth. "Is it over?" I asked.

"Yes," she said.

"Did you see if anyone fell in?"

"I was the last one out. We're okay. We're all okay."

Alice rushed over to us. She gave me a hug. Her drumsticks pressed into my back. When she pulled away she looked at them and laughed. "I'm glad you're okay, Sarah. That was scary!"

Johnny strolled toward us. "We can't hide this from Dad, can we?"

"Not unless we rent a backhoe and fill the yard in a day," I said. I looked behind him and saw Ms. Slovinsky in a pink robe, her hair in curlers, glaring at us. Her glaring didn't bother me one bit. The band rocked and we had saved the party from certain disaster. Adrenaline was coursing through my veins. I felt like I could just jump up and fly into the air if I wanted to, but I had work ahead of me: I had to make the backyard nice and sunny so that sinkhole dried up and went back to normal.

Only one thing interrupted the sound of my thoughts. The whinny of a police siren tearing through the neighborhood. And it was stopping at our house.

THIRTY-FIVE

THE COPS led me out of the car and into the tiny Doolittle Police Station. They seemed nervous. Not much crime happens in Doolittle Falls, and when it does, there are usually five people in capes on the scene before the cops have time to start their sirens. Johnny and his two police escorts entered right after us.

We walked past a few desks, some closed offices and a very sad ficus tree. I could hear Johnny struggling as they dragged him behind me. "Stay strong, sis," he shouted to me. "We'll get out of here."

"You too, bro," I said as we turned sharply and entered a small interrogation room. There was a metal table in the center of the room bolted to the floor with a thick hook on its top. On the side closest to the door were three wooden chairs and on the side near the wall a folding chair. They sat me down in the folding chair and undid my handcuffs. "Sorry about that," the fatter of the two officers said. His badge said O'Grady. "Protocol," said the other officer sternly. His name was Walters.

"So is everyone okay?" I asked.

"What?" Officer Walters responded.

"At the party. I'm worried after what happened. Did anyone get hurt?""You're a good kid," O'Grady said. "First question isn't about why you're here or if you'll get out or begging us not to tell your parents. Real good kid."

"Everyone's fine," Walters said. "As far as we know. Some sprained ankles, a few cuts and bruises. Nothing major."

"Oh thank god!" I said.

"Attica, Attica, Attica," Johnny screamed from the other room.

"Your brother on the other hand is a real piece of work," Walters said.

"So, why am I here?" I asked.

"That party of yours drew a little attention," Walters said.

"But, I didn't think you arrested kids for noise complaints," I said.

"Well, booze to minors and all that," O'Grady said.

"But there wasn't any booze," I said, hoping they didn't know about Johnny's power.

"Seriously, no booze?" Walters said. "How dorky are you? When we used to throw down, it wasn't a party without at least two kegs."

"No kegs," I said.

"Hmm," Walters responded.

"Look. It wasn't our call, kid. Whenever there's an unauthorized use of powers, we got to bring you in. Our chief made the call," O'Grady said.

"Normally we'd just break it up," Walters added.

This situation sucked. Why hadn't the bracelets worked for Rosa? They worked during all the practices. The weight of the situation fell over me. Dad would kill me. And Johnny. I hope we wouldn't be expelled. Or get a record. A terrible thought crossed my mind.

"You're not going to send me to juvie?" I asked, on the verge of tears.Walters and O'Grady laughed. "No, no. Not at all. Just need to clear it all up, file a report, and you should be on your way. With your parent's escort of course," O'Grady said with a smirk.

"Not getting out of that one," Walters said.

"I'll never snitch pigs," Johnny shouted from the other room.

"Are you sure you two are related?" O'Grady asked.

"I ask myself the same question all the time," I replied.

A man in a brown suit poked his head in the door. "We need to talk," he said. "Sure, Chief," Walters said. "Please give us a minute."

The two of them got up and walked out the door. They left it slightly ajar so I could see out. Behind the Chief were two men in black suits with dark sunglasses on. They looked like members of the Secret Service Paladin Division. *This can't be good*, I thought.

They spoke in whispers but I could tell they were arguing. The detectives were incredulous about something and kept raising their voices. I heard them say, "Are you serious?" "This is crap" "She's just a kid." The last one made me really nervous.

Finally Walters said, "Fine!" loudly in protest and walked back in the room with O'Grady. "I'm sorry about this. It's BS," Walters said.

"Walters!" The chief castigated.

"Ugh," he groaned. "Look, you'll be fine, okay? These two men from the federal government want to talk to you. It shouldn't be too bad."

"We'll keep an eye out for you, kid," O'Grady said.

"Okay," I responded, but I felt more like I was reassuring them then they were comforting me.

O'Grady patted me on the head and the two of them left the room. The two men in the black suits walked in and closed the door. They had no names tags and did not introduce themselves. They both had severe faces, with sharp noses and high cheeks. They looked strong and compact. The only distinguishing features between the two were their eye colors. One had green eyes the other brown.

"You're in a lot of trouble," Brown Eyes said.

"A lot," Green followed.

"Why? It was just a party. So Rosa's bracelets failed. The police officers said it was nothing," I said.

"Nothing?" they said in incredulous unison. "Terrorism is nothing," Green followed. He shook his head.

"Terrorism?" I gulped.

"Unauthorized use of powers in public, threat to human lives. Could have been a disaster, Ms. Robinson," Brown said.

"And known affiliation with known and wanted terrorists," Green said.

"Are you referring to my mother in this case, sir?"

"Lady Oblivion. Not only are you a blood relation, you have known contact with her. And have been seen fighting alongside her," Brown said.

"We'll have plenty of time to discuss this further, Ms. Robinson. But for the safety of this town and this nation, you will have to come with us," Green said.

"But can't I call my dad? Or my lawyer? Or my best friend Alice?"

"Terrorists don't get lawyers," Green said.

"Or dads," Brown added.

"Or best friends." Green reached into a brown briefcase and pulled out two metal circles. They were not attached by a chain like the other handcuffs. They had no hinges. Just solid rings of metal. He slid them over my hands and they got tighter somehow when they reached my wrists. He pressed a button and a blue glow emanated from them and a bolt of blue shot between them and stayed there. My hands were immobile, and then my body.

"I ... Can't ... Move ..." I said slowly, my mouth freezing shut.

"That's the point," Green said as I froze completely still.

Brown got up and pulled something out of his pocket. I tried to turn to see it but couldn't turn. Then he pulled it over my head and the world turned black.

THIRTY-SIX

WHAT WAS scariest was that I couldn't see. It felt like forever. I tried to scream or cry or make some noise but they blasted some music so it drowned me out. They picked me up and carried me to a car or van or something. One of the people chained me to something else and then put something on my wrists and my neck. It felt thick, tight, and heavy. We drove and drove and drove. We hit a bump and I fell into something soft, person-shaped.

"Johnny?"

"Hi, Sarah," he said.

"Can you move?"

"A little," he said. "I was able to loosen the cuffs with some alcohol."

"Can you help me out?"

"I'll see what I can do."

I felt his hands move jerkily on my wrists. There was a slight searing sensation around the cuffs. Some tension released in my body. I was able to move slightly. With my shoulder, I jerked the bag on my head up and wriggled so that it fell off.

"Nice moves, Houdini," Johnny said. His bag lay on the floor next to him. "Thanks. What's happening here? I'm scared."

"They're driving us somewhere. And considering they accused me, and I'm guessing you, of being a terrorist, I'm guessing it ain't good. Based on the direction of the wind, and the length of the drive, I would say a maximum security prison for supervillains," he said. "Also, that," he added, gesturing toward the small rectangular window in the side of the van.

Outside the window, I saw the Miskatonic running alongside the road and flow into a large lake. An eight-foot high razor-wire fence surrounded the lake. Behind the fence there was an even taller concrete fence topped with laser gun-turrets, and behind the concrete was a translucent red force field that formed an enormous dome around the lake. The road led to a gate with a guard bunker. There were at least ten guards in black uniforms and balaklavas standing outside the bunker with large laser rifles.

We stopped at the bunker and one of the drivers got out. The back door started to open and I slipped the bag back over my head. Someone shone a flashlight around the van and said, "Yup, all here." He slammed the door shut and shouted, "Good to go," to the front of the car.

I slipped the bag off again and watched as a gate swung open in the chain link fence and a small opening, the exact size of the van, materialized in the concrete wall. We slipped through it and then passed through the red force-field. When the gate shut behind us with a thundering BAM! I caught a glimpse of what all the fences and gun and guards were protecting. An enormous granite pillar stood in the middle of the lake, taller than any building I'd ever seen, taller even then the cliffs the Academy were built on. It was perfectly cylindrical, and midnight black with flecks of silver and gold. A huge, rectangular, white concrete building crowned the pillar like wedding cake toppers. Barred porthole windows ran up the sides in long lines. I put the bag back on my head. We were totally screwed.

It was the Luther. And we were its newest guests.

THIRTY-SEVEN

I WANTED TO bust out of my chains and make a run for it. I had no idea what they were going to do to me but I knew it was no good. There was bile in the back of my throat. My face contorted as I tried to hold back tears. I dug deep within myself, deep enough to build a tornado strong enough to rip the town in half, but I'm sure whatever I could produce was a dinky little one, burbling outside our bubble. Johnny saw me straining and pointed down at the bracelets they had put on me. "Power reducers," he said.

I looked at them. They looked like J5's necklace and Christy's. The bracelets reminded me of Rosa's bracelets. It was the hit PeriGenomics product, made to get everyone under their control. "You okay?" Johnny asked.

"MmHmm," I mumbled, trying not to let him know how scared I was. Fear was contagious, and if I was scared, he would get scared, and I would get more scared. I put on a brave voice "Are you okay, Johnny?"

"I am for now." The door opened suddenly. A rush of cold air blew in with the smell of tobacco and pine needles. A deep voice bellowed, with slight irritation, "You bagged them? You bagged them! Why the hell would you bag them?"

"Direct orders from Secretary Glanton, sir," Another voice said. It sounded like our drivers.

"They're teenagers. You can't bag 'em. I don't care if they came directly from President Bergeron, you know how much trouble we could get in?"

"They did, sir," the man said, stammering.

"Did what?"

"Come from President Bergeron. That's what the secretary said when I asked. The orders."

"I'm not taking the fall if this ever comes out. I'd rather take his wrath than be the public face of abusing kids. Take those damn things off, now." They removed the bags. A large spotlight was shinning into the van. It made it hard to adjust my eyes. After a few seconds I was able to see again. The first thing I saw was my breath, white and misty in front of my face. And then the man who was kind enough to take the bags off. He was wearing a black tactical vest and black rip-stop cargo pants, the same outfit they all wore. He was tall. Six-five easy. And broad, with thick arms. He had no nametag. None of them did. I thought he might be ally, but when I looked at him for compassion he was just as cold as the others. A severe, unflinching face, with thick lips, a deep brow, and sharp cheeks. "This way, prisoners," he said to us.

"Who are you?" I asked.

"Why are we here? What are even accused off?" Johnny asked.

"Terrorism," he said, bluntly.

"We have rights. You can't do this!" Johnny said.

"You don't, and I can. Now if you don't shut the hell up I'll put those bags back on your heads." We shut up. The only thing worse than being dragged into the Luther was being dragged in without the ability to see what was going on. I was terrified. Not only because of what was happening but not knowing why and having no control.

A terrible thought crossed my mind. They could do whatever

they wanted and no one would know. No one would stop them. But why would they want to? What had we done? Why did the Secretary of the Bureau of Superhero Affairs care about Johnny and me? And why did the President give him so much power to take us from our homes. They were two of the most powerful men in the country. And we, apparently, were their enemies.

All because of a stupid house party.

They led us out of the van and marched us down a dock on the shore of the lake. There was a large gray boat moored to the dock with a long metal ramp coming off it. They led us up the ramp and sat us in two seats on the deck, then locked us to the chairs. Two guards stood watch over us with large laser rifles while the rest of the crew prepared the ship for launch. The man, who had been nice for an instant, supervised everything. He seemed to be in charge. The boat slowly chugged to life and sailed toward the Luther. I had no idea where it would land. The base of the prison looked like a solid block of granite. The only entrance seemed to be over a hundred feet in the air.

We were close enough to the edge of the ship to see overboard into the water. It was dark, and hard to see, but there appeared to be something beneath us in the water as we got closer to the prison. Bubbles popped on the surface of the water. There was some kind of structure underneath us in the water, but it looked deep. We passed over something with a light in it and finally I was able to see an entire network of underwater cells with prisoners in them. They were in large glass bubbles moored to each other and the bottom by thick iron chains. I attempted to lean over to get a closer look. I saw a smirk on one of the guards' faces but ignored it. Something was getting closer to the surface. It was glowing blue and was hard to make out. I leaned in and suddenly it shot out of the water. It was enormous. I reeled back. My heart beat out of my chest. I watched as an incandescent shark with thick rows of sharp teeth flew in the air before arcing back in the water.

"They love the taste of swimmers," one of the guards said. The other laughed.Johnny struggled against the chains to reach out his hand toward mine. "It'll be okay, sis. We'll be fine," he said. It was not convincing. When the boat got close enough to the base the captain called someone on his walkie-talkie.

"Ready for the pick-up," he said.

"Ready. Drop em in," the voice on the other end said.

"You're not dropping us in the water are you?" I asked the guard.

"Yes," he said.

THIRTY-EIGHT

W E SAT chained inside clear blue bubbles floating in the water. The boat sailed back to the other shore. I could see Johnny in his bubble next to mine. I tried to focus on him and not the sharks circling around us. They poked at us with their noses and snapped their enormous mouths. I was scared at any moment our bubbles would crack and they would devour us whole. Taking just enough times to sink their large teeth into us before gulping us down. I started to cry and gripped my necklace. Why was this happening? The bubble rocked back and forth and I felt a sinking in my stomach. The water level dropped until the bubble was on the surface of the lake. I looked up and saw a large cable connected to the top of it. There was one connected to Johnny's, too. They had docked with a little metal piece at the tops and were hauling us up. Suddenly a shark jumped out of the water and hit the bubble full force. It shook violently and swung in the air like a pendulum. I shrieked but the shriek just echoed back at me. Johnny looked on in horror. I finally composed myself and mouthed, "I'm okay." It didn't help. He still looked terrified and angry. I was worried he would attack the first guard he saw and get us in even deeper trouble.

The lake got smaller and smaller below us. I could see the lake and the security complex on the shore and the boat docking. I looked up but couldn't tell where we were being taken. The wall of the Luther was dark granite and then suddenly turned into a slate gray. We started passing windows and I could see inside the cells of other prisoners. They were all in the same pristine white jumpsuits with collars around their necks and matching bracelets around their arms. The same PeriGenomics bracelets they put on me. I bet PeriGenomics built the entire prison. I regret ever getting involved with that awful corporation. I wished Sam had nothing to do with them. But I was worried that, maybe, he had already too much to do with them.

The prisoners paced their cells, which were small, featuring a metal toilet and a single bed. There seemed to only be one person per cell. There were no bars on the doors but some kind of invisible forcefield. Still, it seemed more humane than I'd expected. They had books and posters.

We reached the top of the Luther. The entire bubble was clear and I could see the sheer drop back down to the water. At the top of the Luther was an open-air dock of sorts. The bubble popped through a circular opening in the floor and the floor closed beneath it. I looked over and saw that Johnny's bubble did the same. The floor was shaped like a clock, with circular openings for more bubbles, and large hoists with coiled wire to pull them up. Maintenance men in blue jumpers detached the chain from the bubble and opened them up. Guards came over and led us out.

My feet were shaky at first and they didn't give me time to get adjusted to standing on solid ground, they just pulled me back up when I slipped. They led us to the center of the platform, through an automatic door, and into a room where more guards sat at a desk with a large sign that said, "PROCESSING" on it. When they saw us, the guards' faces twisted up into a question "Umm, what's going on?" one said.

"Who are they? They look like kids?"

"We are kids!" I shouted. "They are abusing us and denying our rights. We don't even know why we're here."

"Please, call the papers. Tell anyone. This is illegal." Johnny added. "This isn't right." I felt a sharp pain in my lower back and was frozen solid. I tried talking but couldn't. They must have hit me with the freeze stick again.

"Great, now we have to wait for them to thaw," one of the guards that led us in said. "No, they're light. They're easier to move now. And not complaining," said the one brandishing the freeze stick.

The guards at the desk were still confused. "You can't do that," one said.

The guard with the stick walked over and handed them a piece of paper. They held it up to the light, then picked up a red phone and made a call. After a few, "Yups" and "Uh Huhs" and "Yes Sirs," they hung up. "Okay," they said. "But I'm handling this one with kid gloves. None of the usual stuff. I'm not going to be the face of the next Westbrook."

Westbrook was a notorious juvenile prison for kids with powers that had rampant abuse by the guards. The exact word I did not want to hear. The world only learned about it after two kids died and three ended up in the hospital. And after a two-year investigation, no one was ever blamed and the place was shut down with a few superficial reforms at other facilities.

They led us through a scanner and ran a large wand over us. We had already been patted down before, and all metal and possible weapons taken away, so none of their machines binged. Then they led us into a large rotating device that circled around us, faster and faster with each rotation. It was black and red, and moved so fast it became a nauseating blur. Finally it stopped and we were led into separate rooms. They threw a white jumpsuit at me.

"Put that one when you thaw. I'll be back in an hour. Knock if you un-thaw sooner," one of them said and left. Somehow I had gotten through with my necklace still on. It was the only source of comfort. The only thing I still had. I looked up at the cameras in the room. When I could finally move, I took pains to put the clothes on without showing any parts of myself naked. A skill I learned in the locker rooms at camp. Westbrook was infamous for other abuses as well in their girls' ward. The cameras reminded me of it. Once I was in the jumpsuit, I knocked on the door and the guards came in. One of them stood next to Johnny. My brother looked like a giant stick of gum in his onesie. One of the guards noticed my necklace and reached out to grab it, but I screamed no and clutched it. "I'm sorry, I have to take it," he said.

I started crying. Uncontrollably. I didn't know why my necklace was the one thing that set me off, the one thing that made me feel real feelings. It was my connection to the world. It was my connection to my mother. It reminded me of things bigger than me in the world. I held it so tight it dug into my hands, the grooves scratching my skin. The guard looked nervous. He didn't want to pry it loose, I could tell, but had some sort of obligation to. He walked back to the other guard while I crumpled onto the floor in a ball of tears. Johnny rushed over to comfort me. The guard tried to grab for him but he dodged and crouched by my side.

"It's going to be okay, Sarah," he said. "And you need to be calm."

"Calm?" I roared. "Calm? Johnny, I can't 'be calm.' They're trying to lock us away for more reason. We're in a Kalfka-esque nightmare."

Johnny patted my back. "I feel like it's more akin to Brazil, you remember that movie? But, yeah, you have a point."

"Plus," I sniffled, "guys always want girls to stop crying, to not make any noise. What's the saying? Well-behaved women never make history? I'm not going to behave right now."

"I get it," Johnny whispered into my ear, "but play cool for now. The thing is, we have to let them think that they have the upper hand. It's so we can get our own upper hand. Does that make sense?"

The guards were arguing amongst themselves. One of them

claimed that it was the rules, and I had to give it up. The other was suggesting some form of lenience, considering the situation. He called it cruel and unusual malignancy.

Johnny squeezed my hand and had one more thing to say. "Sarah, we'll get through this together. We always do. After Mom. After George. After Dr. Mann." Man, that list was long, I thought. "I don't know how, but as long as you think we can, we can. But I'm going to need you to believe in our powers. In us as a team."

We were against the ropes. My brother was the only person in my corner. I couldn't even remember how mad I was at him earlier. He was absolutely right. If we were going to get out of this, we'd have to work together. I wiped tears from my eyes with my cuffed hands. Little did I know, it was only going to get worse before it got any better.

THIRTY-NINE

THE GUARDS led us to a bank of elevators in the center of the floor. There was a giant sign above them that listed the different sections of the prison and the floor for them, which read:

Mental Health Unity: Floor 50-45

Low security: Floor 44-40

Reinforced Titanium: Floor 39-30

Non-biologics: Floor 30-25

Heat: Floor 24-15

Cool: Floor 14-0

Aqueous: Floor 0—5

Non-Ferrous/ Non-magnetic: Floor ‑6—11

Non-conductive: Floor ‑12—18

Anti Gravity: Floor ‑19—26

White Noise/Mind-Control: Floor ‑27—37

Maximum Security: Floor ‑38—48

M.O.E: Floor ‑50

They called someone on their walkie-talkies and a few minutes later two elevator doors opened. Each elevator was just big enough for one person apiece. They didn't look like regular elevators. The floor was a thick plastic circle and there were no walls, just a red force field. It wasn't attached to any cords or rope, but somehow levitated. Johnny and I were put in separate elevators. The second I stepped on the sphere it started to descend. It moved quickly through a long tube. I could see through the floor all the way down to the bottom. The only lights were cast off by each floor.

I was hoping we would stop quickly after starting, and be deposited in the low security floor. No such luck. I kept descending and descending until, finally, the elevator slowed down. To my chagrin I could see I the bottom of the tunnel right under the elevator. We had landed at either M.O.E, whatever that was, or Maximum Security. Either way I imagined it wasn't good.

The doors opened on complete blackness. Four hands reached in and grabbed me out.

"Johnny are you there?"

"Yeah," he said.

"Quiet prisoners," the silence shouted at us. "No Talking in Max."

So we were in Max, not M.O.E. "I guess it could be worse," I thought. M.O.E. Terrifying.

They marched us down a hall that was dimly lit by yellowish light shining out of porthole windows. My whole body felt tired. Like the floor, in addition to inhibiting my powers, was draining energy from me. Not like I could see any weather outside the Luther anyway.

After walking for ten minutes, I was tossed in a cell and the door slammed behind me. It was small. Ten-foot-by-ten-foot, with a hole in the corner, a roll-out mattress against the back wall, and a small window that looked out into the black hall. There was a small slot at the bottom of the door. I closed my eyes. Made a wish that a friendly cartoon mouse would come in that slot and befriend me. I was already feeling like I had prison madness.

I tried talking and then shouting but no one heard me. No one came. I was trapped. I banged on the walls. Tried slamming into the door. Screamed at the top of my lungs. But my screams just bounced back on the walls. I felt so useless. If I was outside, without the stupid bracelets, I could have lifted the whole prison off its base with the force of the wind I would make, especially feeling this feeling of rage and powerlessness. I only hoped Johnny was doing better than me.

I slumped against the wall and cried for what seemed like hours. After a while I finally fell asleep, only to be awakened by a strange light coming off the walls. They seemed to glow, light yellow at first, then a brighter white. I guess they were mimicking sunrise.

I had nothing to do but think. I tried to figure out what landed me in the Luther but came up blank. If it was because of Dr. Mann it would have happened months ago. It seemed silly that the party was a big enough crime to get us here. Did anyone know about us? Where we all over the news, like Mom, labeled terrorists? Or had we just disappeared? Dad must be going crazy. I wondered if anybody would do anything. Maybe Alice could get Freedom Boy to do something. Yes, that was it. He would ask the right people what happened and find out the truth. I'd be out in no time.

The fake sun rose and set twice and I gave up all hope. I paced endlessly, cried for long spells, clutching my necklace, and shouted. I was going crazy. I started hearing voices. Some screaming. Some talking calmly. I couldn't separate them. It was just voices all over the room. My mind was unraveling. I knew that this was what happened to people, alone in a solitary prison. They went mad. Their brains couldn't handle the loneliness.

How long could I last? I divided the day by the light from the walls and the food pushed through the slot, indistinguishable brown mush. I skipped the first two meals and was so hungry by the third I ate it all down in one gulp. The voice said, "Good. Eat. You need to eat."

The third day something finally broke the monotony. I heard a speaker in the hall broadcast "Code Red! Code Red! All staff to floor M.O.E. I repeat, Mission Objective Exterminate is Code Red. No terrestrial weapons. Full protection. This is a code red." Footsteps ran down the hall. I guess that mysterious M.O.E floor was below us. But I'd never heard of a villain named M.O.E. It just reminded me of The Three Stooges. I spent the rest of the day thinking about what or who he or she was. It had to be someone or something dangerous, if it was kept in the bottom of the Luther. Some monster lurking beneath me. A giant robot. A dragon. That bartender on The Simpsons. I didn't have much to do on but at least it kept me occupied. Moe moe moe.

I woke up on my fourth day to a disgusting sight. My food came through the slot and, before I could get to it, a rat came in after it. It eyed the food and I grabbed for it. This was not the cute friendly cartoon rodent I fantasized about. I knew between the creature and myself I could win, but I was so freaked out I shrieked and it dropped something and ran away. I figured it was some gross rat thing and ignored it, but a few seconds later the rat came back and gently nosed the thing toward me. I had no idea how Alice did it, talking to all of the animals. Some of them were so skittery and gross.

It was a small metal capsule, the size of a pinkie finger. I reached for it and the rat backed up against the wall. I turned it around in my hand. It seemed to have some kind of cap. I pulled off the cap and a scroll of paper and tiny pencil fell out. I picked up the scroll and read it.

Hello, my name is Roland the Rat. I was sent here from Alice, who is very worried about you. She has sent around thousands of Rats to look for Johnny and Sarah. If you are Sarah, she is really sorry you fought and feels terrible. And she hopes you are doing okay. You can get through this, whatever it is. If this is Johnny (Sarah, cover your eyes), I love you so much and miss you more than anything. I will not rest until you and Sarah are free. Okay, Sarah, you can look again. Here's the rundown. No one knows where you are. There are some rumors, but nothing solid. The last thing we knew you disappeared from the police station. No media coverage no nothing. We finally got one reporter interested and Amnesty International is offering to help us. Please write to tell us what's up on the backside and we'll get you back in no time.

   -Alice

I grabbed the pencil and scribbled down as much as possible. Roland took it and ran off. I wished him luck. I guess we had two chances to get a message out, one from me and one from Johnny. It made me want to bury the hatchet between all of us. Life was too short to resent two people for falling in love, I thought. I felt my heart grow three more sizes inside my chest. It was the right thought to have.

A few hours later, while I was clutching my necklace, I noticed it was starting to glow blue. It had never done that before. More voices came to me. A chorus of women saying, *What did you do? You made so many mistakes. You're a terrorist. Vile. Evil. You're going to be here for the rest of eternity and you deserve it.* I screamed, "STOP!" It provided temporary relief.

That night, I lay down, trying to sleep with my head against the wall. A single voice came into my head. It wasn't mine. But it wasn't the mad screaming from earlier. "Sarah," it said.

"I know I'm going crazy," I said back, hearing my voice out loud.

"You're not," it replied.

"Am too. And now I'm fighting with the voice in my head, so... extra crazy." "You're talking to a friend, Sarah."

"Sure. Who are you?"

"I can't say. But I'm a friend. And a member of the Djed."

I perked up. "How do I know you're real?"

"There's no way. Anything I tell you, you can't confirm so you must already know it inside yourself. And if you know it, it could be your own head. But, I have one way of showing you that I am not the voice in your head. I'm the one making your necklace glow. Count down from five. At one it will glow bright purple."

I chose to humor my own insanity and counted down. Five...

four… three… two… one. I placed the necklace in my palm. In the dark, I could make out a color and a glow. Purple. It turned purple! "You're real," I blurted. "How are you real? How are you talking to me?"

"My powers are stronger then their machines. But listen to me. I don't have much time. Your mother is free but much of the Djed is in prison. It started with Innsmouth and has gotten worse since President Bergeron. We were rounded up after his election and taken here."

"How can I get out of here? What can we do?" I asked.

"The only way out is through fire." I rolled my eyes. Just like the Djed to give me a proclamation and koan instead of an actual solution. Any sort of secret supergroup always ended up sounding as vague as a horoscope. "I think you might have a chance of getting out, but you may have to wait. When you are free: Help us. Save the country."

"How? I can't even throw a good party without the cops breaking it up."

"The key is Innsmouth. Show the world Innsmouth and they will see the truth.""Why? What really happened there?"

"Your mom and others tried to stop it, and when they couldn't they tried to reveal it. It's not what it appears. Everyone on the PeriGenomics board not being hunted is guilty. They were secretly doing—AAAAAAAAA!" he shrieked. The voice pierced my head.

He was trying to tell me everything and he failed. I couldn't stop thinking about his pain. Someone was doing something to him. I held my ears but the screaming didn't stop. I hit my head into the wall until I slumped into unconsciousness.

A wet nose woke me up. I shook, a searing pain, behind my eyes. It was Roland the rat. He had returned. He smiled at me. I sat upright. There was some dried blood on my head.

Roland gave me another note. It was shorter. *People are finally paying attention. You were on the news. The police and government are denying knowing where you are. Stay strong!*

Finally, some good news. They couldn't keep us here forever. Alice was fighting to free us. They would have to admit where we were and then we would be let out and it all would be behind us. I felt happy for the first time since the police grabbed me from the party.

And then, for the first time since I was thrown in my cell, the doors opened.

FORTY

"**Y**OU'RE LETTING me out, right?" I asked. "I know you are. The press is skewering you. You'll be sorry you ever did this!" I shouted defiantly.

"I'll be back, and you'll be sorry!" one of the stone-face guards squeaked, mocking the way my voice cracked. They brought me down another corridor, pushing me into a room where I had to sit in a chair at a table. The room had one overhead fluorescent bulb. The table was metal and painted black. There was a camera on a tripod in the corner. The guards seemed frightened of the room, treating it gingerly. They didn't want to spend more time in it than they had to, for work's sake. They stayed in the hall while I moldered inside.

I heard the noise of footsteps clacking down the hall, and a tall, thin man wearing a long red robe swept into the room. He was flanked by a much shorter man in a dark black robe. The guards took that as their cue to leave. "We'll be back in an hour," one of them said.

"I'll need one of you to stay. They requested film," said the black robe. He looked like a sidekick, short and stout compared to red robe.

"I thought they didn't want any record of this," the guard said.

"This tape is for a very special person," the man in the black robe replied.

"What are you going to do? Why are you filming this? Who the hell are you?" I shouted. It was time for these men to know that I existed. That there was a person in the balance.

The man in the red robe raised his hand toward me and the next words I was going to say died in my throat. My mouth sealed shut. I tried to open it but couldn't. I felt it and I had no mouth. Just smooth skin. I shouted but a loud MMMMM just echoed in my esophagus.

"I'll cover you on Tuesday if you take this," one guard said.

"Fine," he replied, and his compatriot ran out before he could change his mind. The guard walked over to the camera and flipped the switch to on. His hands were shaking. "Hello Sarah," the man in the black robe said. "So nice to meet you. My name is Onyx Rivers and this is my friend Phobetor. He doesn't say much." Phoebeter nodded. "I'm here to make a movie with you. I do this type of work to serve my country. I've been informed that you are a terrorist and supervillain and I want to make sure you have no plans, already in action, that could harm people."

"Now speak," Onyx said, and Phoebeter made a line with his finger across my mouth.

"I swear. I'm just a kid. I have no evil plans. I don't know why you think this. I'm innocent. I'm…"

"I was hoping you'd be more cooperative," he said. He looked at Phoebeter, who proceeded to run his finger backward and my mouth disappeared again. "But, let's be honest, I was hoping you'd say that." Phoebeter held his hands up and my chair tilted backwards and hovered above the ground a few inches. Onyx Rivers walked up to my side and indicated for the man with the camera to follow him. Onyx looked down at me. "I'm not completely unlike you, young Ms. Robertson. I too was considered a Misshape for most of my early life. But I knew my powers were great. But there is a difference between the two of us. I chose to use mine for good, whereas you and your family have chosen the less righteous path."

I tried to shout at him to tell him he was wrong, but I couldn't scream. I had no mouth. I thrashed, wildly, trying to tell him the truth, but my hands were pinned to the table, and starting to hurt as they stretched out, unable to move with my body. "Would you like to know what those powers were?" he asked. "The ones I had to show were extraordinary."

I nodded no, emphatically.

"Oh don't be shy. Sure you do," he said. "Everyone does." He made a circle with his right hand, held it up to his mouth, and blew through it. A large bubble appeared, like a soap bubble, and floated upward from his hand. He then made small puffs and tiny bubbles emerged from his hand. "You see, people thought I wasn't good for anything but party tricks. My guidance counselor suggested I become a clown for children's parties. But my power isn't making bubbles. It's making foams. And everyone around me was too stupid to be able to teach me the power such foams held."

He put his hands together and slowly spread them apart. As he did, a meshwork of tiny bubbles, like you'd see in a soap bucket at a car wash, appeared. But when he moved his hands, instead of slipping off or popping, they followed the path of his hand—which unfortunately, was going toward my face. He took a long strip off bubbles and pulled them across my nose, covering it. Panic shot through my body. My eyes opened wide. I couldn't breathe.

He pinched his forefinger and thumb together on both hands, and created bubbles that expanded and contracted as he spoke. "You see, foam is just air trapped in a thin liquid membrane. The liquid can be anything and the membrane can be anything. You can separate explosives gases from each other by a micron of water, or smoke, so people can't see. In your case, what's being trapped in those bubbles in oxygen. Not all of it, but just enough to keep you conscious."

He looked at Phoebeter who made my mouth appear again, and I screamed for him to stop but a layer of foam muffled the sound. Onyx River pulled out a pin and popped one of the bubbles and a small scream emerged. My scream. He continued to pop bubbles, and tiny screams burst with them. I was on the verge of passing out when he put his hand on my bubble mask and a rush of oxygen came into my lungs. "You see? Very useful." I nodded. "Now, do you have anything useful for me?"

I wanted to tell him anything to make him stop. "What? What do you want?" I said. "I don't know anything. If I did, I'd tell you."

"Hmm. Better trained than I thought," he said, and then he lifted my chair back up. "Well maybe my friend will have more luck with you."

Onyx stepped back and joined the cameraman and Phoebeter stepped forward. He made a strange gesture with his hands, drawing them upward, and my hands followed them, like I was his marionette. He placed them on the table with his invisible strings and they felt bolted to the table. Then he placed his hands on my temples and disappeared. Then the room disappeared with him. A blinding white light flashed in my eyes and I closed them tightly to block it out. When I opened them up I was in my bed at home. I blinked twice and rubbed my eyes.

As I got out of bed, something felt strange about my room. Everything was where it should be, my humidifier on the desk, my books piled up against the wall, my emergency rain bucket by the bed, but they all seemed, I'm not sure how to put this, aged. Like they had been untouched for years. There were some cobwebs inside the humidifier, a patina of rust on various metal objects like my chair, and wooden things like my desk and bedframe were slightly rotted. It wasn't extreme, just slight enough to be noticeable. The light in the room was also weird. Like all the warm tones had been blotted out and the world was gray and blue.

I went downstairs but the house was empty. Dirty dishes piled up in the sink. It smelled acrid. The windows were broken and weeds and plants grew into the house. The carpet was damp. The TV broken. There was graffiti all over the walls in Hamilton's style. It said, "get out" and "just breathe" over and over again in red and black letters. I turned to see more of the house and when I turned more of the graffiti filled the walls. I felt like Hamilton was in the room, just out of range of my vision. I turned faster but couldn't catch him, only traces of his outline. For some reason, I wanted to see him right then. More than Sam or Freedom Boy. I barely thought about those two. I spun around until the entire house was dripping with thick black paint, which slid of the walls and started flooding the room. It came up to my feet, then knees, until I had to trudge through the paint to get out of the house.

The town was empty. It was my Doolittle Falls, but also foreign. All the angles of the streets were off. Things that had been torn down years ago looked new, things from other towns were lined up where they shouldn't have been. The nuclear reactor from Innsmouth sat in the distance, right where the Harpastball field once was. One of the reactors was pristine, billowing white smoke. The other was charred and crumbling, thick purple smoke pouring out of it. I remembered the voice in my head's words and walked toward it.

Hamilton's graffiti was sprayed on: *You'll c-r-a-p yourself!* I heard Alice's voice. "It's been a long time." I looked over. She was standing next to me, a genuine surprise. Her face was gaunt, pale bluish, her eyes were black and sunk into her skull. She wore her Halloween outfit but it had become ratty, the tunic threadbare. The animals glued to her seemed to be moving. I screwed up my face to take a closer look. They were no longer made of foam and paper mache, but were alive. There eyes were red and they were trying to escape from her but couldn't. They were glued to her costume by their feet and they struggled faintly to get loose. Alice didn't notice them.

I wanted to point this out, to ask her to save them, but instead said in a calm voice, "Long time since what?"

"Anyone's walked these streets."

"Where are we?"

"Doolittle Falls, of course," she said. One of the squirrels began to gnaw at its own leg.

"But it seems so strange," I said.

"Nothing strange about it," George said. He walked on my left, in quick neat steps. He was half invisible, and half there. Invisibility floated over his body like a cloud, disappearing sections of him and making them translucent. "Just time and neglect. People don't care for Heroes much these days. The ones left at least."

"But why is this happening. What did this? What can I do?"

"Oh, Sarah, you did this. Don't you remember?" George said.

"No. No, what did I do. Can I fix it?" I asked.

"Of course not," Alice said. "You've been dead for years."

I sprinted toward the reactors. I knew that they held the key somehow. But as I ran I heard footsteps behind me. Dr. Mann and Alice were chasing me. And behind them the crowd grew. Butters, Hocho, Wendy, George, Ms. Frankl, Johnny, my Dad, my Mom. I ran faster and faster but the crowd just got larger. Soon it seemed the whole town was there. I got to the gate at the Harpastball field and it was locked. I forced an enormous gust of wind that knocked down the mob and blasted the gate open. Sitting in the middle of the field were the reactors, one intact and one destroyed. A siren went off. Red lights started blaring from poles, drenching the town in red light.

The mob clutched their ears and writhed on the ground. Dark clouds filled the sky and lightning started to flash, then strike the reactor. I tried to stop it but I couldn't. More and more strikes hit the reactor. It started pouring out black smoke. Everything I did just made it worse. I grew more and more panicked. I used all my energy to dispel the storm, but instead, and enormous lightning ball, the size of a house, shot out of the sky and hit the reactor. The walls cracked at the strike and the crack quickly spread like spider webs throughout the reactor. It seemed to pucker in, and then, an enormous blast of heat and fire shot out in all directions.

I screamed and tore at my skin. The fire raced across it. I watched as it bubbled up, blackened, and tore open, revealing muscle and fat beneath. My body was incinerating before my eyes. Then fell to the floor writhing in pain. It was agonizing. Suddenly, another blinding light came and my skin felt fine. I was sitting at the table in the room, across from Phobetor, the guard was behind the camera, and Phobetor was smiling. "Thank you," Phobetor said. "That was terrific. Great show. Really good brain there."Phobetor turned to the guard, who stopped the camera and gave him the tape like he was a robot. When he handed over the tape he slouched and looked perturbed. "Don't do that," the guard said.

"Or what?" Phobetor said. "Okay, that will be all."

The guard came over and took me by the shoulders. Before we left, Phobetor held up the tape. "Your mother will enjoy this," he said. "Getting to see her own daughter on film."

FORTY-ONE

I FELT SO violated by Phobetor. Every time I closed my eyes I saw that awful version of Doolittle, the mob coming for me, the fire lighting up the sky. I sat rocking back and forth in shock for a day, clutching my necklace. "Are you okay?" the voice in my head said.

"No, are you?"

"I've been better. I have some resistance to them, but they have ways."

"Did they know you were talking to me?"

"No. Just I was talking to someone"

"Have you spoken to Johnny?"

"A little. He's harder to get through to, I'll have you know."

"How is he?"

"Surviving. Did they send you to Phobetor?"

"Yes."

"He's the worst. I've scanned your mind and you seem to have survived unscarred. You're resilient."

"Before you leave again, what was it you were going to say? I've been thinking about it over and over again."

"Shh, I think they're coming." The voice stopped. Moments later my door opened again. Two guards appeared. "Up, prisoner," they said.

"No. I'm not going back there," I protested, my voice getting desperate.

They came in and dragged me out, pulling me down the hall. We passed the hallway where I met Phobetor and kept going. I took a greedy gulp of air. They stopped at the elevator bank. There were two more guards. They had a prisoner, too. He was gaunt and tired looking. His hair looked like a soufflé that had fallen. It was Johnny! I nearly gasped; I was so excited. "What's happening?" I asked him.

"Don't know, they won't tell me. At least we're not going back to that room." "You too?"

"Yeah," he said, sadly. They threw us in the elevators, which whisked us up to the fiftieth floor, one below the top. The door opened on a large sign reading "Mental Health Ward."

Next step, institutionalization. I patted my brother with my handcuffed hands. "It's okay. We're not crazy," I said. The unit resembled a hospital, if a hospital had all the hospitality of a prison. The patients shuffled around, looking at the floor, their hands and legs shackled. There was a TV in the corner showing cartoons, and orderlies walking around serving pills. It was all very surreal. But it felt like they weren't there to drop us off but march us through. Were they trying to show something to the patients? It was then that I spotted him. Or rather them. All four of them. Dead-eyed, sullen, heads down. Doris was sitting apart from Butters and the other two Spectors, but they were all there. "Butters!" Johnny and I shouted.

He looked up slowly and squinted his eyes, but it was like he didn't recognize us. Whatever they had him on, it was heavy. He put his head back down. The Spectors made no movement. As soon as he put his head back down the guards brought us back to the elevators and up to the top floor. Butters was a warning.

When we got to the top we were met by more guards. They led

us to the outer perimeter where we had first entered the Luther. It was where the bubbles found the building. The sky was gray. It was windy and cold. I could see all the way to Doolittle Falls and across the valley that the Miskatonic cut through. There was a helicopter on a helipad that jutted out from the floor above the lake.

The guards held us up and a man in a suit appeared. It was J4 himself. He had a hard face. No expression. A cold face and dead blue eyes. "You know who I am," he said. "So I'll skip the introductions. You're being released. But if you mention this experience to anyone you'll be taken back immediately. I know you must have many questions. You will get no answers. You are owed nothing. And you owe gratitude. So…"

He paused and stared at us. "Did you hear me? I said you owe gratitude."

"Thank you," I said.

Johnny refused. J4 waved his hand and one of the guards dragged him to the edge and held him over the two- hundred-foot drop. The helicopter blades were so loud it was hard to hear. "Did you say something?" J4 shouted.

I mouthed, "Thank you!" at my brother.

"Thank you!" Johnny screamed.

"What was that?"

"THANK YOU?" he screamed.

J4 moved his hand and the guard brought him back. I noticed, when he waved the hand, that he wasn't wearing his collar. "Very good. I hope to never see you two pieces of trash ever again."

He walked to the far end of the platform, mounted a jet scooter, and flew south. Five Secret Service agents on jet scooters surrounded him. The guards took us into the helicopter and flew us home. The chopper landed in our school's football field. They took off our bracelets and flew off.

I hugged Johnny as tightly as I ever had. We wanted to call everyone to let them know what happened but had no phones. We walked home as fast as we could. Our legs were too cramped to run.

When we got home, Dad rushed to us and squeezed us tightly. The TV was blaring in the background. "Thank god!" he said. He looked about ten years older, like the difference between a president at the beginning of their term and at the end of their term. The TV caught our attention. The broadcaster said, "Bane of Innsmouth," and "Janet Robertson, former Dean of the Hero Academy."

We looked at the screen and saw Mom, in cuffs, being taken in by the police to the Luther. A smiling Freedom Man and Freedom Boy stood behind her as she was carted off. There was a reason we were released.

Mom, number one on the Luther's list of supervillains at large, had surrendered.

FORTY-TWO

LATER THAT night, Alice picked us up. I had wondered whether things would still feel tense when I saw her, but it was obvious that all was forgiven. Time in hell really puts things in perspective. She took us to Hamilton's, which had been converted from an art studio into a makeshift operations center for the Free Johnny and Sarah project.

They were all eager to talk to us but I couldn't hold back any longer. "Johnny, we need to tell them that awful thing we saw," I said.

He nodded.

"They have Butters," I said.

Betty let out a gasp.

"Where?" asked Alice.

"At the Luther. He's in the Mental Health unit. All doped up."

Betty was about to faint. "What are they doing to him? What are they doing to my Butters?"

"I don't know," said Johnny. "It's not that bad in there."

"Well, it's not great, but it's nothing like the prison floors," I added.

"We need to get him out," Betty said to the room and me. "Now."

How? Everyone asked, with their mouths or their eyes or both. "I don't know," Betty said. But we need too."

"I think they showed us him as a warning," I said.

"Of what?" Betty said. "We all deal with stuff."

"I don't know. What they can do. That they still have people we love."

"Well I'm getting him out. Now." She was ready to write letters, to storm the barricades. I shuddered to think of Betty meeting the Luther, a land without any rules"Betty don't," I said, trying to grab her wrist as she stormed off. Johnny held me back. They were still messing with us, even outside their awful prison.

"So," I said, "what have you guys been up to?"

At one table, Tape Deck was dissecting the bracelets Rosa wore. One of them was half disassembled, its smooth plastic surface opened to reveal a patchwork of tiny metal pieces and circuits. The other no longer resembled a bracelet at all, it was spread out across the table, each piece with a pencil scrawling next to it. "What's going on here?" I asked her, surveying the transistors and boards. She picked up a piece with his tweezers, a small black box with tiny red wires leading out of it, and held it up.

"This," she said, dramatically, "is a satellite controlled transmitter. It is wired to turn the device on and off, so someone can remotely control it from anywhere in the world." Johnny came over, his arm laced around Alice's hip like he would never let go."Wait," I said, "that means... shoot, Rosa, come here!" This was big news if it was true.

Tape Deck validated my thinking. "Yup. The device worked fine. Someone just turned it off during the show. It wasn't an accident that happened. It was planned.""But who, why?" Alice asked.

"I don't know, but from the look of it, someone who worked at or for PeriGenomics. This has their tech written all over it."

"Sam?" I muttered to myself.

"This whole thing was a set up. They wanted that earthquake so they had an excuse to get us," Johnny said.

"But why would they want to arrest some kids?" I asked.

"You saw last night, for Mom. We were bait for the big fish. They wanted to use us a bargaining chip."

"I have something else to show you," said Alice. She took us over to a table that had photographs spread all over it and a computer in the center with tiny cameras attached to rubber bands.

"What is all this?" I asked.

"Operation Alvin," Alice said. She smiled to herself. "I've been fitting these little cameras on squirrels and chipmunks and having them spy on PeriGenomics for me. I figured after what Tape Deck found they might see something damning."

I picked one up and turned it in my hand. "Wow, these are pretty cool."

"So what you got?" Johnny asked.

She pulled up a few files and opened them up. They were grainy pictures, some in color, some in black and white, of the PeriGenomics buildings. People walking in and out, trucks dropping off supplies, picking up things. Nothing special.

"That," she said, and pointed to a small figure. She pushed a few buttons and the figure got larger. He was wearing an elaborate costume, like a Hero, and walking past PeriGenomics employees like some regular shlub. It took me a moment to figure out who it was.

"Holy what," I blurted. "I know that face. I fought that face!"

"Admiral Doom in the flesh," Alice said. She pulled up picture after picture of the Admiral walking into and out of PeriGenomics. It was clear that he was not attacking the place or putting some crazy hex so they couldn't see him. It was mundane and banal. Pictures of the Admiral parking his car (a Honda Civic), the Admiral walking in with coffee, the Admiral sitting with coworkers at a picnic table eating a sandwich, the Admiral talking to the top brass at PeriGenomics. It was obvious. He wasn't a supervillain at all. He wasn't out to steal whatever he stole at MIT, he wasn't out to take down PeriGenomics and wreak havoc throughout Doolittle Falls. At the end of the day, Admiral Doom was a regular guy. He was a PeriGenomics employee.

FORTY-THREE

"WAIT," JOHNNY said. "You mean to tell me that Admiral Doom is a confederate?""What does this have to do with the Civil War?" Marcus asked.

"No, not that kind of confederate. He's a fake, an actor, not an actual villain but a prop villain."

"That's what I'm saying," I replied. I knew Johnny was reconstructing his old conspiracy wall in his head, the one he kept hidden in his room, moving around suspects, locations, newspaper clippings. In all his research he had not uncovered this one crucial piece of information. I didn't find it, either. It must have been well hidden.

"So what's that mean?" asked Marcus.

Kurt replied, "It's not that hard, Marcus. All those attacks and crimes were faked.""What's in it for him, though?" Marcus asked.

"It wasn't him faking it, it was him working for PeriGenomics. Don't forget he walked in there like any other employee," Betty said.

"So the Doom Raid Drills, and the shelters. All fake. All to build up this Admiral Doom thing," Wendy said.

"It make senses," Johnny said. "What better way to build up his reputation than to create a fearful response. And make sure it gets in the papers. Not every day, but just often enough so we don't forget."

"It's about freedom," said Alice. "Remember the machine they tried to destroy our powers with? The machine made by PeriGenomics? Remember all those stories of the environmental damage, the treatment of workers, et cetera? Every time one of those came out, Admiral Doom grabbed a headline and took over the airwaves. If we're worried about him we're not worried about what PeriGenomics."

I remembered my own encounter with Admiral Doom. What had been the reason for that one? Was it for Freedom Boy's PR team?

"It's also about power," said Kurt. "What better way to show that Heroes are necessary than to invent supervillains. I bet they're all made up. Just a way to give the world a reason to keep these people around and let them run the place."

Everyone was ready to riot. The vibe inside the Free me & my brother campaign headquarters was tense. Johnny blurted, "Kurt, it's not a conspiracy across the world. Heroes have been around for thousands of years and PeriGenomics is much older than the Admiral Doom attacks. Doom's only been around for three or four years at most. Really his first big attack was…" he trailed off.

"What? What was it?" asked Marcus.

I looked at my brother, a terrible realization dawning. "Mom," I said.

In unison, we blurted, "We have to go to Innsmouth."

FORTY-FOUR

EVERYONE STARED, dumbfounded, at Johnny. Was he serious? Betty broke the silence. "What the hell are you talking about Johnny? That place is a nuclear disaster. We'd be irradiated."

"Well, what my idea presupposes is… is it?" he asked. "Really?"

"Yes," said Marcus. "Of course. Didn't you see all the news footage and photographs?"

Johnny paced around the room. He looked like a mad person. "How do we know that's real? They made up Admiral Doom, and he's a person. Why not the disaster itself? If it was what they say it is, why the secrecy? Why the subterfuge!" His hands punctuated each remark. I wasn't going to butt in, in this case. Johnny and I had ties to Innsmouth, emotional ones. We had something in the idea that it was all faked for the media.

"Has anyone actually seen it? We live less than a hundred miles away and were fine." He turned to Kurt. "You were from there. Did you actually see anything?"

"Can you have children?" I added, trying to bother Kurt.

"Nope," Kurt said. "I didn't see anything, Johnny." He said my brother's name, pointedly. "One minute the power goes out and the next minute the police and army are banging on every door. They just evacuated us and carted us out of town. Gave us ten minutes to get whatever we wanted and could fit in our hands." He looked angrier than usual. "It was the worst day of my life."

"See?" said Johnny, pointing at Kurt. "He was there and he saw nothing. No smoke. No explosions." He sounded crazy. But crazy enough to be right. It didn't add up. "Okay," I said. "So if we go there, how do we find our way around the place?" "I can show you," Kurt said. "It would be good to learn the truth. And get some of my things back, assuming they haven't burned it."

"That place is locked tighter than Fort Knox," Alice said.

"There's got to be more than one way in," Hamilton added. "Let me at it. You can't lock down a whole town."

"I'll ask Dr. Ravela for Geiger counters," I said.

"Sounds like you're going, Sarah," Johnny said. "I'm going too. Anyone else?"

FORTY-FIVE

MARCUS WAVED the wand of the Geiger counter in front of him with long sweeping motions. The bright yellow machine in his right hand pinged rapidly and the needle pushed off the scale. According to the machine, the level of rads was increasing with each step closer into town. At the gate it had pulsed at a slow steady rate. After we cut a hole with Kurt's wire cutters and stepped inside, it shot up to dangerous levels. If we kept going, we would be exposed to enough rads to give us instant cancer. As it was, we were probably causing some long-term damage. I didn't care. I wanted to know the truth about my mother.

We stopped just beyond the gate, afraid to move closer. This wasn't superpower radiation. This was long painful death radiation. Silently we looked at each other. Tape Deck, oblivious to our concern, walked forward.

"I knew it," she said. She put her hands on her head like she was calling the gods. "What?" I asked, frozen in place.

"The Geiger counter. It went up too high and too fast. Even if there was an incident, it's still miles off. There would be a curve upward, not a cliff." Tape Deck shook her head. "Faker than my mom's Berkin bag knockoff."

Tape Deck pulled something out of her briefcase-ish purse. It was one of the Doolittle High Geiger counters but this one was different. It was inside a green glowing metal box with the label, Palacorp printed on the side. Palacorp was one of PeriGenomics' competitors in the superweapons field. Tape Dec'ks machine pinged once every few seconds, at a steady rate, and the needle stayed close to zero the whole time. "I don't get it," Marcus said. "Why is mine going crazy and yours barely registering anything?"

"Does that block radiation?" Alice asked, pointing to the box.

"Not exactly. It blocks something else," she said. "Are you really that dense, Marcus?" I shook my head in time with Tape Deck. Marcus sure could miss the obvious sometimes.

The town of Innsmouth came into view. It was exactly as we'd seen on the news. Completely devastated. The buildings were burned to char; the whole town was like a music video about being depressed where everything was rendered in shades of gray, black, and brown. The world was dead. No birds flew. No squirrels scurried. The grass looked like ash. Cars were abandoned in the middle of roads, their doors opened, swinging in the breeze. The air smelled of sulfur and tar. My eyes started to water. I covered my face with a tissue.

"What exactly does that thing block," I asked, "because if that's not a radioactive wasteland I don't know what is."

"Powers," Tape Deck said. "It blocks powers."

"Are you sure it works?" Johnny asked.

"Yes. This casing isn't enough to block any gamma waves, so if there was radiation it would read it."

"Trust it with your life?" I asked.

She thought about it for a second. "Yeah."

"Trust it with our lives, sure?" Alice asked.

Hamilton rolled his eyes. I wanted to roll my eyes, but I felt just as paranoid as everybody else. "If I trust it with my life I definitely trust it with yours. Besides, it's not like you can do anything if I'm wrong. If Marcus's counter is right in a few more steps we're all dead. But also if he's right, in a few miles, our skin will be peeling off. So if we go forward we're going to find out soon enough if we have hours or decades left to live." Tape Deck took a breath and smiled. "But I'm pretty sure we're going to live."

She walked forward, bravely. We stood frozen behind her, shivering. "Don't be scared, guys. It could be a false signal sent out to trick the machine. Or someone with powers like mine that can control Geiger counters messing with it. But, considering that," she said pointing to the destroyed town, "if there is no radiation that means there was no disaster. Or no nuclear disaster. So most likely it's a psycho-neural field over this whole region. The field would warp the reality inside so that we only saw what he wanted us to see."

"Wouldn't someone need to be here to do that?" I asked. Someone like the J4 family. Or Pheobeter. Johnny looked pale. "Yeah, we've met people who could do that," he said. The bulk of the group, save Tape Deck, was still standing in place.

What Tape Deck was saying made sense, and we all believed her. She looked so happy in the great non-radiated beyond. I thought she was fine, a couple of paces ahead of us, but she was slowing down. She wasn't going to sacrifice her life for this experimentation. It was going to take someone to break the spell, and I took the first step. I took the first twenty actually. I zoomed past Tape Deck into the radiated atmosphere, and I felt completely fine. Tape Deck followed closely. Everyone else stood still. Johnny was about to charge ahead but when I saw him move, I shouted, "Wait!" He paused.

A plan came into my head. "How about Tape Deck and I go forward, and if we don't turn into a puddle of radioactive goop, we'll come back to get you guys." My gut knew that we were fine, but I didn't want everyone else to freak out.

"We're all in this together?" Johnny said, but the rest of them seemed nervous. "Okay, new plan," he said, grabbing Marcus's Geiger Counter and walking toward us. "Me, Sarah and Tape Deck walk into town. If we don't turn into goop we'll get you." "Fine by me," said Alice.

Hamilton looked pissed. He wanted to be part of the fun. "No point in us all dying," he said, but I knew he was disappointed.

FORTY-SIX

THE THREE of us made our way through brambles and forest until we hit a road in the suburbs on the outskirts of Innsmouth. The regular Geiger counter was beeping like crazy. Tape Deck assured us that, if it was right, we didn't have much longer to go. Her special one continued its steady syncopation, never skipping a beat, reading background radiation.

All the trees on the street were dead. They were burnt down into dark husks, their branches seared off, their bark cracked and ashy. All the grass was dead. The remnants of bushes, just wilted nests of black, dotted the road. The first house we saw was nothing but charred beams and melted siding. We could see the structure, the rooms with their black beds, the black shower stall, the ash that was once a bookshelf, the pool of plastic that was once a television, from the road.

"Interesting," Tape Deck said. "The burn pattern. It's off."

"Looks burned to me," Johnny said.

"Yes, but not nuclear disaster burned. It would be from a firestorm, which would push outward. That just looks like a housefire." Tape Deck smiled, confident in her knowledge of nuclear disaster. I was less well read on the topic, but I felt like she was telling the truth. I was trying to be very, very quiet so that I could listen to my instinct. It was starting to talk to me.

We walked by more houses, each burned in a similar way, and each inspection from Tape Deck came to the same conclusion. When we got to a suburban block that looked like our own, it had house after burned house. Johnny used a map on his phone to tell us where we were going. But in this neighborhood, the Geiger counter beeps got faster and I felt a sudden pain in my stomach. I put my hand on it and the pain grew worse. It was sharp.

I looked around and saw that Johnny and Tape Deck felt it as well. Beads of sweat formed on my forehead. My body felt flushed. I spit up a little on the ground, and when I wiped my mouth I saw my skin was starting to turn red.

"What's happening?" I asked.

"Radiation poisoning?" Johnny said. He was too busy puking to say much more. I felt something sticky come off my head. I looked down and the skin was starting to peel. It was bleeding and raw. *How long do we have,* I wanted to ask, but I couldn't get the words out. My body slumped to the ground, too sick to move. Heating up, melting, coming apart. I tried to make noises, groaning, moaning. I wanted to go out of this world the way I came in.

When I felt like I couldn't even keep my eyes open, that I wanted to die rather than feel any more pain, I saw Tape Deck jump up like she was fine and walk over to me. She seemed pretty spry considering his skin appeared to be sloughing off. She grabbed my hand and her other hand held up the box that had contained his Geiger counter, empty now. I put my hand in the box. It was oozing with blood, dripping red, but inside the Geiger counter box, it was fine. As soon as I took it out, it morphed, becoming grotesque again.

"What's going on?" I groaned.

"I was right," she said. "This is all fake. But there isn't a field. Someone has to be doing this. Someone knows that we're here and wants us to leave."

Have you ever had one of those dreams where things change so completely and seamlessly that you feel like it would be wrong to point them out? Like, one minute you have a rubber chicken in your hand and the next minute it's an enormous knife. You didn't put down the chicken and pick up the knife, one didn't morph into the other, what once was, was no longer, and what now is, has always been. I hated those dreams.

But those dreams were the only things on my mind as I saw J5 and Christie emerge from the darkness. They were just standing there, watching us writhe in pain. One minute there were dead trees and the movement of the wind. The next, the two stood there, looking at us. "Fine, fine. You caught us," said J5, materializing in thin air next to his sister Christie.

"They didn't catch us. They would have never figured it out," Christie said.

"We'll it doesn't matter either way. We'll play with them for a bit and then call our dad to pick them up."

"I don't see why you had to reveal ourselves to them. You're no fun." Christie said, in a little girl whine.

"Oh, I'm sorry," he said, grabbing her by the chin. "But if we don't waste our powers on that, we can use them to have even more fun."

"Promise?" she asked.

I tried to get to my feet, but he waved his hand and it felt like a ton of bricks fell on me. I fell to the ground, pinned in place.

"I don't think you'll be going anywhere soon," J5 said.

"I swear to god I'm going to..." I protested, weakly. But my powers didn't work here. My feelings felt like nothing, echoing the desolate landscape.

"Oh will you shut up," J5 said, and closed his hands together like a duck, shutting my mouth as if I was a puppet. J5 took his free hand and adjusted Christie's metal necklace, opening it up and pressing several buttons I couldn't see. She beamed as he did this.

Her excitement worried me. "There you go," he said. "Good as new."

Christie walked toward us and raised her hands. We lifted off the ground. Could she do that? We started to rise, faster and faster, until I realized something. "Guys, it's all in your head. This isn't real. It's like the—aaaaaaahhhhhh!" We plummeted to the ground. I kept telling myself that this isn't real, it isn't real. But even if it's fake, 130 miles per hour still feels fast. We hit the ground with a loud painful thud and Christie jumped for joy.

"Nice job Christie," J5 said. "Now, can I get back to doing what I was trying to do."

"Fine. It's so gross though," she said.

J5 looked at us with his evil grin, squinted his eyes, and my skin burned. He lifted one finger up and our fingers followed his into the air, then he delicately put it on his arm and pinched. We did the same, but while he pantomimed pulling his fingers across his arm, we grabbed a piece of irradiated flesh and ripped it off our bodies. It was like a long line of pain. And disgusting. I'd had enough. Mind control or not, this had to stop.

I placed one hand on the ground, pushed myself up, and walked toward him. I moved slowly, like walking through sand, each step an immense amount of effort. Christie and J5 laughed. I saw Johnny and Tape Deck beside me, doing the same. Then, J5 and Christie put both hands up, and slammed them down. It felt like a boulder to the chest. I fell backwards, back where I started.

"Okay, no more games," J5 said. "That was just a warm up. By the time the cops come you'll be begging to be put back in the Luther."

"Ouch," said Christie. "What was that?"

"I don't know," J5 said. "Probably just an—OUCH!" He screamed. Christie put her hand to her neck and when she looked at it was covered in a speck of blood. J5 yelped grabbed something that had gathered at his side, lost in the tails of his elaborate jacket. He pulled something to his face. It was gray and furry and had a long bushy tail.

"Ew! Disgusting! What the hell?" Christie screamed.

"I think it's a squirrel," he looked at us. "Is this you? Stop—"
But he was cut off. In an instant, a cavalry of squirrels launched
themselves at Christie and J5. The creatures had them running in
circles. In an instant, they were covered head to toe in gray furry
and a frenzy of tails. I saw Alice pop up behind the mayhem with
a cavalry of Misshapes. Johnny stood up and brushed himself off,
"Took you long enough."

"The thing to say is nice job," I said.

Alice threw herself at Johnny. He took her affections gratefully.
I was shocked at how not grossed out I was, in this case. Heck, I was
even grateful. "I told you squirrels are great," she said.

FORTY-SEVEN

ALICE TOLD the squirrels to sit on Christie and J5. They were like a furry prison. Tape Deck adjusted their collars with a small screwdriver, setting the controls to maximum. "After that, they'll be lucky to control their own minds," she said. "Though there was something a little strange with the collars."

"Strange how?" I asked.

"Remember how Rosa's bracelets had a RF off switch. They had something similar. It wasn't just a power dampener, it seemed to be in communication with something or someone."

"Any idea who?" Johnny asked. He still looked uneasy on his feet. They hadn't done any physical damage but their sick games made us a little uneasy and jumpy. He looked like he just got off a long boat ride, or a rollercoaster.

"No. It was encoded somehow. I'd need to… or I could… but maybe."

She continued talking in half sentences to himself until Alice finally cut in. "What? What do you need to do?"

"If I take off one of their collars and hook it up to my tablet and run the signal directly through my router, I can use my computer to see what it's talking to. If, that is, it's close." We all thought about it for a moment. We'd seen what they could do with their collars turned as low as possible. Pulling one off would be risky. Very risky. We'd still have Christie and J5 locked away in squirrel prison, for however long they would stick around, but who knew what they were capable of if we provoked them.

"Hold on," she said. She walked over to the furry prisoners and pulled her tablet out of his bag along with a bunch of wires and some wire cutters. She snipped and twisted and connected wires until there was a braid running from the collar to the tablet. J5 screamed in protest but once Alice said something in squirrel, his monologue was interrupted by a truly goofy yelp.

"Just keep quiet, and you'll be fine," Alice said.

"Look at this!" said Tape Deck. Alice and I looked at the screen and it showed a map with red blinking dots overlayed at various points on the map. "Those are transmission points. The fabulous twosome is connected to them." She typed away at the screen for a few minutes and then unplugged it. Without explaining why, she got up and walked farther along into town. We followed Tape Deck as she looked for something.

We got deeper and deeper into Innsmouth. The town was utterly destroyed. Each house we passed was less and less intact, until finally, there was nothing but black shadows where houses once stood. Everything was char and ash. The air was hard to breathe and tasted noxious, the soot got in our eyes and covered our skin. There was a charred brick schoolhouse, which was just a single wall, a sign that said Innsmouth High, and piles of blackened bricks. We walked past it. On the street, ahead of us, there was a telephone pole. It was the only one on the street and was badly burned, but surprisingly, seemed sturdy. Tape Deck walked right toward it, looking at the tablet as she went. When she got to the pole, she checked the screen again, and then looked up. "That's it," she said.

"That's what?" Marcus asked.

"One of the transmitters," she responded. "Help me out." Marcus walked over to Tape Deck and put her on his shoulders. Tape Deck reached up to a black box with her wire cutters. The box seemed untarnished, smooth and black, even though the pole had been burned. If it was plastic it should have melted, I thought. Tape Deck tried and failed to reach the lower wire on the box. Marcus let her down, grabbed the wire cutters, and sized up the pole.

"Well, this looks like a job for a chicken man," he said, then swung his arms wildly as his sides and lifted up a few feet off the ground. He flapped and flapped harder, a panicked look came across his eyes, but his face remained still. With one quick movement, he waved the cutters and snipped the wire, before plummeting to the ground. We ran over to make sure he was okay. Johnny helped him up. We were all looking at the ground to help him, so we didn't really see the magic happen.

The town emerged slowly as if from a mist. Hazy outlines of buildings appeared. The burned bark of trees dissolved into bright browns and birch whites. Melted plastic morphed itself back into solid shapes. Slowly at first, so the town felt like a dream. Something half-remembered. Entire buildings popped up where once there was ash. Telephone poles, mailboxes, doghouses, street signs, playgrounds. Birds appeared in the sky. Squirrels on the trees. Innsmouth rose from the ashes before us and after some moments of adjustment, settled back into itself.

It was a shocking sight. We looked at it in wonder and then collectively thought: "What?" But then there was Tape Deck. She had a big grin on her face. She was doing a little dance of joy, moving her shoulders back and forth.

"Congratulations," I said. "You did it! But what was it?"

"Innmouth was a neurotransmuted net," she explained. "There one across the whole town, sent out by these transmitters. It makes everyone that looks at the town think it looks destroyed."

"So it's like our mind is playing tricks on us, collectively," I said.

Tape Deck nodded. The town looked like it had been in a state of decay long before the evacuation. It's downtown was not too dissimilar from Doolittle Falls, filled with one lone row of dense three story buildings in a New England style and one white steepled church that stabbed jaggedly into the sky. But it seemed like it had already been shuttered before the people left town. Windows were boarded up and "for sale" signs were hung in front of trash-strewn interiors. There where a few shabby looking stores, bars, pawn shops, and a Stop and Shop with a broken sign.

It was starting to sink in that there was no Innsmouth disaster. Johnny was right. All the photos and footage had been faked. But if there wasn't an explosion what were they trying to cover up? And why did they frame Mom for it. The answer, I was certain, would be found at the two white towers in the distance. The pinging of the Geiger counter continued at a steady pace as we proceeded to walk toward the reactor.

As we got closer, weird inaccuracies popped up: the electrical lines appeared to have been cut at regular intervals, several large towers had been uprooted and left on their sides, and a few of the power stations appeared burned. The weather was still. It was like the whole space was devoid of any energy.

When we arrived at the gate in front of the power plant, a car came racing behind us. The sound cut through the air and we all dived for cover, looking for a place to hide.

"Stop what you're doing and put your hands behind your heads," a voice said through a megaphone. "Now jump up and down and quack like a duck." I

turned around to see Kurt behind the wheel of a half-built mustang. "You guys look ridiculous," he said. "Check it out, my cousin's car still works and had gas. Plus, this megaphone. Very official."

"Hey," Johnny said. "Wanna help us with this gate?"

"Hell. I've always wanted to do this," said Kurt, ducking his head back in the car. The engine let out a loud growling noise and we could only see Kurt's glowing eyes behind the wheel. The growl turned into a squeal and a cloud of white and black dust shot up behind the vehicle, which took off like a racehorse. Just as the smell of diesel fuel and burning rubber hit my nose, it plowed into the center of the gate. Sparks flew everywhere, the chain snapped with a loud crunching noise, and, finally, the gate popped open with a loud shriek and flew off into the parking lot.

We followed behind the car, breaking up into teams to search each building. Some of the doors were off their hinges so it was easy to get in and look around. The outside buildings, one and two story square structure, were mostly offices. All the power was disconnected so we couldn't check the computers and the files we looked at didn't seem out of the ordinary.

"Don't you think it's a little to easy for us to get in?" Alice said.

"Yeah, especially if there's all this radioactive stuff around. Couldn't someone just steal it and make a bomb?" Marcus asked.

"Wrong type of materials," said Tape Deck. "Fuel for bombs is different. Also, they probably moved it all or sold it. Doesn't seem like they were in a rush to get out." We were coming up empty. As we were about to leave, we heard Tape Deck shout out, "I found it!"

She was standing above a large black box, which had been hidden under a false floor. "The last transmitter!" she said. She knocked on it and a hollow noise rang out. We looked around for things we might be able to smash it open with, but everything just bounced off of it. After a lot of hitting, kicking, and pulling it wouldn't budge. I got sweaty trying to pry it open with a makeshift lever someone had found, and grabbed a bottle of water and took a sip. I looked down at the bottle and realized we did have one way in.

I handed the bottle to Kurt and eyed the metal tube. He nodded. He took the water and poured it through his hands and over the tube. It oozed over the surface slowly. "Do the honors," I said to Tape Deck, giving her a hammer. She grabbed it and with all her force swung down at the tube. It shattered into thousands of tiny black pieces, revealing the thin flimsy cables below. She pulled out the cutters and snipped them one by one. We looked around the room, but nothing had changed.

"I thought that transmitter was going to do something," said Tape Deck.

"What does a transmitter do, anyways?" Hamilton asked.

"Maybe something happened outside?" I said.

We went outside and saw the fruits of our labor. Something we hadn't seen before. A large building, sitting right next to the reactor and an enormous tank with a giant gaping hole in it, which had, as far as I recall, not been there last I checked.

FORTY-EIGHT

DESTROYING THE transmitter made the building and tank materialize. Rising from a concrete base at least fifty feet off the ground, the tank was a smooth cylinder in theory, but now it was a silver can of beans where someone shot the top off. The building was two stories high and seemed to be made completely out of solid steel. There were no doors, no rivets, to anything. Just a smooth, enormous block of metal. We walked around it, looking for some opening or even a space we could try to break open. Nothing.

"Great, another dead end," Johnny said. "We were so close."

He knocked his head against one of the walls in frustration. It made a loud echoing noise. Johnny continued to knock his head against the wall. I walked over and tried to stop him. After a moment I was able to get him to relent. "Did anyone else hear that?" Johnny asked.

"Hear what, the drum solo with your forehead? Alice said.

"No," Johnny said seriously. "The voice." He grabbed me and Alice by the back of our necks and pressed our heads to the wall. The minute my head touched the metal I heard something. It was low. Barely audible. But definitely a voice. Very flat. Like a robot trying to say something.

"Quiet," I said. "Put your head on the wall. Maybe together we can make it out." We all stood leaning against it, quiet, listening for some mysterious person. As each person put their head on the wall it grew louder. Finally, the voice came through clearly. It was telling us to do something. It was telling us to open the building. Tape Deck pulled out a notepad and started scribbling down instructions. I kept hearing the word wind over and over again. Something about strong force over the eye and wind. When Tape Deck was done I grabbed her notepad. It said nothing about eyes or wind.

"Do you think he's telling us different things? Mine was about the wind," I said. "Mine was about some device I needed to control," Tape Deck said.

"I didn't hear anything," said Alice.

"Neither did I," said Marcus.

"I'm supposed to turn water into a high potency alcohol. He gave me a very specific formula," Johnny said. "It's like whoever it is can read our powers." Hamilton just stood in the corner, not suggesting anything. I wanted to know what the voice said to him.

Tape Deck looked down at her notes and measured out an exact distance down one of the lengths of the building. She stopped, turned, and placed her hands against it. Her hands sunk a little into the wall and a door appeared. There was a red mechanical eye in the center of the door. Below the eye was the phrase 'Retina Scan.'

"Who's supposed to do what?" Kurt said. "I don't have anything until Johnny does his water thing."

"I think it might be me," I said. "Mine said something about an eye."

"And mine didn't?" Hamilton asked. "Nah, I'm just playin'. Pretty sure it's your call, Sarah."

I looked at the eye. It was scanning us. I told everyone to step back and concentrated my energy on it. I was able to use the wind to move the eye. I blew a small concentrated gust and the eye started moving, faster and faster. I kept my attention focused, until suddenly, the eye blinked, once, twice, three times, then uncontrollably. Finally it got very wide with the pupil dilated so the entire circle was red, and it closed for good. A door slid open revealing another entrance, with a keypad, a screen, and a small dial.

"I guess my work is done," I said. "Your turn."

Johnny, Kurt, and Tape Deck walked up to the new challenge. Tape Deck started punching something into the keypad. She was repeating the same pattern of numbers over and over again. Hamilton sent one paintball zooming over to it, but nothing happened. "Long password?" Johnny asked.

"Override code, I think," she said, continuing to press the numbers. She was counting quietly to herself, repeating the number sequence; and then at the end the number of sequences that she completed. When she got to one hundred she pressed the nine key with a flourish and the keypad popped open, revealing an intricate cabin with chips, drives, wires, circuit boards, and small fans.

Johnny squinted and looked down, examining the panel. He moved his head slowly around, trying to take in every section of the computer guts like they were a map he could read. He is not much of an engineer or scientist, unless tuning a guitar counts so I was confused by his actions.

"There it is, just like the voice said." Johnny pulled up a small red wire soldered into a small circuit board in the shape of a compass. He handed it to Tape Deck who held it delicately in her hand, like she was defusing a bomb, and put an eyedropper's worth of water in Johnny's hand.

Johnny's face contorted, turned red, and his alcometer started to blink. Normally it took at least converting a bottle of water to set that off, so whatever he was up to, it was noxious. He slowly slid the droplet of water into Kurt's hand. Johnny popped a pill settling his alcometer—while Kurt cupped his fist and squeezed. After a minute of intense concentration he took the water, which now resembled glassy gum with swirls of white in it, and pressed it onto the circuit board. Tape Deck pushed the substance around with the end of her glasses until it was in position. Johnny pulled out his Zippo, flicked it open, and the other two stood back. He set the flame to low, and slowly, with his arm outstretched, brought the lighter down into the compartment.

WHOOSSHHH!

An enormous fireball shot up. Its flame was blue and it was as tall as my brother. Johnny reeled backward. The air smelled of singed hair. He patted his face to make sure he was okay and Alice ran over to him. By the time she got there, the door was sliding open, revealing the secret interior to the mysterious building. Hamilton shot his paintballs at it, creating a beautiful frame.

Marcus pulled out his phone and started filming.

FORTY-NINE

I'M NOT sure what I was expecting. Maybe an enormous supervillain's lair, or an alien spaceship hovering the center of a room, or a giant box that said, "Secret of Innsmouth" in large letters, or a wall covered with elaborate explanations of a conspiracy with the words "Secret Plans" written above all of them. But that's a lot.

I know it sounded silly, but I was expecting my mom and my dad, sitting at our kitchen table, chatting as if nothing happened. In my heart the secret of the room was that everyone I loved was innocent and they got to live happily ever after.

Instead, I found a room more like a giant hospital ward, filled with rows of beds, spaced widely apart, about forty of them. Each bed had elaborate monitoring equipment, monitors, wires, tubes, accordion bags pumping up and down, a large circle cast a red laser field around each bed. We moved as one, walking up to the nearest bed, and slowly, very slowly, looking at its occupants.

I think I would have preferred to see a monster instead of what I did. It was a kid. Our age. Her face was delicate. Her features lax. She was completely immobile except for the slow rising and falling of her chest, which was in time with the bag pumping up and down next to her bed. She seemed alive but completely catatonic. Not even her eyes moved. I reached down to touch her but was shocked by the laser field and my hand recoiled.

"What do you think happened to them all?" Alice asked.

"I have no idea," Tape Deck said. "But I bet he does."

He pointed down the long row of beds to the opposite end of the room. Sitting upright, eyes open, arms at his side, there was a boy. Staring at us. He seemed to be saying something but we couldn't hear him.

Marcus held up his phone and zoomed in. The boy waved.

"Do you think he's dangerous?" I whispered.

"I don't know," said Tape Deck.

"Should we go over?" Alice whispered back.

"Quentin?" Kurt said loudly. He started rushing over to the bed. "Quentin, is that you?" I'd never seen Kurt excited about anything ever in his life.

When we got to the bed Quentin tried to tell us something but we couldn't hear him. After a few more failed attempts he pointed to a small button next to the bed. Tape Deck pressed it and with a zzzz noise the laser shield retracted into the circle.

"Can you hear me now?!" Quentin screamed.

"Yes," we all said back, covering our ears.

"Awesome. I didn't realize that blocked noise. It's mostly been me. They're not much for conversation," he said, pointing to his roommates. "So you got my messages?" "Messages?"

"Yeah, through the walls. Well, I guess you did. You got in," he said more to himself. "My god, this is awesome." He looked over at Tape Deck. "Glad I got to be a voice in your head, honey." Tape Deck rolled her eyes. He swung his legs over the bed and stood up. As soon as he was up he slid down to the ground. We had to help him back up. "Quentin, by the way," he said when he was upright, then he shook our hands vigorously. He grabbed Tape Deck's hand with two hands over each other, like he really extra super duper meant it with her.

"How do you two know each other?" Johnny asked, pointing at Kurt."Classmates at Innsmouth Junior High and High School," Quentin said. "Well, until Special K got kicked out and got sent to RVS."

"RVS?" I said.

"Retcon Vocational School," Kurt said. "So Q, where'd you get that nifty power?""Which one?"

"The ability to talk through walls."

"It came with the bunch. To be honest I didn't even know if it worked or not. I'm glad it did."

"Wait, you couldn't always do that?" Tape Deck asked.

"Nah," Kurt said. "Q could walk through trees."

"You could what?" I asked.

"I had some phasing abilities," he said. "I could phase through wooden objects like trees, so long as they weren't too big. And wooden doors."

"Just wood?" Johnny asked.

"Yup. And not all wood. I had trouble with oak, which is annoying because everything old is made of oak," he said. "But that's in the past."

I wondered what he meant by that. I was about to follow up when Marcus pointed his phone at Quentin and asked, "So how long have been here?" Marcus called himself a filmmaker lately. I had noticed that he took care to film each part of Innsmouth as we explored it.

"I don't know. It feels like forever. Since the incident, I guess," he said.

"Since the nuclear disaster?" Marcus followed.

"What nuclear disaster?" Quentin asked. He wasn't lying to us. He looked genuinely confused, like a grandma just hearing about the Internet. It was the most baffling reaction. I didn't know what to think about it. Obviously Innmouth had been through… something.

But why would Quentin have no idea about what happened? Quentin held up his hand and a voice whispered "shhhh" inside my head. The same voice I had heard before, in the walls. "Get comfortable, this may take a little bit," he said. "I should tell you the whole story. At least what I know."

We sat on the ground around him. Marcus stayed standing. He positioned his phone and started recording again.

FIFTY

THE STORY of Quentin was more like a monologue. I sat in rapt attention. "I'm not sure where to start the story," he said. "Maybe with the release, or the explosion, or the experiments. I could start by telling you how bad it was for Misshapes in our town. Worse than most, but I can tell you already know all about that."

Experiments, I thought. *What experiments?*

He faced the camera and starred straight at it. "So the experiments then."

I wasn't sure what his powers were but they were strong. He was no Misshape, not by any stretch of the imagination. Even if he didn't go to an Academy, he was too powerful and too controlled to go unnoticed. His telekinesis, or whatever it was, was unnerving. "I can tell you're wondering how a Misshape like me, someone who didn't even impress Kurt over here, is able to talk through walls. Don't worry, Kurt, I don't hold it against you. My powers were weak. Well the answers are in this building and known by a select few." Johnny put his hands together. He looked absolutely thrilled. We were finally getting some answers. Maybe it would even lead to our mom. But I couldn't think about it that way.

"About a year before the incident the Junior High School and High School administrators started recruiting volunteers for a program being run with the support of PeriGenomics. It was billed as a college prepatory class meant to support students in science and engineering, some brilliant STEM program giving the country the leaders in engineering and technology that they needed. It was free, extra credit, and we were told it would help us get into college. All out parents signed up."

"The classes were held in this building. It didn't look like this when we were here. It was set up like a classroom. Rows of desks and a table at the front for the teacher, tables where we could do exercises, and some rooms for examinations and treatments. But that didn't come until later."

"Was the giant blown up tank here?" I asked.

"Yes, but we didn't know it. It was invisible. Cloaked like I expect this building was before you found it. I only saw it once, when they were herding us into the building after the explosion. It was strange." Quentin shuddered. "To think it was there the whole time. It was several months before we realized that everyone in the class was a Misshape. Like most Misshapes, we didn't like to reveal that we were one, or we had powers, but after a few people's powers were accidentally revealed, well, it all just came out somehow." Hamilton smiled at me. There was a familiarity to Quentin's story. We had been there too.

"It was getting harder to hide our powers as they grew stronger. We suspected the food was giving us extra strength, maybe. There were free snacks everywhere: sodas, ice cream, chips, cookies, everything. One of us, Dan, tried to get us all to stop taking the free stuff. He thought they were poisoning us or experimenting or something. We tried it for a week but our powers grew, and new ones emerged. Dan claimed we were cheating. That we wanted the powers and didn't mind the experimentation. Which was true. The following week he was gone from the program. When I saw him in school he refused to talk about it, but he said he was glad he was out."

"After that, things got weirder. They started giving us daily physicals and monitoring our vitals while we explored our new powers. A few more people dropped out. Or were kicked out, we didn't know. Basically anyone who had a problem with what was going on was gone within days. We were told to hide it from our parents and our friends who weren't in the program. But really, by this point, the only friends we had were in the program."

"After six months of this we still didn't know what was going on, but we were powerful enough that we could hold our own against any Academy kid. Someone started a rumor that they might let us even enter the Academy. But there were other rumors as well. Like they were using us to test new powers, which they would then sell. Or that they would eliminate our powers… and us, after the experiment. That was the scariest. Also, some kids starting complaining of headaches or pain when they used their powers. And then, everyone started getting symptoms. Except me. I was the only one with telekinesis, and I think I was able to use it to control my own brain into minimizing my symptoms."

It was a dark turn. I wasn't surprised. Every Misshape was looking up at Quentin like rapt school kids at the cinema. "And then, one day, while I was walking to the building, I noticed something. It was like it was there and wasn't there. The tower. I told everyone about it but no one else could see it. It was cloaked somehow, and my powers gave me the key to open it, but only for me. I was intrigued but most of the other students didn't care at that point. Their powers were fading and they were getting sicker."

"But checking out the power was the key. They were pumping some kind of gas into the building, which was what changed us. And each day, the levels seemed higher. My powers accelerated while everyone else just got sicker and sicker. I told Dan what was going on, and he said he wasn't surprised. He got a look of profound righteousness on his face. He said that it needed to be stopped. I agreed. It wasn't right. We were like three-eyed fish in PeriGenomics' nuclear waste. Dan and I took it to parental authorities. They didn't believe us. They said we had the flu. The school promised them that, if anything, the PeriGenomics class would make us healthier, once we got over it."

"That's awful!" Alice said. "And so shady. You didn't consent to be experimented on." She was right. It was a complete violation. Quentin took a minute to nod, sadly, and then he continued with his story.

"One day in school, the worst thing happened. The tower exploded. I have no idea why. Whether it was an accident or on purpose. But it was bad. It happened when we were in school. Regular school. The explosion could be heard all over town. At first we expected to look up and see a mushroom cloud. We were told to duck under our desks in case of flying glass or a firestorm. But nothing came. There were no news reports. Nothing. Within a minute of the explosion, while we were still under our desks, men in full body suits and masks came into our classrooms and grabbed anyone in the special class. Half of them were absent. Home sick. We were herded into a bus, where we found our sick classmates. We thought we'd be driven someplace safe. Somewhere outside of town. But instead, we headed right back toward the reactor."

"As we drove we saw cars streaming out of town. People throwing their things in the back seats and making hasty exists. All the main streets were clogged. And as we got closer, we could see a misty gray plume in the air. People lying on sidewalks, choking. Heroes in with full masks and air tanks were flying around trying to help out. There was the head of the Hero Academy with a small cadre of students."

"Mom," Johnny and I said in unison.

"That's right. You're the Robertson kids," he said to us. "She must have been part of the conspiracy. But wait, if she was, why are you here?"

"She wasn't," I said.

"She's in prison right now. The Luther," Johnny added.

A light flicked across his eyes. "Ahh, now I see."

"Which Academy kids where there?" I asked. The question, *What did Sam know?* flicked across my mind.

"I didn't know any of their names. Some of them I'd seen. Mostly I recognized the uniforms. Blue and Gold. Freedom Boy was probably too young, but his dad was flying about, pulling busloads of people out of harms way. Just like your mom. Those creepy mind control freaks were there. L7 or something."

"J5," Tape Deck said. "They're around. Still. Weirdly ageless."

"Go on. Then what?" Alice asked.

"No wait. What where the academy kids doing?" I asked, still thinking *what did Sam know?* The others glared at me but I didn't care.

"Mostly pulling people to safety. Putting out fires and helping people trapped by the fog. Someone was trying to blow the wind back so it wouldn't spread. Did it spread?""No. Just Innsmouth. No killer fog," Marcus said.

"Well I guess he did it," Quentin said.

"He?" I asked. So Sam was there.

"Yeah, it was a he. He was lean, but went by in a flash so I couldn't make him out. By then we were distracted by what happened next." It was Sam. It had to be. Who else was in the Academy then that could move wind? I needed to know the answer.

"Did he look like a surfer?" I asked. I knew I was being annoying. I didn't care.

"Enough Sarah," Johnny said. "Your boyfriend was probably there. Go on."

"They all had on the uniform. They looked pretty much the same. But, yeah, as I was saying, we were distracted because the air started to creep into the bus. We started to shout at the driver, who was in a suit as well and behind a protective cage, to turn around. Stop. Save us."

"And then, one by one, the students started to have seizures. Their eyes would grow wide and black, their hands would clench, they'd convulse violently, then lapse into sleep. I thought they were dying, but I checked and they still had faint pulses. Everyone except me was out by the time we got to the building. I saw men in suits with large laser rifles approaching the bus, and I pretended to seize and pass out myself. I was able to will my body to simulate their reactions, including the heart slowing, using my new powers. I knew I was strong enough to fight off several of the guards, but not enough to make an escape. After the first few weeks awake here, I wish I had tried."

"Awake?" Tape Deck asked.

"Well, yeah. I was so good at self-hypnosis I did in fact lapse into a coma. Or I thought I did. It was a while before I got out of it. They brought us into the building, which had been set-up like a makeshift hospital. I realized when I finally emerged from my coma that they'd made no effort to wake us or help us. Instead, everyone was put in stasis. They came on a weekly basis or whenever something went haywire with a machine to make sure everyone was still alive. They also drew blood and continued their experiments. I decided that the next time they came in I would attack whoever did my vitals and escape, but unfortunately, that was so long ago. We've been alone in here all that time."

He grew concerned suddenly, like he was in a trance from his own story and it broke. "How long have I been here? I can't even tell at this point. A year or so."

We looked at each other, afraid to tell him. Finally, I spoke up. "It's been four years since the incident." I looked at Quentin. He seemed very, very alone.

"Four years!" he shouted, and then fell back onto the bed, shaking his head and muttering. "Four years. I've been away four years."

Johnny put a hand on his shoulder. "I am so sorry."

Kurt was more direct, "Don't worry. They'll pay for this."

Quentin's eyes glimmered when Kurt spoke. I could tell the thought of revenge had been in his thoughts for some time now.

"Four years. So what was the story? How many died?"

We told him the story—the official story—of Innsmouth. About our mom, the evacuation, the fight, the election, our time in prison. He absorbed the information quickly, nodding with each new fact. But he seemed to nod slightly out of beat, just a millisecond before we spoke, like he heard what we were going to say before we said it, but needed the reassurance of our voice to confirm the fact. He'd been virtually alone for four years. I understood it.

While we did this, Tape Deck handed off the iPhone and wandered around the room and looking at the other kids. She pressed buttons next to all the beds, and released them from their laser prisons. I watched her from the corner of my eye. None of the other kids moved at all, not even rolled or groaned. They were in a vegetative state. But she kept going, walking and freeing them, quietly starting a revolution, I thought. When we finished updating Q he thanked us for the information, without commenting on it, and said, loud enough for Tape Deck to hear, "They're as good as dead. It won't help. The only thing keeping them alive is the machines."

Tape Deck turned and said, "Maybe. Maybe not. You're awake. And if they do get better, I don't want them stuck here."

"Well, I don't know about all of you, but I don't plan on staying around much longer. We got our footage and Q here is proof enough. If PeriGenomics didn't know we were here before, they do now," Hamilton said. He pointed up to all the cameras in the room. There were hundreds, lining the tops of the walls near the ceiling. They were all blinking red and pointing down.

"Crap," Alice muttered.

"I probably should have mentioned that earlier," Q said.

We helped Tape Deck finish up as quickly as possible and headed outside. Q was still a little unsteady on his feet so we had to help him walk for a few steps. By the time we got to the door he was well enough to walk with more confidence then any of us. Before leaving I took one look back at all the kids my age lying on their gurneys, hooked up to machines. *This is what they do,* I thought. Experiment on children. Put kids in prison and torture them to get at their parents.

Something dark had been growing inside of me. A black ball of rage and anger. It started in the Luther. The more I learned the bigger it became. I no longer believed the answer would be as simple as getting Mom back, defeating some supervillains and returning to our normal lives. The entire system was broken. From the school principal in a town like Innsmouth to the President of the country. My hand was shaking with anger. The thing that scared me the most was not some foe I'd have to face, but what I might do.When we emerged from the building, we were greeted by a small phalanx of PeriGenomics security officers. They were wearing full riot gear. Their faces obscured behind black masks, their eyes covered in thick reflective goggles, their chests clad in square bullet proof vests, and their legs in sleek military cargo pants. Each one had a Plexiglas shield in one hand, covering their bodies, and a large assault rifle drawn. The rifles' black circular mouths stared at us, daring us to run. In the distance, I could see J4 and Christie, squirrel free, nearly giddy, standing next to a PeriGenomics security officer. This was no workaday officer; however, he was clearly the commander because of his more formal attire and maskless face. Whatever happened next, I knew that we were in deep trouble.

FIFTY-ONE

J5 AND Christie walked to the front of the officers. I wasn't sure if they were real or implanted images, like the town had been, they created as reinforcements. "While I'd love to play some more," J5 said. "These nice men would like to take you away. So, for your own sake, please give up."

"Or don't," said Christie. "It would be more fun if you didn't"

Quentin walked out in front of us and stared at them quizzically. They squinted at him and he waved a hand in front of himself. Their faces dropped in shock. "Why isn't it working?" Christie asked J5.

"I don't know," he whispered back, then stood up straight and stared at Quentin. "And who are you. Another Misshape?"

"You could call me that," he said proudly.

"Well, whatever you're able to do to block our powers won't matter. They still work on the proletariat over there." J5 twisted his hand and a pain shot through my stomach. I clutched it as did the rest of the Misshapes.

Quentin, however, did not. He raised one hand and pantomimed pushing forward. When he did this, J5 and Christie flew backward like rockets, launching off into the distance. They flew so far we couldn't see them. Our stomachs instantly felt better. But even though the initial trouble was gone, it was clear that the troops weren't some mind game. They were real, and their fingers moved toward the triggers of their guns.

We saw the guns fire before we heard the shots. By the time the loud BANG hit my ears I was certain I'd been hit. I patted my body, expecting to find blood, before falling dead. To my surprise my hand came back dry. When I looked up I saw the bullets hovering in the air, sunlight reflecting off them like tiny suspended stars. More BANGS rang out and the air in front of us was filled with these tiny glints of light. It wasn't until we heard the clicks of empty cartridges that the bullets stopped. Quentin waved his hand and the guns flew out away from the security guards and landed in the distance with a loud clatter.

Out in the open for the first time in four years, Quentin seemed indestructible. His powers must have been at an untouchable level. He walked slowly through the hovering bullets. When they touched him the fell to the earth with a tinny clang, like loose change. His body cut a silhouette through the sparkling sky, a tunnel of space forming behind him. He stopped for a moment in front of the terrified guards, examined one bullet, and flicked it away. It shot forward, punctured one of their shields, and cut through the guard's body armor. He fell to the ground, a look of shock still on his face.

The guards tried to turn and run but Quentin scrunched up his hands and they were locked in place. I could see their bodies twitching, unable to move, pushing against some invisible force. Soon he was upon them. He thrust his hands through two shields and they moved through the Plexiglas like water. He placed his hands on the guard's chest and a surge of blue electricity flowed through him and into the guards. Their bodies shot back, black smoke pouring out of their chests and off their heads. I was certain they were dead. They hit the ground with a loud thump and didn't move. My moment of relief turned into terror. I was powerless to stop Quentin — quite possibly our only hope for safety.

He released the other guards and they were on him in an instant, swinging clubs, slashing with large knifes, thrusting with Tasers. He was lost for a moment in the scrum of violence, then suddenly, at once, they all flew outward as if pushed by a great force. He emerged unscathed. Some of the guards managed to get to their feet and started sprinting off. The officer looked at one of them with disdain, thrust out his hand, and shot a red bolt into the man's back. He fell to the ground convulsing.

"Coward," he muttered.

The other guards, seeing this, continued their assault on Quentin, but more timorously. He dispatched them, one by one, until the ground was littered with their limp bodies. I couldn't tell if they were alive or dead. But they were motionless. Not even their chests were rising. The only one standing was the Officer. He had on red leather gloves, which he removed delicately and laid on the ground.

Quentin tried to shoot him with another bolt but he waved it off and it flew skyward. He tried a few more moves but they were all deflected. The officer probably had on some of the PeriGenomics power-blocking equipment or had some ability to block them on his own. Probably the reason he had been put on security for the company. I was worried that Quentin, who had never really used his powers before, let alone faced a challenge, might be no match for him.

After one last invisible push failed, Quentin rushed toward the Officer. Quentin moved so fast I didn't seem him until he was right in front of his opponent. This didn't faze the Officer, who was comfortable fighting others with powers. Quentin swung wildly at him in lightning-quick, untrained swings, easily blocked or ducked under. The Officer, having dodged a wide blow to his head, struck back with a hard punch that sent Quentin sprawling. He hit the ground with the look of shock on his face, which was quickly replaced with amusement. He held his hand to his cheek—which seemed undamaged—got up, and walked slowly toward the Officer. This time he seemed more relaxed. Slack in his movements. Like he wasn't rushing into a fight but taking a stroll down the block to the comic book store on a Sunday afternoon.

The Officer shot some sparks at him and Quentin didn't even try to deflect them. He took them full-on in the chest and didn't flinch. The electricity flowed over his body, blue crackling bols spreading over his skin and swirling in his hands. The Officer tried to hit him again but he just stood there, absorbing the blow. When the Officer pulled back his fist it was bloody and red, but the blood was his own—as was the pain. Quentin, a foot shorter and half the size of the man, took his hands and pressed them against his chest. I thought he would shock him again but instead his hands pushed through the Officer's clothes and continued moving.

It was hard to see but by their depth it seemed like his hands were inside the man's chest cavity. The Officer's once-calm face turned to terror, his mouth unhinged, his eyes widened. Quentin lifted him up into the air, his wiry forearms tightening, and with a quick, powerful thrust, he threw him against a brick wall. The Officer's body hit the wall so hard, the bricks cracked behind him, and he slid down, leaving a trail of blood as he fell. His chest, too, was a pool of dark, thick blood. There was something dark and fleshy in Quentin's hands, which he threw on the floor at his feet.

I tried not to look at it, but my eyes kept flicking on it while my mind kept telling me to stop it. The mass was like a dead animal, gray and red, with its skin removed. I tried not to think about what happened, the violence that I just saw, but the evidence laid there at Quentin's feet. I turned to Alice. Her face was white, bloodless. Hamilton was cowering in a corner. Marcus, his eyes fixed on the viscera, turned and vomited. Tape Deck and Johnny were motionless. Fixed in place, trembling at the horror.

Kurt was smiling. He walked up to Quentin and gave him a huge hug. "So good to have you back man," Kurt said. He released him.

There were bloody handprints on Kurt's back. "Thanks for that."

"Don't mention it. I've been dying to stretch my legs since they've had me cooped up. Still getting used to these new powers."

Kurt eyed the corpse of the Officer. "Got some pretty neat tricks."

"Still learning what I can do. It's amazing. I feel like I'm in tune with the universe. Like every atom in the world is at my command. I can see things. And feel things and move things I never knew existed. It's almost too much." As the two talked, the rest of us exchanged looks of fear. I didn't know how to be a person in this situation. Quentin used his power for evil. He was dangerous and deadly. And he was, at this point, on our side.Johnny unfroze himself. "What's our next step here?"

"Well PeriGenomics is probably going to sending more security. A lot more. So you may want to get out of here." Quentin said.

"Are you coming?" Marcus asked him, in a trembling voice.

He whispered something to Kurt. Kurt smiled.

"We're going to head out of here as well," said Quentin.

"Take my cousin's car," Kurt said. "It's fast and I won't need it."

"Why, where are you heading?" Alice asked, her voice quavering.

"Oh, we're off to kill Freedom Man. And anyone else at PeriGenomics that did this to me," Quentin said. He sounded downright cheerful. They then lifted off the ground and flew into the distance.

FIFTY-TWO

I WAS IN shock from what just happened. It was hard to process. The reality that Innsmouth was not destroyed, Q's story, the horror of what just happened to the security guards. I wanted to turn it into an adventure in my head—the Misshapes' own Documentary—and focus on the future. But I couldn't do it. I was privy to some horror, and I didn't know what to do.

"What do we do now?" Tape Deck said.

"I'll tell you what we do now," said Johnny. "We go to the closest television station we can find and show them what we saw."

Alice was staring at the bodies strewn across the parking lot. She stood unmoving, her hands trembling. "I can't believe it. How could he do that?"

I walked over to her and placed a hand on her shoulder. "It was us or them. He was just trying to protect us. Like the fight with Dr. Mann."

She shook me off and placed her arms across her chest. "But it was so violent. He didn't have to be so brutal. He killed them. He enjoyed it."

"They fired on us, Alice. They wanted us dead," I said. I couldn't believe I was arguing for Quentin.

"But we're better aren't we," she turned to me, tears in her eyes. "Right. We're better than this. We didn't need to kill them."

"We didn't Alice," I said. She was shaking. I pulled her into my arms. "We didn't do anything. We just saved him. *He* did this. We are better."

"We have to tell someone. We need to get help. Maybe we can still help them." Alice was nearly crying. I wanted to cry, too, but I didn't feel anything.

I looked at the lifeless bodies. I wanted to reassure her but calling anyone would just bring more people after us. It was too late for them. I flashed to an image of the hovering bullets. I was about to say something, but distant sirens cut me off.

"I don't think we'll need to. Someone's on the way," Johnny said.

"We should do something," Hamilton said.

"There's nothing to do. The best we can hope for is to make it worth something. To tell the world what happened. These men were pawns, too," I said.

Alice looked at me. "I guess," she said. "So the media's the solution? I don't know, Sarah."

"The news. The papers. Everyone who will listen," I said. "It's the least we could do." Another thought came to me. Even if Freedom Boy had ghosted me again, he deserved to know that Quentin was on the march and that his father was the target. I sent a quick text and an email to him, suggesting that the whole Freedom family could stand for some extra protection and security. Maybe that would garner a response.

"They won't believe us," Marcus said.

"They'll call the cops. What we did was illegal," Tape Deck added. She looked stressed out. "Remember what happened to Donny with his graffiti. Or the Red Ghost. They'll just send a Hero to dispatch us."

"It will be like the Doolittle police after the fight with Dr. Mann. They'll prevent the story from getting out," Johnny said.

"Remember what J5 said, Johnny?" We met eyes. He had been through the same thing as me. Neither of us wanted to go back.

His tone softened. "So what, then. Let this happen. Let Mom rot. We have no other options. What would you do?" I thought about it. The world needed to know about everything. About Innsmouth, about Quentin. About unchecked power and its violence. We had been on the front lines.

We had a duty to the people of Innsmouth, to these fallen men to tell the truth, to our families, to our friends. If the powerful weren't stopped they'd do it again. They were running amok with the country. Because no one had told them no. They'd learned no lessons. I guess it was our job to teach them.

"We can't go to XBS. With Ann Glanton there we'd be in cuffs before we got to the elevator. How about DLF?"

"No," said Marcus. "They're owned by PeriCorp, the parent company of PeriGenomics."

"Well definitely not HRO," said Johnny.

"What about EBC?" I said, "They have a station in downtown Boston."

"The channel with Real Time with Bob Dine?" Marcus said. "Not a bad idea. They did do the expose on the Red Ghost."

"Yeah, but they pulled it before it went to air," Tape Deck said. "Obviously they can be bought."

"Maybe if we go straight to the people on that show. As opposed to the network," Hamilton said. "I believe in us. We can do this."

"At the least, we have to give it a shot," Johnny said, a look of grim determination on his face.

FIFTY-THREE

EBC was in downtown Boston, in a large glass building with a giant EBC logo at the top in glowing blue letters. It took a few minutes with security to convince them we were on a serious mission, and finally a young woman in a pencil skirt came down to speak with us.

She was in her twenties, and spent her time looking at her phone. She was just humoring us with yeses and ummmhmmms. "Look," I said. "We have footage of Innsmouth. It's exclusive. It proves that the whole thing was a sham." Once I said that, she looked up with a twinkle in her eye.

"Well, why didn't you tell me? I could do something with that." I told her that it implicated the President and demanded a meeting with Bob Dine, or at least his head producer. After she saw the footage, she made a quick call and led us to security, where we were patted down, then led upstairs to the offices on the fourth floor.

They were filled with glass walls and cubicles, people staring at computers and running around with iPads showing each other footage and cutting it together. We walked by an "On Air" sign lit up in bright red and could see a newscaster inside reading off a

TelePrompTer.

We sat in a large conference room, one of the few that wasn't encased in glass, and told us someone would be with us shortly. The walls were white and there was an enormous glass window looking out onto the street below. Cars drove past, women pushed strollers down the sidewalks, bikes weaved in between pedestrians, teenagers sat slumped against buildings smoking cigarettes and reading books. The world moved as it always did, oblivious.

I realized what we were doing. It wasn't just for the sake of clearing my mom's name. That was the beginning. We'd be accusing the president, the most powerful man in the world, of covering up murder. Accusing the biggest company in the world, worth billions, of experimenting on people without their knowledge. It implicated the country, maybe even the world's most beloved Hero.

The first person they sent in to meet us was a production intern from Bob Dine's show. Tape Deck hooked her phone to a computer and we streamed the footage. She watched it quietly, growing more concerned with each piece of information that challenged everything she knew about the town. Tape Deck fast-forwarded through the long stretches of walking and looking around. After the building appeared, she picked up Tape Deck's phone and twirled it in her hand.

"Has this footage been off the camera?" she asked.

"It was exported to a safe location, but no, we haven't edited it. It's a live feed," Tape Deck said.

The intern watched as the door opened and the rows and rows of children came into view. She got up quickly and told us she'd be "right back" and left the room in a rush.

"I think we got her attention," Johnny said.

We waited. We watched the clock. With each passing minute I worried that no one was coming back. That security would burst in soon and kick us out of the building. We eyed each other nervously. Just as I was about to suggest leaving, a team of news people came in. They wore suits and ties, mostly men, and one woman in a red pantsuit. Mostly producers and one segment director. We played the footage again and let them fast-forward at their own pace.

As they watched they whispered to each other, pointed at the screen, and took notes. As Quentin told his story, one of them picked up a phone and told the person at the other end that they had a breaking story they needed to run. I looked at Alice and Johnny and smiled. Our story *would* be told. It was worth it.

They closed down the computer and asked us questions about the footage and the town. I was answering the woman in red when a man burst into the room, his face taut with anger, and demanded that all his staff meet him in the hall immediately. They thanked us curtly and shuffled out one by one. We could hear him screaming but couldn't make out what he said. His screaming got quieter as they moved away from the door.

"Maybe we should leave," I said. "I don't like the sound of that."

"I think it might be too late," Tape Deck said, her eyes fixed out the window.

FIFTY-FOUR

WE HEARD the sirens first, then shortly after red and blue strobe lights shone into the windows. Cop car after cop car surrounded the building. Large armored vehicles that looked like tanks followed behind. A helicopter hovered above us. One black car drove to the center of the pack and parked in front of the main entrance. Two figures emerged. I squinted to see them.

"Uh oh," I said.

Everyone looked at me with concern.

A large cop in SchWat gear passed a megaphone to J4. I was shocked to see who was next to him. J4 handed him the megaphone and stepped back. There he was, my old friend. He walked toward the building, like he was walking down the street, like nothing was wrong. He was so at ease I relaxed for a moment, thought it was all a dream. My heart shrank. Of all the things that happened, this was the worst. Watching him walk toward me with the police and SchWat and torturers standing behind him.

I started to step outside but everyone held me back. Alice's hand gripped my shoulder, and Johnny was on my other side. I was shaking with nerves. The wind picked up. Clouds formed into dark masses above us. I was no longer fully in control.

"Don't worry," Sam said to them, "you're safe."

"It's okay," I said, and they let me go.

I reached him midway between the barricade and the news stations. He looked straight at me, his eyes soft and warm, and I stared downward. He started to speak but I cut him off. A world of sadness echoed through my voice.

"You knew?" I said, half asking, half hoping. I looked up. Our eyes met. "Innsmouth. You knew."

With each repetition, I grew angrier. "You knew. You knew. This whole time you knew." I started pounding on his chest. He hugged me close. I wanted to fall into his arms. But that would have been falling into the lie. I pushed him away. "How could you?" I asked. "You know how much I miss my mom. How it ruined my life."

Sam was at a loss for words. The police sirens wailed behind us. Helicopter rotors beat against the wind. Rain started falling. Thick heavy drops.

Finally, he said, "They did so much good, Sarah. And you shouldn't hold it against me. I was a kid. Innsmouth had an accident at their plant. They sent me to save people. That's what I did. That's what I do. I save them. I don't know why they covered it up. I tried to find out but they wouldn't say. They told me everyone would be safer if they didn't know what the town looked like."

"But my mom, Sam!" I cried. "My mom. The fights. And to work for people who were experimenting on kids!"

"I was helping people. That's why I'm here now. To help you. I don't want to see you hurt. And you may get hurt right now," Sam said. "Look, you have one side of the story and a lot of anger. I can tell from the weather. You're emotional, obviously. But your power comes from a deeper place than just your emotions. PeriGenomics are good people. These people behind me? Also good. Law and order serve the public good. They're trying to make sure more people don't get hurt. You saw that last summer. All those lives we saved."

"Lies. All Lies," I said. "If it was an accident then why did they say my mom did it on purpose? Why, Sam?" I nearly fell to the ground.

This stopped him in his tracks. Sweet Sam. Sweet trusting Sam. Sweet stupid Sam. He'd never questioned what happened. Even to himself. Even when it was so clearly a lie. He wanted to believe so it was true. It wasn't malice. I looked at him with new eyes. He clearly wasn't evil or wearing a black hat. He was just lazy. And he didn't know what to say. "I don't know. They have their reasons," was all he could muster.

I kissed him on the lips. His eyes grew wide in surprise. "Sam, thank you. For all you've done. For me and for those people we helped. In a time that sucked, you were my salvation." But I had to lay the hammer down. "Things are different now. If you can't help me, you can either fight me or leave."

"But Sarah…" Sam protested.

"I know. I know. Please," I said, tears welling in my eyes, masked under a downpour of rain. "Just go."

He gave me one last look and turned away. J4 tried to stop him but he continued walking off, past the police and the barricade. When he had disappeared, someone got out of a van, a dark hooded figure, and took his place next to J4, who picked up the megaphone. I slowly stepped backwards toward the building. The rain was heavy, but I could feel control returning to me. With Sam gone, with that big question mark vanquished in my head, I could access my true power again.

"There are many ways we can do this," J4 said with a rain-smeared grin.

I reached behind me for the door and heard whispers of "get inside, quick" coming from the building. The door closed behind me, and as I hid, the man next to J4 showed his face—Phoebtor. And there was a gleam in his eye that showed just how angry he could be.

FIFTY-FIVE

I WAS FROZEN to the floor, paralyzed with fear. Phoebeter was enjoying this, striding purposefully toward the building, slow-clapping, perfectly aware that he was a living cliché. "Johnny and Sarah Robertson," he said. He was gleeful, although his face remained a stone. "I thought I told you that you would not enjoy meeting me again. But here we are. Look at you gluttons for punishment. Just like your mother." He paused. "If you miss her, well, you may be seeing her again if you keep this up."

Johnny shouted out through the window, "Don't you want to know our demands?"

J4 snapped. He lost his composure, his face twisting sideways. "I don't give a god damn about your demands." As he said, "your demands," Phoebeter made scare quotes in the air. He was enjoying this. J4 kept yelling. "*My* demands are what matter! And I demand you turn yourself over immediately or face death!"

"What are we doing wrong?" I asked. "We only wanted to tell the world the truth. There are innocent people locked in their beds here. Innocent people who've spent years moldering for the sake of propaganda."

"Some truths, Sarah Robertson," said Phoebeter, "are dangerous. To the world and to their holder. This one will kill you if you don't let it lie."

I looked to the cops for support but they seemed oblivious. Nearly gum-chewing in their boredom and ambivalence. They were ready to pounce; their guns were drawn. Snipers were on rooftops. I realized that if J4 was there, he must have been controlling what, exactly, the cops were seeing. We could be monsters. After all, if J4 could help make Innsmouth look obliterated to the bone, what else could he do?

It wasn't long before I found out. We were at an impasse. And then Phoebeter pulled a small figure out of the crowd. His hands were bound and his head was covered with a bag. He looked broken, weary. Four women followed behind him, under a spell. There were bags on their heads and their hands were tied. They were all wearing sequined dresses that made a silvery sound as they walked forward.

"If you don't give up immediately, your friend gets it," J4 yelled.

"Not Butters!" Alice shouted.

J4 pulled out a gun and pointed it at Butters' bag-head. "Guys, he's serious," Butters said.

I stared out, looking at the horrific tableaux. Something wasn't right. "You have until the count of five," J4 said. He started to count down. Alice made for the door with Johnny and Marcus, but I grabbed her sleeve.

"No. We can't," I said.

Alice rolled her eyes. "No time —"

"Four…"

"They'll kill him!" Alice said.

"Two. One." J4's voice rang out, loud and mocking. "Last chance, Misshapes!"

"They won't!" I said, just as a shot rang out. Everyone ran to the window and looked out, horrified. Butters slumped to the ground, as did the Spectors.

Everyone freaked out. Howls pierced the room, but I felt weirdly calm. "That's not him," I said. "It's a trick that Phoebeter pulled. But he forgot one detail. Butters controls the Spectors. Butters wouldn't have let them get bound and blinded. And if he was dead, they would've disappeared. It doesn't add up."

"Oh well. I guess you won't have much time to mourn your friend," J4 said. He was mocking us, I could tell.

"I hope you're right," said Alice, shaking her head. "You have to be right, Sarah."

Suddenly, there was a wail so loud we had to cover our ears. Even that barely helped. It was like a baby hawk screaming right in our face. It sounds like the entire world was crying from every corner of existence.

"Where's that coming from?" Alice screamed.

"I don't know," I screamed back, feeling like I was descending into madness.

When we looked out the window, the whole world was starting to melt away. The police disappeared into a pit of magma that was dissolving buildings and streets all the way to the horizon. All that remained was a world on fire with Phoebeter and J4 staring at us. The building still seemed intact, but waves of heat were pouring off the walls.

"Are you all seeing this or is in my head?" Johnny asked.

"No," Tape Deck said. "It's there. A shared nightmare."

"Well, this time they don't have all their cute toys," I said.

I shot of a gust of supersonic wind that blasted them in the chest and knocked them back a few hundred yards. When they landed they hit concrete, not magma, and the world began to emerge again. J4 stood up and pulled something out of his pocket. It looked like a large laser gun. He fired it at us and a blue beam shot out.

"DUCK!" Alice shouted, and we got down on the ground. The laser blasted through the glass and exploded on the wall behind us. After a few moments it stopped, but the walls of the room started to melt. I wasn't sure if it was Phoebeter's doing or the walls were actually melting. He waited while his gun recharged.

"I don't think we can survive another one of those," Tape Deck said.

"Or more of his evil powers," Hamilton said.

"Well, I guess I should get it from him then, shouldn't I?" I said.

I stood up, brushed the dust off my clothes, and leaped out the window. I had no plan; my mind was blank. I just knew we couldn't wait in the building, waiting to be destroyed by two men with scary amounts of power. This time I approached the air feeling like there was ice water coursing through my veins. A stream of wind lifted me up, and I sailed down towards the two of them. If I could reach J4—before the gun reloaded—I could use the force of the wind to knock him down. As I got closer the nightmare got worse, but I tried to remember it was fake. I felt my skin burning, dripping off my flesh, but I refused to look down. I was gaining on them. The gun was still red. Fifty yards. Forty yards. Thirty yards. I was almost there when, suddenly, it turned green, and he clicked the trigger.

FIFTY-SIX

I CLOSED MY eyes and braced myself, trying to will the beam away. It was involuntary. I didn't have time to get out of the way, I was going too fast, and I didn't want to see it coming.

When I opened my eyes, J4 was no longer standing up holding a laser gun. I fell to the ground with a thud, my aerial wind dispersing behind me. The gun lay broken on the ground and Quentin was holding J4 above his head, while Kurt was pressing his hands against the bluing temples of Phoebeter. A moment later the two men deflected the assault and were on the offensive. Quentin and Kurt clutched their heads and fell to their knees in pain. Phoebeter and J4 stood over them, concentrating their energy.

With their focus on the two boys, the world reappeared from the hellscape that Phoebeter had constructed. The police cruisers and SchWat wagons were all still there. The police were statues. J4 must have hypnotized them somehow. I noticed, gleefully, that Butters and the Spectors were just an illusion. Wherever he was, he was safe.

I continued to lie on the ground, feigning unconsciousness, but quickly scanned the ground for some kind of weapon that I could use. In the distance I could see two police guns near two hypnotized officers. I focused all my energy on that small point behind them and the guns blew forward, nailing J4 and Phoebeter in the head. They hit with an almost inaudible boink, and the two of them fell over.

Kurt and Quentin got up, shook their heads, and picked up the guns. They pointed them at their unconscious adversaries and I shouted "No. Fight fair."

They turned to me. Quentin looked almost hurt by my protestation. "Why?" he said. "They tried to kill you. They tried to kill us."

"Alice was right. We're better than that. They're no longer a threat," I said. "And there's no honor in stabbing someone in the back."

"They will be," said Kurt, pointing to the gun at Phoebetor's head. "Besides. We saved you, we have the right."

Quentin raised his free arm, placed it on Kurt's gun, and pressed it down to the ground. Kurt didn't protest, though he looked visibly disappointed.

"She saved us, too," Quentin said. "Only fair."

"Fine," Kurt muttered. He spit on the gun and tossed it against a police cruiser. It shattered into a million frozen pieces. As they scattered across the pavement, the officers started to come out of their fug.

"Maybe it's time we get going anyway," I said.

We flew back to the building and found Johnny, Alice, Marcus, Hamilton, and Tape Deck all waiting outside.

"Nice moves," Alice said.

"Thanks. I got a few more if you're interested in getting out of this place." Things felt like they were getting nearly normal with my favorite friend.

We watched as the police came to life. They clutched their heads and looked around in disbelief. It would only be seconds before they noticed the two unconscious government officials—the ones they were ostensibly supposed to protect—and the seven of us smiling and alive. I summoned an enormous cloud, as large as I could muster out of all the lingering anger and rage, and launched a torrent of baseball-sized hail on the barricade. Someone got hit in the face and it gave them a bloody nose. Seeing this, the rest of the cops took cover in their cars from the hail. I made it so there was a small patch of sunlight around the most important people in my life and the two borderline terrifying wounded animals that we had taken in. As angry as I was with Sam and everything that he stood for, I still respected what he had taught me.

We piled in the back of Johnny's car and took off.

FIFTY-SEVEN

HOME WOULDN'T be safe. Not for us and not for Dad. There was also a high probability that he had been taken in by PeriGenomics for the sake of leverage.

We headed to the control station by the old mill, our defacto secret headquarters, to regroup. Johnny parked his car in the woods, as far as it would go, and we covered it with leaves and branches. When we were done it looked like an old car covered in forest detritus.

"I don't think that's going to fool anyone," I said.

"Probably not. But they might miss it in a quick scan," Tape Deck said.

"Well, maybe I can help," said Alice, who let out a few small chirps.

Squirrels surrounded us, ready to do Alice's bidding. She chirped a little more and they set to work covering the car in twigs, branches, and moss. Pretty soon it looked like, well, not a tree or a bush, but like a large nest made by a gnome, or something a large forest creature might have regurgitated. Most importantly? It did not, however, look like a car. Alice reached into her pocket, grabbed a handful of something, and tossed it out along the ground. She noticed me looking and said, "Peanuts. They love em."

We walked through the forest to the dilapidated building. Someone had written "George's Station" over the door. It looked like Hamilton's handwriting. Seeing that reminded me of how dangerous what we were doing was. The price we may have to pay.

I picked up my phone to call Betty, but Johnny grabbed the phone from my hand.

"I wouldn't do that."

"Why?" I asked.

"They can trace it. They'll be here in a minute," Hamilton said.

"How can we tell her where we are? What's happening to Butters?" I asked.

"Do we even want to?" asked Alice.

"Why not?" I asked. "Aren't we stronger together?"

"Yes. But right now she's safe. The minute we bring them into this we put them at risk," Tape Deck said.

I hadn't realized it but they were right. We were dangerous to be around. I wanted everyone to be there, to help. But we were wanted by the police, the government, anyone and everyone. "Look, guys, if you want to go, we can go. No worries." My message was for Marcus. I didn't think he was up to it. And I didn't want Hamilton to be further involved. If there was anybody out there who inspired something like hope for me, it was Hamilton. Marcus and Hamilton got the hint, and they set off for their homes.

"Sarah," Hamilton said as he strode out of the mill. "Take care of yourself." He squeezed my hand. I squeezed back. I felt a charge surge from where our hands touched, and heard a bolt of lightning in the distance. "I expect to see you again, Sarah."

"What do we do now?" I said.

"We go after them," Quintine replied.

"How? Where? It's not just some small group of villains. It's an entire system. There are so many people involved in this and we're so few," Alice said.

"We should run," Tape Deck said. "Get out of here."

"And go where?" Johnny asked "Even if we can escape, then what? They're going to keep coming. There's no stopping them."

"We can't stop them if we don't try. We need to go on the offensive," I said.

"Attack them? They're the Bureau, they have the government and most major Heroes," Alice said.

"We have some of our own," I said, looking at the assembled troops. I didn't trust Kurt and Quentin, but at least they were fighting on my side. "And we can get some more."

"Sarah, you just let Marcus and Hamilton go. Who else do we have?" Johnny said."Mom," I replied.

"But she's in prison," Alice said. She made a face after she said it, realizing how lame she sounded.

It was time to tell our scraggly team about my big idea: "Not if we break her out.""At the Luther," said Tape Deck, incredulous.

Quentin and Kurt looked at me, a devilish gleam in their eye. Johnny, Tape Deck, and Alice didn't look as happy.

"That's about it," I said. "We get Mom and we get Butters back. And we fight.""Sister, you are crazier than I thought," Johnny said.

"I'm in," Kurt said.

"So am I," said Quentin.

I looked at Johnny. "Do you even need to ask?" he said.

"I'm not sure about this," said Tape Deck.

"Neither am I," said Alice.

"That's okay. I don't want you to come." I said. I meant it. I wanted as few people as possible to pull this off. Tape Deck looked relieved. Alice, however, seemed more concerned than before.

"Can we talk?" she said to me, then looked at Kurt who was looming, unsteadily. "Alone. Just you, Sarah."

We walked outside and she grabbed my hand, leading me away.

We headed off into the forest until the control station was out of sight. She turned to me.

"Sarah, this is crazy. Crazy. It's a death mission. Once you do this, you will never be the same." Alice grabbed my hands and looked in my eyes. "You don't have to do this. There are other ways."

I looked at her, evenly, and said, "It's the only way. We need her help."

Alice repeated herself. "Once you do this you can't go back."

I appreciated what Alice was saying. I knew that it was important. But she talked, offering me another way, and I just couldn't see it. "You were at the TV station too. I think it's already too late for that," I said.

"But this is a whole other level. The Luther, Sarah. The world's most notorious villains are held there. It's the most secure place on earth and for good reason. What if you let one of them out by accident?" Alice grimaced, looking sick to her stomach. "Anarchy could ensue."

I shook my head. "I'd rather have that anarchy then what we have right now. We're not living in a democracy. There are people in there who just told the truth."

Alice got desperate. "They'll label you a terrorist. A supervillain. A traitor."

"I know."

"And they'll be right. You're going after the most powerful people in the country. The president, even. You're seventeen years old. You have a future ahead of you, and you're teaming up with Kurt. And Q." Alice shook her head. "You saw what that monster was capable of—and he has no remorse. He's scary, Sarah. He'll stop at nothing, no matter who gets in the way."

"Maybe I need a little of that right now." I knew it was flip.

"Sarah, this is serious. There's no turning back from this. No going to school the next day, walking down the street. Normal is over. Kurt could care less if people die. And Q has already killed."

"I need them. I can't do this alone. And once my mom is out she can help us sort it out. But all those people that will accuse us of heinous crimes are already making that case. And right now, we need to fight back. I've made up my mind."

She started to cry. "I know you have. I just don't want to lose you. And I don't want to lose Johnny. I just want to play in the band and hang out like teenagers and not been involved in these violent struggles. I wish there was some other way."

I hugged her close. "Me too," I said. "Me too. I'll try to talk him out of it. I know how much he means to you. We can just sacrifice one Robertson to the cause."

She wiped her eyes and regained her composure. "Thanks. It won't work, but thanks. If you're going he's going."

I grabbed her hand and we headed back to the mill.

When we got back inside Johnny looked at me then Alice. Alice gave him a pleading look that said "Don't" and his eyes softened. But he turned to me and gave me a resolute nod. Seeing this, tears leaked out of Sarah's eyes. He came over to comfort her, then, with his hand wrapped over her shoulder, he said to me, "So I take it you have a plan, sis."

My eyes narrowed. I had no plan. But if I didn't try, I would regret it for the rest of my life.

"Yes," I said.

FIFTY-EIGHT

Some may call me a villain. Some may call me a hero. That's not my concern. I know I was serving justice and that's all that mattered. If a Hero was someone who imprisoned the innocent and controlled people for their own end, I had no interest in being a Hero. And if a supervillain was someone who fought for the wrongfully accused, for the victims of a corrupt regime, for the tortured—then I am proud to be called a supervillain.

We assembled by the River, a few miles downstream from the prison. Alice had summoned the Misshapes to bid us goodbye. It was come at your own risk, but everyone came. People offered to join in but we told them no. It was especially hard to convince Rosa not to come.

Alice went over to bid Johnny goodbye. I'm guessing he got a similar speech as I did, but his involved more tears, desperate hugging, and making out. He stood resolute. But I wouldn't have held it against him if he backed out. In fact, I kind of hoped he did. He had more to lose. He had Alice. I didn't have anybody. But if this didn't work, Dad would be even more crushed. He would be a shell of a man. I worried about that, and it's why I wanted Johnny to say no, to leave.

Alice and Betty were crying. We were about to go over into the mill to set up our final plans. Hamilton came over and pulled me aside. He dragged me into the woods so nobody would see us. "I have something to show you," he said.

He pulled me over toward a tree, stopped me short, and kissed me. I was shocked at first, but then I relaxed into it. He had soft lips, slick with paint drippings, and I felt like I could melt into him. "I wanted to make sure it was real. That it wasn't a mistake. Please, come back alive," he said.

He pulled off his glasses and kissed me again. When he pulled away, my face was covered in blue paint. I ran my finger through it, setting up some war paint on my cheeks in the negative space. We laughed. He wiped my face clean with a cloth he kept in his back pocket, put his glasses back on, and we went back to the group.

My heart was fluttering. Johnny looked at me with a smile. "You got a little paint on you," he said, pointing at my chin.

I wiped it off with my hand. "Are you ready?" I asked.

"Yes," he said back.

"And you two?" I said to Quentin and Kurt. We turned to the river. Johnny cuffed my shoulder. "Here goes nothing." The air was still. I felt like I was on the edge of a cliff, like that day that Sam taught me to fly.

Johnny pressed a few buttons on his PeriMedics machine and it pumped medicine into his blood. He thrust his hand into the river. I could see him straining, his whole body a ball of muscle. I put on my earphones and waved my hands in front of the Miskatonic. The hand waving was for show, but it helped me channel my energy. The whirl started slowly. Whisps of wind and air circling each other. It grew in bulk quickly. Johnny pulled his hand out of the water and tossed a lit match into the surge.

"All yours," he said before the river burst into flames. They danced along the surface, red and orange demons floating above waves of heat. Then it hit my whirl of air and shot up into the sky. "The most metal thing I've ever seen," Kurt said.

It was an enormous vortex of bright red, like a demon's finger. Walls of fire circled each other, turning anything into their path to tinder. One tree leaning across the river got caught in a whisp and it went from black to gray to nothing in an instant.

"Wow, sis," Johnny said. "What the heck is that?"

"A fire tornado," I replied calmly. The flame lit up the faces of the Misshapes, flicking yellow and red across their faces. Alice began to clap. The rest joined in.

"Go get em," she shouted. They cheered us on in a chorus of whoops and wails. I felt the energy like a surge of love.

The tornado jumped up another notch, moving downstream. Large flames leapt into the air. I felt the glee of someone finally doing the right thing. The tornado veered West in the direction of the Luther.

Quentin was the first to lift off and, with a strong upwind, I was able to get all three of us off the ground. Three people was the most I'd ever done, but it wasn't much more difficult than myself.

We joined Quentin in the air, following the path of the river with the fire tornado leading the way. It was my job to keep the tornado on the correct path. I couldn't feel anything too extreme—pride, lust, disgust—I had to stay passionate and even-keeled, a difficult balance. Despite the rushing wind and surge of adrenaline the tornado was looking good. It was our way in. And our way through the giant force field that was coming into view. As it got closer, I remembered what the man in the cell next to me said. "The only way out is through fire." And if the tornado didn't work, nothing would.

The prison loomed in the distance, beyond the lake, and beyond the shield. One we broke through we could fly to the roof and hunt down Mom. Soon enough we would see her. Suddenly, I heard a loud whooshing noise. I looked to my left and right, expecting an attack or some kind of projectile flying at us. But there was nothing. When I looked ahead, there were two figures heading towards the tornado. It took awhile before my eyes could adjust—these two loons went straight for the flames, nearly hiding in the glare—but when I could see, I knew exactly who it was: Sam and Freedom Boy.

They had teamed up. They had teamed up in an effort to take me down, to convince me to do something completely different. "What are you doing here?" I asked.

"We're here to help," Sam said. "We're here to stop you before you do something stupid. Something you can't take back."

"There's another way. A better way," said Freedom Boy. "A way of peace."

"No. There's not. And you can afford to say that." He looked hurt. I didn't care. He was part of all of this. His face grew stern.

"Sarah," Freedom Boy said. He was yelling. There was an edge to his voice. I wondered whether he would end up fighting me if I didn't stop.

"You can't do this, Sarah," Sam added.

I looked at both of them. I had been so in love with those two that I couldn't even see straight. And now that they were here, acting like they cared about what I did, I realized something very powerful: I didn't care what they thought. "I don't recall asking your permission, boys. And from what I remember, you two don't handle tornados too well." I shot forward with Johnny, Kurt, and Quentin, our fire tornado burning molten hot magma ready to tear the Luther apart.

In the distance, I could see their eyes grow wide. The flames were reflected in them. And beyond them, the prison beckoned.

The Misshapes will return…

ACKNOWLEDGEMENTS

Thanks to Jason Pinter - publisher, editor, marketer, and general champion of the misshapes - this book would never have seen the light of day without you. Thanks you for your dedication, passion, kindness, and most of all, patience.

Kudos, hi-fives, and best wishes to the strongest team around: Amy Sprung, Tommy Wallach, Jon Ronson, Abigail McDonald, Katey Parker, Owen King, Lisa Lucas, Rachel Syme, Georg Pedersen, Alex Asher Brown, Chris Watters, Sean Michaels, Dr. Caitlin Crowther, Alexandra Roxo, Rachel Cantor, Sean Howe, Isaac Tilton, Daniel Tilton, Jason Diamond, Marisa Meltzer, Joe Coscarelli, Isabel Gardocki, Michele Filgate, and John Scalzi. To my Cabal for the crucial online love and safe space for venting. Stephanie Valdez and the wonderful Community Bookstore, Amanda Bullock and the team at Housing Works Bookstore Cafe, and our lovely local Word Bookstore. Additionally, we'd like to thank our parents, siblings, nephews, and nieces for support. Our book has been championed by amazing school librarians across America and we'd like to thank them for their support.

And Broken Lands, for giving us a place to write.

ABOUT THE AUTHOR

Alex Flynn is the pseudonym for Stuart Sherman and Elisabeth Donnelly. They like garrulous Irish writers, *Pushing Daisies*, *Axe Cop*, and anything involving "The Tick". Donnelly has written for the *New York Times Magazine*, *The Boston Globe*, *L.A. Times*, *Paris Review Daily*, *GQ* and many more. Sherman is a bioethicist, health policy analyst and a former contestant on the game show *Who Wants to be a Millionaire*? They live in a hollowed-out volcano in Brooklyn.

Visit them online at www.TheMisshapes.net.